INEVITABLE SECRETS

THE INEVITABLE SERIES | BOOK TWO

KADE CHAREST

This book is dedicated to Tonya Barrett.
When I wrote Inevitable Inheritance I hoped that someone out there would like it, maybe even love it. And I am forever grateful that Tonya did.
Tonya without you this book would never have been written. Everytime that I wanted to quit I thought of you, and how you were waiting eagerly for the completion of this story. You kept me going when I thought it wasn't worth it.
So Tonya, here it is. I hope it was worth all the waiting.

ONE

THE LINOLEUM under Taylor's silver, strappy, multi-thousand-dollar shoes was incredibly ugly. It was a brown, patterned mess and between that and the smell of whatever it was that hospitals smelled like, Taylor thought she was going to be sick.

The shine of the hideous floors reflected the glare of the ceiling light into Taylor's face as she sat, arms crossed, leaning forward on her knees. Taylor examined the tiles and tried to lose herself in the buzzing of the fluorescent light. She was desperate to think about something, anything else besides the fact that Derrick was in emergency surgery for a gunshot wound, but the floor wasn't a very helpful distraction. She swallowed her fears down, but they just rose again in her throat all acidic and burning.

He hadn't moved. He had just laid there on the ground, totally still, his face void of color. Despite her attempts to distract herself she kept going back to her last view of Derrick, still despite her calls to him. Motionless even when the medical team had arrived and loaded him onto a stretcher and then into a waiting ambulance.

As Derrick was being loaded into the white box, Taylor had scrambled to her feet. She was ready to follow as he was wheeled away, but Henry interjected. He threw one of his arms around her and stopped her from getting into the ambulance. Instead he loaded Taylor into an SUV that seemed to have appeared out of nowhere and climbed in beside her as the ambulance doors were slammed shut.

"Go!" Henry shouted to the driver, which sent the vehicle screeching loudly away from the chaotic scene.

"What are you doing? I need to go with him!" Taylor demanded, trying to shove past Henry's immovable frame and get to the door handle. "Get out of my way! Let me out of here!" she shouted, her voice becoming shriller as she made no headway in her quest to get out.

Henry gripped the sides of Taylor's arms. "Taylor!" he shouted, giving her a gentle shake, allowing her to focus on him and silencing her. "I am taking you to him," he said slowly and firmly, pulling Taylor out of her frenzied state momentarily.

Taylor looked up and realized their car was in fact tailing the large white box with flashing lights. "Is he okay?" she asked Henry desperately, hoping he had some insight that she didn't.

But Henry remained stoic in his answer. "I don't know," he answered truthfully, "but they are all working very hard in there to try and make sure he will be." Taylor felt a tear fall from her eye at his omission. They didn't know—no one knew if Derrick would be okay.

"Wait, where's Marty?" Taylor asked in a sudden flare of panic.

"The Fletcher family security team got her out of there," Henry answered flatly as he scanned the world around their car.

"Good," Taylor said, "that's good." Marty was safe. Taylor gave herself seconds to absorb the one shred of good news she had.

And now, hours later, she sat in a room with hideous linoleum tiles, wipeable plastic furniture, and horrid fluorescent lighting, hoping with every fiber that Derrick was going to pull through this. She smoothed her hands down her ball gown and scanned its current state—bloody. There was so much blood on it, Derrick's blood. Once again, a shiver ran down her spine as panic took hold. She looked at the clock and saw over two hours had passed since she had arrived and still she knew nothing, had heard nothing. Doubt rolled in and she shook her head quickly trying to brush it away, but instead it brought hot tears down her cheeks.

"He's gonna be okay, Mrs. Preston-Fletcher," Mick said from his post beside the doorway.

Taylor had forgotten he was even in the room he was so quiet. She tried to muster up a smile for him but her face wouldn't comply. "Thanks Mick," she acknowledged hoarsely, as more tears careened down her cheeks.

The huge man came over and crouched before her, and still he was a foot higher. "I'm serious, Taylor," he affirmed to her. "Mr. Fletcher would never leave you," he said as he stooped his head lower to look in Taylor's eyes. "He loves you. I have never seen love so strong in anyone. He would never leave you like this," Mick said nodding his head at Taylor.

Taylor felt her chin tremble and then her head went naturally to Mick's shoulder and his arms enveloped her. Taylor let all the tension inside of her go and she sobbed into his suit. How could she not have told Derrick that she loved him sooner? How could she have ever denied that she loved Derrick? Regret was eating away at her as she sat there, hoping and praying she was going to get the chance to tell him how much she loved him.

The door to the room swung open and crashed against the wall behind it, sending Taylor jumping away from Mick in surprise, and Mick spinning around and drawing his well-concealed gun at the intruder.

"It's me!" Charlie called out, hands up. "It's just me!"

Mick rose slowly, keeping Taylor shielded behind him, harnessed his gun, and went back to the door, closing it behind Charlie. He took his post as if he had never moved.

"Taylor," Charlie said as he took her in. By his tone Taylor could only assume she was a huge mess. Charlie crossed over to her, his shoes clicking on the ugly linoleum on the way, and took Taylor into his arms. "How are you?" he asked.

Taylor could only shake her head in response, as she didn't trust her voice.

Charlie leaned back, pulled a handkerchief from his pocket, and wiped Taylor's cheeks as he kept an arm around her. "Have you heard anything?" he asked as he smoothed the fine linen down her cheeks.

"No," Taylor whispered.

Charlie nodded, but Taylor didn't miss the way his eyes shot over to the wall clock and widened a bit. "Taylor, why don't we take you home to change—"

"No," she said a little louder this time.

Charlie was silent for a moment, seeming to try and choose his words. "We don't know how long they will be, sweetheart," he explained softly. "You may be sitting here for a while and you might be more comfortable—"

"Charlie," Taylor cut in softly but firmly, "I appreciate your concern, and I love you for it, but I will not be leaving this hospital without my husband."

"But—"

"She wants to stay, Charlie," a stern voice cut in, and Taylor turned to see Todd standing beside Mick. Charlie huffed but nodded, admitting defeat. Taylor locked eyes with Todd and saw something in them but she wasn't sure what—compassion, sorrow? At that moment she felt a weird connection to Todd. He must have felt it, too, because he looked away. He couldn't ever let that stony facade down, Taylor mused.

Taylor shook her head a little to clear it. "Did they find the person?" she asked Charlie.

The resignation that appeared on Charlie's face answered her question before he even spoke. "No one," he said shaking his head slightly.

Great, so some crazed gunman with unknown intentions was

running wild on the street, Taylor thought. "So we don't know how or why this happened?" Taylor asked as panic welled inside of her.

Charlie hesitated for a fraction of a second but finally answered. "No," he confirmed, "the police have no leads."

Taylor dropped her head into her hands and dragged them down her face. "They were shooting at me," she declared finally.

"Now Taylor, you don't know that," Charlie soothed, patting her back.

"We really can't prove anything until we find this lunatic, Taylor," Todd chimed in. "It—" He cut off as his phone wailed through the small room. "Hammel. No comment," he said and hung up.

"Who was that?" Taylor demanded.

Todd opened his mouth to speak but his phone once again started ringing. Taylor turned to Charlie for answers, but his phone also started to ring. Taylor watched in horror as this back and forth went on for several minutes. When a lull happened both men silenced their phones.

"Was that the press?" Taylor demanded. The two men exchanged a look and finally Charlie gave her a somber nod. "What do they want? Huh? To know what happened, what Derrick's status is?"

The hysteria in Taylor's tone silenced the men. "Did they ask if he was dead? Because he isn't," she said firmly, but the tears came down her cheeks anyway. "He isn't dead and he is not going to die. He is going to walk out of this place and, and..." Taylor's voice cracked and she stopped to take a deep breath, "he is going to be fine!" she declared.

A noise at the door had Taylor shooting her gaze there and finding a woman dressed in hospital scrubs and an operating room cap looking back at her. Her face was grim, and suddenly Taylor wasn't sure anymore.

TWO

"MRS. FLETCHER?" the woman asked and all Taylor could do was give a slight nod. The woman made her way over to Taylor. She sat beside her and gave Taylor a small smile. "I am Dr. Lyles," she introduced herself. "Your husband is alive," she shared as Taylor deflated into the chair, relief washing over her in a cool wave, "but he is critical. I can't say for certain that he will survive. The bullet severed a major artery. There are many complications that can go along with that so we are going to be closely monitoring him for some time."

Taylor absorbed all the information, "Where did the bullet hit him?"

"In the chest. It missed his heart by millimeters."

Taylor nodded, "Wh-when can I see him?"

"He is being brought to the surgical intensive care unit now. They are going to need a little while to settle him in. He is going to be on a ventilator to help him breathe until he stabilizes," she explained. "As soon as he is all set, we will let you come in, okay?" Compassion shone in her eyes, but it was not without wariness. Taylor could tell the doctor wasn't sure Derrick would make it.

But Taylor was sure.

"Thank you," Taylor said. "Thank you, Dr. Lyles, for helping him."

"Of course, Mrs. Fletcher," she said, patting Taylor's hand and getting up.

He is alive, Taylor thought and felt a weight leave her shoulders. She would get another chance to tell him she loved him.

"This is good news, Taylor," Charlie said next to her, a glow to his face now, but all Taylor could do was nod in response. She watched his phone illuminate as a call came in, and watched Todd look at his own glowing screen. They both ignored them.

"Do you want us to call Marty?" Todd asked.

The fog that was surrounding Taylor's head lifted a little at the mention of her sister-in-law. She shook her head hesitantly at first, clearing away the haze, and then more surely. "No," she said the word coming out as more of a croak. Taylor cleared her throat and tried again, "No, I will." Taylor reached around for her phone. "I—I don't know where my phone is," she said uncertainly.

"You left it at home, Mrs. Preston-Fletcher," Mick reminded from the doorway.

"Oh yeah," Taylor said absently, realizing it was not the first time they had discussed this since she had been stuffed into this little room.

"Here," Todd handed her his phone, "use mine." Before Taylor could take possession, the screen lit up with another incoming call, so Todd snatched it back.

"Use mine," Mick said pulling his phone from his jacket pocket and passing it to her.

"Thanks, Mick," Taylor said taking the phone and dialing in Marty's number. It was funny how the mind worked. There were just some things that would always be clear—song lyrics, social security numbers, and phone numbers memorized long before smart phones.

"Hello?" Marty answered quietly hesitant, very un-Marty like.

"Marty?" Taylor asked, the quiver in her own voice hugely apparent.

"Taylor? Oh God, how is he?"

Taylor swallowed and felt fresh tears slide down her cheeks. "The doctor just came in," Taylor said, stopping to clear her throat, "and he is out of surgery."

"Oh, thank God," Marty breathed.

"But she said he was still critical, and, and..." Now that Taylor was relaying the message to Marty she found the meaning of the words soaking in. "And, she said the bullet severed a major artery—"

Marty's gasp was a reflection of how Taylor felt. "But they were able to repair it and now they are moving him to intensive care."

"Will, I mean, do they think he will be okay?" Marty stammered out.

"She said, she said that, uh, she wasn't sure he will survive," and with that Marty let out a sob, and it was in that noise that Taylor found her strength. "But he is going to survive, Marty," Taylor said firmly. "He is going to pull through this and walk out of here," she said clearly. "Do you hear me?"

There was sniffling and some ragged breathing on the other end, and Taylor had to wait, but finally Marty said, "Yes."

"He won't leave us."

"I know," Marty said, but Taylor could tell she was having trouble believing. "I want to come, but I'm scared," she finally said. "Rog said it was too dangerous for me to go out right now because the paparazzi is in a frenzy."

Taylor nodded, and then realized Marty couldn't see her. "I will go and see him and then call you again, okay?" she said softly. "Try and get some rest, and come in the morning. Deal?"

"Deal."

"Marty?"

"Hmmmm?"

"He is going to get through this," Taylor reminded her.

The silence on the other end was pounding. "I believe this only because I know he would never, ever leave you, Taylor. He went too long without you to leave you now. Keep me posted. I love you."

Those three words were like a knife in Taylor's chest. "I love you, too," she answered, having an easy time saying it to Marty, and once again having immense guilt over all the times she should have said it to Derrick. She ended the call, passing the phone back to Mick. "Thank you," she whispered, suddenly flooded with emotion again.

The events from just hours before played in her head like a bad movie. One second she was smiling at her husband and the next, well, the next second...

A clearing of a throat pulled Taylor from her highlight reel of last seeing Derrick, wounded and bleeding on the ground before her. She looked up to find Charlie and Todd looking at her and she had the feeling it wasn't the first time they had attempted to get her attention. "We are going to find a place for you, *in case* you need some rest," Charlie emphasized.

"Do you want us to make a statement?" Todd asked.

Taylor shook her head. "Not until I see him," she said, "and maybe not even then." She wasn't sure she wanted to share her private business with the press. It hadn't seemed to go well the small amount she had shared before. She thought it was going to make things easier but instead it only seemed to result in more popularity and her husband shot.

Charlie looked unsure. "Maybe we—"

"No comment. Got it," Todd spoke up as he put his hand to Charlie's back to get him from the room. Once they were gone, Taylor was again alone in her thoughts. She dropped her head into her hands and tried to will away any doubt, to will herself to stay positive. She thought about Derrick's father now. About how Simon had asked her to keep Derrick happy. She raised her eyes to the ceiling. "Sorry Simon," she muttered, knowing she wasn't doing a really great job holding up her end of the bargain. She missed Simon, and she really missed Delia. Besides her mother, Delia Fletcher was the best woman she could think of, and having her here would have made things easier all around.

"Are you a princess?"

Taylor whipped her head up to find a small face peeking into the waiting room behind Mick, who looked as baffled as she felt. When the little figure moved to make her way around him, Mick went to stop her. Taylor waved her hands to let him know it was okay, allowing the tiny little girl to move towards her.

"Are you?" she asked as she approached Taylor and tilted her head.

Taylor searched the little girl's eyes, sweet little brown orbs that took in Taylor's gown and perfect hair. Taylor also saw the IV in her arm and the thinning hair on her head. "Am I what?" Taylor asked in a fog, unclear if she was dreaming or if this was actually happening.

"A princess?"

"N—Uh, yes. Yes, I am," Taylor said and she saw something light up in those brown eyes. A smile came to Taylor's face at the joy on the little face in front of her.

"I knew it," she breathed at Taylor, and then her face scrunched up as she took in Taylor again. "What's on your dress?" she asked curiously.

Taylor looked down. Blood. Derrick's blood was on her dress.

"Uh, it's uh—"

"Paint," Mick offered from the doorway.

Taylor smiled at him gratefully and nodded, looking back at the little presence in front of her. "Yes, it's paint. They were painting my castle and I was careless and got some on my dress."

The small child nodded, accepting that answer. "How come you are here?"

"My prince is sick," Taylor said easily.

The girl's face became somber. "That sucks," she said, and Taylor laughed. "You are beautiful," she said and reached out to touch Taylor's face. "That's how I knew you were a princess."

Taylor felt warmth surge from the inside. "Well, thank you," Taylor said.

"I wish I was beautiful," she said and dropped her hand from

Taylor's face to her own arm, which, in addition to the IV, had bruises.

Taylor slipped off her chair and onto her knees before the child. "You are gorgeous," she said seriously, in shock that someone so young would think anything but wonderful thoughts about herself.

The child looked at the floor. "I'm sick, too," she said.

Taylor took her fingers and slipped them under the chin of the little tot, tipping her head up to look at her. "You are a beautiful young lady," Taylor said.

The girl shook her head, "No, I—"

Taylor placed a finger over her lips to silence her. "You have eyes that shine, and one of the best smiles I have ever seen," Taylor said. "And you are confident and inquisitive which are qualities that only smart, kind, and strong people have. And I know, because I am a princess and I have met lots of people," Taylor said.

The little girl smiled once again. "Yeah?" she asked hesitantly.

"Oh yes," Taylor said.

"There you are!" exclaimed a voice from the doorway, and a woman tried to enter the room but was stopped by Mick. The woman shot the huge man a death glare. "That is my daughter," she said and looked back to the little girl. When her gaze connected with Taylor's the woman's mouth hung open. "You're, you're—"

"Mommy, I found a princess!" the little girl exclaimed.

The woman nodded at her daughter. "That's, that's wonderful sweetie," the mother said numbly, still staring at Taylor. She shook her head and looked down at her daughter, "But you can't run away like that."

"Your mom is right," Taylor said, "you can't just leave and not tell anyone. It scares people, trust me," she said.

"Okay, I won't do it again," she promised solemnly to Taylor.

Taylor nodded and stood, taking the little girl's hand and walking her to her mother. When they had taken a few steps the little girl tugged on Taylor's hand and then motioned for Taylor to bend over. When Taylor was bent at her level the little girl took her face in her hands. "Your prince is going to be okay," she said to her seriously. "Princes never leave their princesses behind," she promised with a nod.

Tears filled Taylor's eyes. "Thank you." She gave the little girl a hug, then walked her over to her mother.

"Say thank you, Delia," the mother reminded.

"Delia?" Taylor asked the little girl's mother who nodded, and then Taylor looked at the little girl. "Your name is Delia?" she asked, seeking further clarification.

"That's me," the small child nodded proudly. "Thank you, Princess."

"Thank *you*, Princess Delia," Taylor said and curtsied to the little girl, earning a giggle.

"Thank you," the mother said, still in surprise. "She likes to explore," she explained.

"It was my pleasure," Taylor said and waved as they walked away.

Delia, Taylor thought looking up to the ceiling. "Please let that be your way of saying it will be okay," she muttered.

THREE

DERRICK'S EYELIDS were weighted down with bricks and his body felt like a limp noodle. He was trying to wake up but he just couldn't. And damn, did his chest hurt. There were voices all around him. He heard a lot of murmur and chatter but none of it was familiar, none of the voices was the one he wanted to hear. None of them was Taylor's.

He went to take a deep breath but something was in the way, and then a loud horn went off, and he was coughing trying to clear away the blockage.

"Try to relax, Mr. Fletcher," someone said, wiping at his brow. It was a kind voice, a feminine voice.

But it was not Taylor's voice.

Derrick fought harder against the weight on his eyelids and opened his eyes, pushing to try and get up. He was in a brightly lit room and there were people dressed in scrubs all around him. He was easily pushed back down.

"It's okay, Mr. Fletcher—you're safe," the female voice said to him a little firmer and louder this time. "You're in the hospital. I'm your nurse."

A hospital? Derrick was so confused. Where was Taylor? He tried to ask but something gagged him, making him cough.

"You have a tube in helping you to breathe," the woman said. "We are going to give you medicine to help you relax."

Derrick shook his head in defiance and someone came in and pushed his head down. What the hell had happened? Where was Taylor? Had it all been a dream? Had she never come back? Or maybe she never left?

Panic seized Derrick as he realized he must have OD'd after the tattoo parlor. That must be why his chest hurt, from that stupid tattoo. And Taylor didn't know he loved her.

He had to find her.

Hands clamped on Derrick's limbs as he attempted to get up again. "Give him something," someone ordered.

"Derrick?" a voice came from the distance and he stopped. It was Taylor. Derrick turned his head and saw a foggy shape across the room.

"Mrs. Fletcher, I don't think—"

"Let her in," the woman who said she was his nurse ordered. "He calmed down, so let her see him."

The figure came closer and Taylor filled Derrick's gaze. Derrick felt relief flow through him, and as Taylor took his hand and touched his cheek he relaxed back onto the bed.

"It's okay, baby," she said, tears filling her eyes, "it's okay. You're gonna be okay," she said nodding, her voice thickening with emotion.

The hands of all the nurses and techs who had been trying to hold him down left Derrick's limbs. Once he was free he reached up and wiped away a tear from Taylor's cheek.

"I love you," she whispered and turned her head and kissed his hand. "I love you," she repeated, looking at him.

Derrick felt his eyes fill with tears, and Taylor shook her head. "Are you in pain?" she asked in a sudden panic. Derrick shook his head, only to wince as he shifted to try and get closer to Taylor.

"Mrs. Fletcher, he needs to rest," the nurse explained gently.

Derrick gripped her arm and his eyes went wide. She couldn't leave—they couldn't take her away.

"It's okay, Mr. Fletcher," the woman assured him, "she is going to stay, but we need you to rest. You have been through a lot tonight and we need you to heal."

"I'm not leaving, Derrick," Taylor promised him. "I'm staying right here, okay?"

Derrick nodded and grabbed Taylor's hand, bringing it to his face and rubbing it on his cheek. Something on her hand hit his face and he moved her hand to his view to look at it. His eyes went wide when he looked at her rings on her finger.

Taylor laughed. "Did you forget?" she asked as he started to blink more, his eyelids becoming weighted down like before. "Just go to sleep, we'll talk about it when you wake up. I'll be right here," she assured him. Then Taylor looked intently into his eyes and said, "I love you, Derrick Fletcher." Slowly, Derrick's eyes drifted closed, even as he tried to fight it, and he was pushed back into sleep.

TAYLOR WATCHED Derrick drift off to sleep and once his eyes stayed shut, she kissed his forehead.

"Mrs. Fletcher?"

Taylor turned to the nurse speaking to her as the other staff emptied from the room. "Please, call me Taylor."

The nurse nodded. "Of course," she said smiling. "I'm May, and I will be your husband's nurse for tonight. I'm going to get you a chair and some blankets so that you can stay close by. We may need you to step out when we move him. He obviously needs you," she said, smiling.

Taylor looked back at Derrick. "I need him just as much," she said, her voice wavering a bit and tears sliding down her face.

"Oh sweetheart," Nurse May said, taking Taylor into an embrace. She was an older woman, and her soft frame was made to soothe. "He is going to be okay," she assured her. "His vitals are stable and we are going to keep them that way."

"Thank you," Taylor muffled into May's scrub shirt, grateful for the reassurance.

The woman leaned back. "Can I get you something to change into?" she asked. "I mean don't get me wrong, this is stunning," she said motioning to the ball gown Taylor still wore, "but it can't be comfortable."

Taylor shook her head. "I'll be fine for now," she said, looking back at Derrick. She watched his smooth brow and his steady breathing courtesy of the tube in his mouth. There were bandages, tubes, and wires all over him, but none of that mattered. Because despite all of the scary-looking machinery around him, there was a blip-blip-blip on the monitor and that meant he was alive. Derrick was alive and he had seen her and she had told him she loved him.

Everything was going to be okay.

Taylor looked over to the doorway and found Mick standing just inside. "Mick, can you text Marty and let her know he is okay?"

"Already done, Mrs. Preston-Fletcher," Mick said.

"Thanks, Mick," Taylor smiled at him as the nurse wheeled in a recliner chair and pulled it close to the side of Derrick's bed. "Thank you very much, May."

"No problem, Taylor. I will be in and out a lot. Try to rest as much as possible," she said gently.

Taylor sat in the chair and rested her head on the bed right next to Derrick's arm. She took in a deep breath of his scent and fell asleep instantly.

———————————

"MRS. FLETCHER," a voice said, accompanied by the light pressure of a hand on Taylor's shoulder.

Taylor cleared her throat as she opened her eyes and found May, the nurse from the night before, waking her. "Yes," she said, then became aware of her surroundings and flipped her head to Derrick. "Is everything okay?" she asked, suddenly panicked, taking Derrick in and seeing he looked exactly the same as he had when she fell asleep.

"Oh yes, we just need to take an x-ray of Mr. Fletcher and reposition him so we need you to step out for a minute."

Uncertainty flooded Taylor. "Do I have to go? I want to stay with him—"

"Taylor, it's okay," a voice from outside of the room chimed in. Taylor turned to the sound and found Marty giving her a small smile. "He is going to be okay, just let them take care of him," she said with a nod.

"Marty," Taylor said with a smile, and then turned to the nurse. "Can she just come in and see him, and then we will step out?"

"Okay," the nurse relented, "but just a couple of minutes, please."

"I understand," Taylor said. She didn't want to throw her high-profile status around for special favors, but she would push for her sister-in-law to see her critically wounded brother. Taylor turned to Marty and found her rooted in place, just outside the doorway with Rog behind her.

"Marty?"

Marty just shook her head in response. Taylor walked over to her, "What's wrong?"

"I don't think I can see him like this," Marty whispered.

Taylor nodded her understanding. It wasn't exactly Derrick's most shining moment. "That's okay—"

"No, it's not," Marty said. "I need to grow up and go in there," she argued. "I need to tell him I love him just in case—"

"He will walk out of here," Taylor interrupted.

Marty bit her lower lip. "Yeah, but, well, I just need to tell him."

"Then let's do it," Taylor said, pulling Marty forward and into the room. She led Marty to the top of Derrick's bed, and stood behind her. "They said his vital signs are stable."

"When will he wake up again?" Marty asked, her forehead

furrowed as she looked her brother up and down. "He is so still. He is never this still. Is he okay?"

"They sedated him. He was trying to move too much when he was awake the last time. To help him rest they gave him some medicine," Taylor explained, trying to recall and reiterate all the information May had given her. Marty reached and grabbed Derrick's hand, giving it a squeeze. "They said once things stabilize, they will try to wean him off of the life support."

"I'm sorry, Mrs. Fletcher, but we need to do his x-ray now," May said from the door.

Taylor nodded, and turned to see Marty lean down and kiss Derrick's forehead. "I love you, big brother." Marty came back to Taylor, grabbing her arm.

"Should we wait in the waiting room?" Taylor asked May.

"Taylor, Henry secured a private area for you to wait," Mick informed her from the doorway. Taylor turned to find Rog and Luke beside him. "I have already given the staff the number to the room. When they are ready they can call for you."

"Henry was here?" Taylor asked, completely dumbfounded.

Mick gave a quick nod and started off down the hall. Taylor and Marty followed, Rog behind them while Luke stayed stationed at Derrick's doorway.

They were brought down a long corridor to an elevator. Along the way, they passed multiple security guards and police officers and Taylor was certain their presence was thanks to Henry. Marty and Taylor were ushered inside the elevator as soon as the door slid open, and Mick slid a key into the panel and turned it, holding it in place and hitting up.

"Are we going to the bat cave?" Marty asked Taylor in a whisper as both women watched in confusion.

"No, no. The bat cave would be down, we are going up," Taylor said analyzing the situation.

"Oh, you're right," Marty agreed. "Who has a hideout up high?"

Taylor shrugged, "Ironman?"

"Well shape up, Tony Stark, the Fletcher girls are coming over," Marty joked, her overtired status clearly taking over.

The elevator dinged and the doors opened to a darkened floor that lit up as soon as Mick stepped out. Taylor went to follow, but Rog stepped in front of them.

"Stay here," Rog said in his deep voice as Mick unsheathed a gun and walked around.

"Should we tell them that they are really no match for Ironman?" Marty asked and Taylor laughed. It felt really good to finally laugh and soon they were both cracking up. Mick returned less than a minute later, rolling his eyes and smirking as he took in Taylor and Marty's giggle fest.

"All set," he said motioning for the two women to follow him.

"What is this?" Taylor asked, exiting the elevator and taking in the polished marble floor and ornate crown molding in the space before her.

"Executive suites," Mick explained. "For the hospital's, uh, more elite clientele."

"And we have this—"

"At your disposal, Mrs. Preston-Fletcher."

"Of course it is," Taylor said with an eye roll. She wondered how many people were trekking back and forth to visit their loved ones while her spoiled rich ass was up here.

Mick led them into the lit space and it was a huge, open floor plan suite right in front of them.

"Taylor, why don't you and I head to the bathroom. I can help you get out of that dress," Marty said, way more at ease with this whole penthouse arrangement than Taylor was. Her discomfort with excess was her mother's doing. Elizabeth Preston was never quiet about how easy they had it compared to blue-collar, hardworking families.

Taylor looked down, shocked to see that she was still wearing her dress.

"Did you honestly forget you were wearing it? It's like ten pounds of material and it's covered in sequins," Marty said dryly, rolling her eyes. "Okay, let's go. I have a bag of goodies to dress you down, Princess." She pulled Taylor over to a bathroom, in true Marty-take-charge fashion, and Taylor followed without question. She knew it was her way to cope—Marty needed to be in control of something or she would go crazy.

They made their way to a bathroom, and both said a collective "wow" when they turned the light on.

"It is so white in here," Marty said squinting. "I think I just lost a retina."

"It's blinding!" Taylor agreed, shielding her eyes and blinking, trying to get her eyes to adjust.

In the sterile white bathroom, Marty staggered over to the counter, blinking her eyes, and started to unload her bag. Taylor stood and just watched. "We should probably get all the bobby pins out of your hair first," Marty remarked, "so you can actually shower."

Taylor bit her lip and recalled how long it had taken to get all the pins in. Would it take just as long to get them all out? They had already been away from Derrick for at least fifteen minutes and she was eager to get back to him. "I think before we do that we should go back and check—"

"Taylor. It is six-thirty in the morning. You haven't eaten or washed, and have only slept about an hour and a half against a bed. You need to get cleaned up and eat something before you go back in there."

"Marty," Taylor said, agitation starting to eat at her, "I will—"

"Taylor, my brother is downstairs in a medically induced coma. I am doing what he would want you to do. And *he* would want you to shower, eat, and sleep. I'm conceding on the sleep thing because I don't want to fight all day with you. Now sit down. Let me take the damned pins out of your hair, get you out of the hemorrhage dress, and get you cleaned up so you can eat and we can go back to see Derrick."

She had a point.

"Well, when you put it that way," Taylor said, rolling her eyes and sitting on the closed toilet lid.

Marty heaved out a breath. "Thank you, I didn't want to have to move on to my plan B."

"And what was that?"

"To slap the shit out of you."

Taylor let out a sigh and bent her head to allow Marty access to her hair. Marty stepped behind Taylor and went to work plucking out the pins holding her hair in place and dropping them into the sink. The rhythmic ping-ping-ping sound of the hairpins hitting the stone sink had Taylor hypnotized and her eyelids felt very heavy.

"I'm glad he found you," Marty murmured after several minutes of silent work.

Taylor jumped a little at the sound of Marty's soft voice, which was good because it stopped her from falling forward in sleep, and goodness knew what was on those floors.

"Found me?" Taylor croaked, and then she cleared her throat. "I think more like we were thrown together by our Moms, but I'm glad too," she said spinning the diamond around on her left hand. She needed to move or she was at risk to fall asleep again.

"No, I mean found you in the coffee shop."

Taylor froze for a second, then turned her head quickly, but it pulled her hair because at that moment Marty was pulling a bobby pin out. "Ow!" she yelped. "What do you mean, Marty?" Taylor asked as she tried to catch her sister-in-law's downward gaze. When she wouldn't meet her eyes and tried to go back to pulling pins out, Taylor grabbed her arm. "Marty, what do you mean?"

Marty flicked her eyes to Taylor's. "I know, Taylor," she said. "I know you were in that coffee shop in the middle of nowhere. And I know that Derrick found you there."

Taylor flapped her mouth opened and closed searching for the right words, "H-how did you—"

"Derrick told me," Marty said, dropping her gaze to Taylor's hair. "He told me after he found you."

That did not sound right. Derrick had said he hadn't revealed where she was to anyone. "I don't understand," Taylor said, shaking her head.

"Well, he probably had no idea that he told me," Marty said quickly. "I found him drunk in his apartment after he had found you and I thought he had gone back to his party ways. I mean, he had been so straitlaced after Dad told him he was sick and I thought maybe he just went back to it, you know?"

All Taylor could do was stare. She couldn't even acknowledge what Marty was saying.

"I hadn't heard from him in days. He wouldn't answer my calls or texts or anything," Marty recalled. "And I found him, bottle of whiskey in his hand and just, just a mess. Like worse than I had ever seen him. He didn't even know I was there for a minute or two. I had to literally shake him a little before he would look at me, before he would talk to me."

Taylor watched Marty as she recalled the story, "Wh-what did he say?"

Marty had been staring at her hair but now she looked at Taylor, her eyes full of pain. "He said, 'I found her, Marty.' When I asked who and he said 'Tay', I asked where you were and all he would say is somewhere that made you happy. He wouldn't tell me anything. So I got another bottle for him."

Taylor gaped at her sister-in-law and all Marty did was shrug. "I know how to make him talk, and he was already there anyway," she defended. "So I handed him the other bottle and he eventually said you were at a small coffee shop all tucked away. He just kept saying how happy you looked, how happy you were," Marty said, shaking her head and looking away again. "I even said we could go and get you but he got so mad. He said you were happy and that was what he wanted."

"Derrick said no one knew where I was," Taylor repeated, still in disbelief that Marty had known all this time.

"He passed out and I left. I think he thought he dreamed it,"

Marty said. "It broke me to see him like that again, Taylor. I hated you," Marty said leveling her own gaze at Taylor. "I'm so sorry, Taylor, but I had no mom, I knew something was going on with my dad, and now I thought Derrick was going back to the way he had been—a spoiled closed-off dick. I knew you would make him okay and you weren't around and he was just protecting you."

"Marty—"

"But he was okay, you know. Monday came and he went to work and kept coming to dinner, but he was empty, he was missing something. And I tried to get him to date and he would just blow me off or avoid me. Then he brings you back and it was like he came alive again. It was like a Derrick I thought was gone came back and he was going to finally really live the life he had wanted for so long. And now...and now..."

"Marty, he is going to be okay," Taylor said, grabbing onto Marty's forearms as she watched the tears fall down her cheeks, her own eyes filling up, too.

Marty cried but nodded. "I know that. I really do. But you know how I know, Taylor?" she asked meeting Taylor's stare. "Because he would never, ever leave you. He just loves you so much."

The tears fell down Taylor's cheeks at a steady stream now. "I know, Marty, and I love him, too," she assured her.

"I know," Marty said through a strangled sob and then reached in and hugged Taylor.

It felt good to have someone else to cry with, to talk with, Taylor mused. She wondered how she had done it all on her own before.

"I had to get that out," Marty said into Taylor's shoulder. "But I love you, Tay. I don't hate you. I never did. I just wanted my brother back."

"I get it," Taylor said, nodding.

"Okay good," Marty said, giving her a final squeeze. "I'm glad we talked that out. Now let me finish getting this stuff out of your hair and get you in the shower, because lady, you stink."

TAYLOR GOT out of the shower and dried with a towel that had overdosed on starch. She was surprised they stocked a fancy place with horrible towels. It reminded her of her time away from the Preston world, away from the life she had now.

She went to the bag Marty had left her, a huge Louis Vuitton duffle, and was quite nervous about what Marty may have thrown in there. Taylor slowly unzipped the bag and peered hesitantly inside, as if something might jump out at her, but heaved a sigh of relief at what stared back at her.

The bag was stuffed with leggings and jeans and comfy-looking shirts, all matched up in individual bags. Below the clothes there were a few shoe options, which Taylor and her feet were glad to see were not stilettos but a variety of flats, and a toiletry bag with her phone inside. Of course the toiletry bag had a boatload of makeup in addition to deodorant, hair ties, and brushes. Taylor grabbed a hair tie, ignored the foundation bottles and mascara wands, and threw her hair up in a pile on her head.

She hastily grabbed a set of clothes and her Tieks flats and got dressed in record time. She struggled a little because her skin wasn't completely dry. She just wanted to get back to Derrick. So she tugged, yanked, and jumped up and down into her clothes, tucked her phone in her pocket, and got it done.

Taylor hopped out of the bathroom in a multitasking attempt to put on her shoes and smacked right into Henry's chest.

"Jesus Christ, Henry," Taylor said as she grabbed the wall to stabilize herself.

"Sorry," Henry said stoically, gripping Taylor's arms to help keep her up. "I heard you coming out," Henry said.

"It's okay. I'm just a little jumpy," Taylor said. "Where's Mick?"

"I sent him home. He needed to rest."

Taylor nodded. "Oh good, he looked exhausted," she agreed.

Henry raised his brow to Taylor. "You look like you could use some rest, too," he remarked, but Taylor ignored him.

"Where did you go?" Taylor asked him.

Henry was quiet for a second. "I was double-checking the security of Preston Corp and the penthouse."

"Oh good," Taylor said, "and things are okay?"

"They will be."

"What does that mean?"

"I want to take you back down to see Derrick," Henry said leading the way toward the door and effectively distracting Taylor from his remark.

As they approached the elevator the chime sounded and Charlie appeared with Arthur, the Fletcher Enterprises advisor.

"Oh Taylor, glad to find you," Charlie said.

"What's wrong?" Taylor asked, panicked. She realized this was becoming her go-to response whenever someone was looking for her.

"Oh nothing, nothing dear," Charlie soothed. "I'm sorry if I startled you."

"Derrick is okay?" Taylor asked.

"Yes, we just saw Marty down there with him. He is just as you left him, the nurses said."

Taylor slowed down her breathing. "Okay." Nodding slowly, she allowed the information to sink in. "Okay."

"But we have another matter," Charlie said.

"Oh Lord. What?" Taylor asked, suddenly feeling very weary.

"We really do need to release a statement," Charlie said. "The rumors are swirling and if they continue, they could really be harmful to Preston Corp and Fletcher Industries."

Taylor furrowed her brow, "What sort of rumors?"

"Well the silence from both corporations has people surmising that Derrick has not survived his injuries."

Taylor closed her eyes to try and calm herself. Fucking press and their need to dramatize anything. They do it for viewers and ratings and have absolutely no regard for the fact that she and her family were actually people. How dare they speculate on the fact that a statement had not been released.

"This is unbelievable," Taylor said with her eyes still shut.

"I understand that it is distressing to hear them say this and that you do not want to have them intruding in your personal life, Taylor," Charlie sympathized. "But with saying nothing they will continue to put their own spin on this so that it benefits them the most. And, unfortunately, tragedy draws far more viewers than truth."

"Yes," chimed in Arthur, "and the more detrimental things they say the more destructive it is to the companies."

Taylor heaved out all the air in her lungs and opened her eyes. "Fine," she said through clenched teeth. "Release a statement saying that Derrick is in stable condition and that he is receiving the best care. And that we appreciate privacy in this matter."

Charlie nodded, already typing into his phone.

"Would you like us to make the same one for Fletcher Enterprises?" Arthur asked.

Taylor looked between the two men, dumbfounded. "That isn't my decision, Arthur. Fletcher Enterprises is run by—"

"Derrick," Arthur interjected, "who can't make any decisions right now."

"Okay, well, then it falls to—"

"Martinique," Arthur finished for her, "who has deferred her responsibilities to you."

"She what?!" Taylor asked, completely blindsided. In that same instant her phone started ringing. Taylor glanced at it quickly and then answered.

"Marty," she said through her teeth.

"I'm sorry, Taylor, but Arthur came to me and I panicked and I didn't know what to do and so I deferred to you. I mean, you know how I am with the press. I can't just release a statement. And he said no hashtags! And then he started talking about business meetings and shareholders and I just shut down and said who does it if I can't and then he said you and, well, I thought that might be a way better idea than me," Marty rattled out.

Taylor heaved out a breath when Marty finally stopped talking. She couldn't get mad. Poor Marty was, in fact, way out of her element in major business dealings. Taylor understood since she had been out of her element herself just months earlier.

"I will take care of it, Marty, don't worry," Taylor said. "How is Derrick?"

"Same as when you left, just resting," Marty reported. Taylor was beginning to wonder if this was a coached response, cooked up by her advisors to try and keep her in check to make decisions. She was eager to get to Derrick and see for herself that it was actually true.

"Okay, good. I will be there shortly," Taylor hung up and turned back to Charlie and Arthur. "Fletcher Enterprises can release a joint statement with Preston Corp," she told them and both men nodded their understanding. "Now, Henry, we can go and see my husband," Taylor said turning to the hulking frame waiting by the elevator.

"Just a moment, Taylor," Charlie called after her, "we have some pending business meetings that we need to reschedule and review."

Taylor spun on her heel, which was a lot less dramatic in flats than in heels, but it stopped Charlie from speaking, nonetheless. "Let me make this clear. All business dealings which require my presence or signature are on hold until my husband leaves this hospital. Is that clear?"

Charlie's eyes went wide, "Now Taylor, you can't, you can't just stop a billion-dollar business in its tracks."

"Charlie, I am not needed for every decision. Things are all set in motion. But anything that requires me is on hold. Deal with it." And with that, Taylor spun back and jabbed her finger into the elevator button, causing the doors to open immediately. When Taylor got inside, she noticed that Charlie and Arthur both looked like they were about to have a stroke.

"Well at least they are in a hospital," Taylor muttered to herself as the doors shut.

FOUR

THE ELEVATOR ARRIVED at the third floor and Henry led the way to Derrick's room. Taylor followed, her head down. She didn't want to make eye contact, or be noticed if at all possible. She just wanted to see her husband.

"Mrs. Fletcher?"

Well, so much for not being noticed.

Taylor turned in the direction of the person calling her name, but her view was suddenly blocked as Henry shoved her behind him.

"I apologize," the man said, and Taylor peered around Henry just enough to watch the man show a badge hanging around his neck. "Detective Watts," he said, introducing himself, "I wanted to ask you a few questions about last night."

"Oh, of course," Taylor said, as she threw a glance over to the doors that led to Derrick's unit. She wanted to help in whatever way she could, but she also wanted to see her husband.

"I understand you are eager to see Mr. Fletcher," the detective said, seeming to read her mind. "I promise this won't take long."

"Okay," she said, relieved that he understood. She followed the detective to an alcove in the hallway to speak more privately. It was still quite early but the hospital seemed to maintain a constant hustle and bustle all around no matter the hour. "Do you have any leads? Have you found anyone?" she asked once they were out of the main pathway.

"We are still looking, Mrs. Fletcher."

She nodded, disappointment filling her.

"Is there anyone you can think of who might want to harm you or your husband?"

Taylor shook her head, "No."

"No one?" the detective pushed. "You're sure?"

"I honestly can't imagine anyone who would want to shoot at us," Taylor said.

Detective Watts looked unconvinced. "Business rivals? Upset employees? Old lovers?" he offered.

"No."

"That doesn't seem entirely truthful, Mrs. Fletcher," Watts said, giving her a chastising look. A look that put Taylor immediately on the defensive. "You realize that there are threats daily on social media to your company, as well as you and your husband?"

The hair on Taylor's neck stood up. "Yes, Detective, I am aware that my company and family are threatened daily on social media," Taylor returned the snarky tone back to the man. "My security is on top of this and monitors each one," Taylor said nodding her head to Henry. "I take it very seriously."

The detective nodded, "And you don't think any of those people would set out to attack you? We need to cover all potential avenues, Mrs. Fletcher, including the threats you receive on social media."

"I think that if you see them as having any possible involvement it should be something *you* need to follow up on," Taylor countered, her tone reflecting her irritation. This conversation was definitely not as enlightening as she had hoped.

Watts threw his hands up in a 'calm down' fashion. "No need to get excited, Mrs. Fletcher, I am trying to help you here."

"Well, you don't seem to like the fact that I don't know who would want to attack us."

"I just want whatever insight you may have," the detective said, now appearing amused by Taylor's response. "Tell me, are you and your husband having any marital issues?"

Taylor's jaw dropped. "What?" she gasped out in disbelief.

"Any disagreements? You seemed to marry fairly quickly after your engagement came to light."

Taylor narrowed her eyes at the detective. "How does how quickly I was married have anything to do with finding the person who shot my husband?" Taylor asked.

The detective shook his head, "I have to say I am not surprised at your lack of cooperation. Seems to be a Preston family trait."

Taylor raised her brows, shocked that flames were not shooting out of her eyes to engulf the detective. "I fail to see how you doubting my answer equals lack of cooperation," she replied. She also doubted how well the police were going to be able to handle solving this matter with this approach.

"I think you are not being forthcoming with information, Mrs. Fletcher," Detective Watts admonished. "If I don't have your full cooperation with this investigation, I will never be able to track down who did this."

Taylor dug very deep in order to maintain her composure. "I am sorry you feel that way, Detective, but I am being as transparent as possible."

"Are you, though?" he asked snidely. "You were gone for a long time, Mrs. Fletcher. It was, how many, five years before you came back to take over your family's company."

A chill went through Taylor and she hoped she was masking it with her exhausted facade. "Yes, I took time away," she responded as evenly as possible.

The detective attempted to stare her down. "Where were you exactly?"

"How is my time away relevant to your investigation?" Taylor softly demanded.

"Well, since your return there have been many deaths, so the question of where you were and what you were doing could be a key factor here."

"Are...are you accusing me of something, Detective?" Taylor asked, horrified.

"Should I?" the detective countered as Taylor stared at him, her mouth agape.

"I—"

"That's enough," a stern voice echoed through the hall and all parties turned to see Todd steaming towards them at full speed.

"Hello again, Mr. Hammel," Watts said dryly. "I was just reviewing some things with Mrs. Fletcher."

"I am quite sure you were," Todd said through set teeth. "From now on, all questions go through our lawyers instead of accosting her on her way to her husband's bedside."

"Of course, of course," Detective Watts said, his tone dripping with sarcasm. "I thought that Mrs. Fletcher would want to cooperate in the investigation to find out who shot her husband, but obviously I was mistaken."

"But I—" Taylor was cut off before she could finish her explanation.

"Your lack of compassion and use of scare tactics on a vulnerable woman have been recognized, Detective Watts," Todd said and pulled Taylor away from the man and down the hall.

"Don't you ever get tired of defending and protecting the above-the-law Prestons, Hammel?" Detective Watts questioned their quickly departing backs.

"Are you okay?" Todd asked her at the doorway to Derrick's room. Taylor couldn't answer because she really wasn't sure. One thought kept coming back to her from her encounter with the detective. "Todd, do people really think I tried to hurt him?" she asked as she looked in on her husband, tubes and lines coming out of everywhere.

"People believe things that help them make a story connect, Taylor. It helps them feel better about why something happened. They just want answers to things."

"But how can they find who really did this if they are focused on me and where I have been?" she asked in a hushed tone. Panic started to seize her.

"Taylor, they will be looking at whatever angle they can to get this thing answered and squared away. You are the only target they have right now."

Taylor rubbed her forehead and looked at Derrick again. "What if they try again? How are we going to figure out who did this to him? Are they going to figure it out?" she asked in rapid-fire succession as tears dripped down her cheeks.

Todd's face was a stone facade now. The face Taylor was used to from Todd. He said nothing.

A voice came from behind him. "Let the police do their job, Taylor," said Charlie, who seemed to appear from out of nowhere. "They will figure out who has done this."

"But how can I keep him safe," she asked looking at Derrick yet again. "How can I keep him from harm if they aren't looking for who really did this and instead just trying to blame me?"

"We will make sure you have plenty of security with you at all times," Charlie assured her as he pulled her into a hug. "Please do not worry, Taylor, we are on top of it."

Taylor stayed wrapped in Charlie's embrace, but her mind was in an absolute tailspin. She got it now. She totally got how Derrick had felt when he kept pushing security onto her, on wanting her to be in a bubble, on his obsession of keeping her safe. He had gone years without being able to speak with her to ensure she was okay. She could see how painful it must have been when he couldn't talk to her. What if she lost him? What if this was it? What if the last time they had actually spoken to each other was with him bleeding out on a red carpet?

"Taylor? Are you okay?"

The voice was all warbled and the room was spinning. Suddenly Taylor was pushed into a chair, her head between her legs, and Marty's voice was there in her ear, telling her to breathe.

Her mind went back to the plane, when Derrick had done the same thing to help her get through the onslaught of anxiety that was being thrown at her. She realized that as bad as she had thought that was, this felt infinitely worse.

She had to do something. She needed to figure out who had done this and why they were doing it. Was she the target? Or was it Derrick all along? Was it someone just looking to be noticed? And how were the police ever going to be able to devote enough time to it?

She couldn't let this go unsolved.

And she realized she needed to get a freaking handle on herself because there was no way she was going to figure anything out with her head between her knees.

Suddenly Taylor sat herself up. "I'm okay," she said clearing her throat. "Really," she said, her voice steady even though she was shaking inside. But she knew she needed to assure the group before her that she was fine. And she needed to assure herself a little bit, too.

"Have you eaten, Taylor?" Charlie asked.

Taylor shook her head.

"Tay, you've gotta take care of yourself," Marty chastised.

"Well that's part of the problem," Charlie said tenderly. "Why don't you go and get something to eat."

"I'm not leaving him again," she said firmly.

Charlie nodded, totally unfazed by Taylor's rash interjection. "Fine. We will have food brought to you."

"Okay," Taylor agreed, "and Marty also, please."

"Of course," Charlie said. "Now about a statement, Arthur and I wanted to make sure—"

Taylor pinned the older man with a death glare.

"I guess we could just go ahead with what you gave us if that is what you want, Taylor."

"It is," she said. And with that, Charlie, Todd, and Arthur went off to forage.

Taylor got up, crossed the room, and touched the side of Derrick's face. "Hey there," she said, feeling his stubbled cheek abrade her palm. She kissed his cheek and touched her forehead to his. "I love you."

Taylor sat down by Marty and the two women leaned into each other as they looked over Derrick.

"Taylor, as much as I want to just sit here and stare at that shit-head with you, I am wiped," Marty admitted. "I'm gonna head up to the Ironman tower and just relax for a bit. Is that cool with you?"

"Of course," Taylor said. "If we don't take care of ourselves, we are no good to him, right? You rest, and I will have them bring food to the ivory tower."

"Okay, but if..."

"If anything changes, I will come get you," Taylor vowed to Marty before she could even ask the question.

Marty nodded and looked over at her brother, while Taylor looked at Marty. She saw the bags under her eyes, the fatigue on her face, and was sad for how much Marty had endured in just a few months' time. Then she rolled her eyes when she realized how much she had also been through in that time.

Taylor watched Marty go over and kiss Derrick's forehead. "Heal up dork, and btw your B.O. is horrendous," she said as she came away from him with the most disgusted face. "Seriously, Tay, he needs deodorant or Febreze or something. It's bad," Marty stage whispered to Taylor.

Taylor smiled at her sister-in-law. "I will get on it," she promised. "Now go get some sleep."

Finally alone with Derrick, Taylor pulled her chair over to his bedside, the weight of the world on her. She looked at him, his eyes closed, his breathing so rhythmic. She heard the clicks and the beeps of the monitors and machines around them. She took a deep breath, wrapped Derrick's hand in hers, and placed a soft kiss on his palm. Taylor wanted to be positive. She knew he was doing well, but the picture before her did not look very good. Taylor was so wrapped up in her thoughts she did not notice Henry until he crouched down next to her. She turned when Henry spoke. "Taylor, I think—"

"Hello Mrs. Fletcher, my name is Dr. Merk and I am the pulmonologist taking care of your husband while he is on the ventilator," a man stated coming through the doorway, looking immediately at the monitor with Derrick's vital signs on it. His appearance stopped whatever Henry was about to say, and instead sent him back to standing position behind Taylor. "Mr. Fletcher has done really well overnight," the doctor remarked, not once looking at Taylor.

"Um, well, that's good to hear," Taylor watched as the man left the monitor, walked over to the machine pumping air in and out of Derrick's lungs, and touched some buttons. "Uh, doctor, what exactly are you doing?" Taylor asked the man who had retreated into himself just as quickly as he had come in.

"I am adjusting the settings on this ventilator so that Mr. Fletcher here can exercise his lungs," the doctor clarified, completely focused on what he was doing.

"Exercise them for what specifically?" Taylor asked with some concern.

"To breathe on his own," the man said as though this were the most obvious answer. He finally looked at Taylor as if she was delusional and then left the room as quickly as he had come in.

Taylor looked at the door the man had exited, then at Derrick, still fast asleep, and finally at Henry who just shook his head and shrugged with an equally baffled expression on his face.

A nurse entered the room, took one look at Taylor, and shook her head. "Based upon the baffled and horrified expression on your face I can tell that Dr. M has already graced you with his presence," she said. "I'm Polly, Mr. Fletcher's nurse today."

"Uh, yeah, hi," Taylor said, still in a fog. She shook her head, "I'm sorry. Hello, I'm Taylor."

"Hi there. So let me just explain what the heck is happening here. Mr. Fletcher is doing well. His x-ray is clear and his blood work shows he doesn't really need to have the tube to help him breathe anymore. So Dr. M has adjusted the settings on the ventilator to allow Mr. Fletcher to exercise his lungs. He can breathe on his own with the tube in and then we can check and see if we can take the breathing tube out of him today."

Taylor felt her stomach knot up with anxiety. "Is he ready to do this on his own?"

"He is," Polly assured her. "It is better for him to have it out. The longer it's in the more issues associated with it. Of course, we will monitor him as he is weaning from the ventilator, and if he gets too tired the machine will kick in." She walked over to the IV pumps around Derrick's bed. "I am going to start lowering his sedation, so he may start moving more, start waking up a bit. But from what I hear you are more soothing to him than we are so if you could stay close by, I would appreciate it."

"No worries there, I'm not going to leave him," Taylor promised.

"Yes, based on what I've heard it seems you two have a great bond," the nurse said smiling at Taylor. "Oh, and don't worry, the surgery didn't interfere with his tattoo."

"Tattoo?" Taylor said.

"Yes, it is near the surgical site but it didn't ruin it," Polly said. Someone from the desk called out to Polly, and she leaned out the door. "Shoot, I have to take that call. I will be right back but just flag me down if you have any questions."

Baffled, Taylor stood and leaned over her husband. He had stray lines left here and there on his side from where he had been tattooed. He had said he had gotten rid of the big chunk of it but left the stray lines to remind him of what he had been through and how far he had come. Also because the removal, as he had described it, "hurt like having your balls kicked and set on fire."

Taylor pulled the horrible hospital gown aside and scanned the side of his chest, looking around the small bandages. And then she saw something. Something she had thought was leftover, just some scratches, but when she got a little closer, she saw it was tiny, drawn out cursive in gray ink. The tattoo *Always Taylor* was tucked under his well-defined chest muscle.

"Fuck, Derrick," Taylor muttered and then rested her head on his arm. She felt him move and quickly picked herself up. "It's okay babe, it's okay." He relaxed at her words. She brought her hand to his face, leaned down and kissed his wrinkled brow and watched it smooth. She would keep him safe. Everyone she had left would be safe, she vowed.

Because, always.

FIVE

DERRICK FELT a sharp sting in his wrist and he jolted and tried to shout, but there was something in his throat. He coughed but it wouldn't clear so he reached up to pull it out. But he was stopped.

"Derrick, you have to leave that in a little longer," the sweetest voice said.

Derrick pushed up his eyelids, fighting the weights that held them down and looked into beautiful blue eyes.

He tried to say her name, but it just made him cough more.

"It's okay, it's just a tube to help you breathe, babe." The way she said it he was sure was supposed to soothe him but it only made him panic more, alarmed that he needed a tube to help him breathe. "It's coming out soon, okay? You are doing so well. I promise I will explain everything. Just give me a few minutes, please," she pleaded.

Derrick was a sucker for anything Taylor wanted so he gave a small nod in reply. Derrick watched as a tear slid down her cheek. He reached up and wiped it, his forehead scrunched with concern.

"I was scared," she admitted. "So scared you wouldn't wake up. I love you so much," she choked out and laid her head on his chest to cry, one of her hands snaking up to touch his cheek, the other holding his arm.

Derrick pulled his arm free, and wove both arms around his wife. His chest hurt like someone had just kicked him but he didn't care because the feeling of Taylor crushed to him was better than any painkiller.

IT FELT like three years later to Derrick, but finally they removed that horrible tube. The first thing out of his mouth was, "I love you always, Taylor," and he watched her dissolve into a puddle and cry. Taylor started to kiss him on his cheeks, his lips, his eyes, and his forehead. All the while she said, "I love you" to him over and over again.

A thousand kisses later, Taylor pulled back and looked at him, just smiling, her eyes coated in tears.

"What happened?" Derrick croaked out. Taylor swallowed hard and walked him through everything that had happened at the Gala.

Derrick's stomach knotted up as Taylor spoke. He felt sick for having put her and Marty through all that. But the fact that someone could have hurt her, that it could have been her instead of him, was suffocating. When Taylor explained that the amount of clothing he'd had on, along with the phone in his jacket pocket, had helped protect him she looked relieved. But he wasn't. Because Derrick knew she wouldn't have had that. If anything the information made him more nauseous.

"But you are okay," Taylor confirmed, interrupting Derrick's mental wheels. "Even though this horrible thing happened, you are okay and I get to tell you I love you. Because I do, Derrick. I love you so much and I am so sorry I didn't tell you sooner. That was dumb. But you are okay and I swear that I will tell you as many times as possible every day because you are my happily ever after."

To hear her say that she loved him, and that he made her happy, made him euphoric. Derrick had never thought of himself as a softy, but he could feel his eyes burning as Taylor professed her love for him. "I love you, Taylor," he whispered back, his voice suddenly hoarse. Taylor kissed his lips, her own lips wet from tears.

She laid her head next to his on his pillow for a long time, whispering "I love you's". The staff would come in and out around them and still they stayed this way, looking at each other and smiling as the doctors and nurses remarked at how well he was doing. A while later Derrick exhaled and said to Taylor "I want to go home." Taylor laughed through her tears at him and assured him that she was taking him home as soon as he was well enough.

But he didn't just say it once and stop. Oh no, he kept on saying it. In fact he wouldn't stop repeating it.

And so twenty-four hours and a million "I want to go homes" from Derrick later, it was way less cute than it had been the first time. Taylor was about to snap.

"Derrick, I know you want to go home, but as I have reminded you seven hundred times, you were shot. It isn't like it was a papercut and we are all overreacting. They had to do emergency surgery to get in there and clip a major artery so you didn't freaking bleed to death."

"But I am fine now," he replied stubbornly.

Derrick literally heard Taylor grind her teeth in response. When her phone rang, she looked down and then back to him. "I am going to take this. I will be back. I love you, please get some rest," she said on her way out.

"I'm not tired!" he yelled to her back.

DERRICK WAS furious as he watched Taylor walk away. He wanted to walk away, too, damn it. He didn't freaking care if his chest hurt every time he took a breath. This bed sucked.

He caught Mick's eye after he had shouted after Taylor. Get rest? What was he, a cranky toddler? Derrick was certain the huge man was smirking at his behavior, so he looked away to try and relax. But he found himself looking out the window. The sun shining outside was totally mocking him, as he was forced to stay inside. Derrick closed his eyes to calm himself.

When Derrick opened his eyes again it was dusk. He checked the time on the generic wall clock, confirming he had slept through the entire afternoon.

"You know if you keep bitching and moaning about leaving, you might just drive her away again," a voice said from the corner of the room.

Derrick whipped his head in the direction of the voice and found his sister sitting there, with a stack of papers and notebooks in her lap. "I am *not* bitching and moaning," Derrick defended, "and I didn't drive her away in the first place."

"You sure about that, Ken Doll?" Marty taunted with her eyebrows cocked.

Derrick glared at Marty. "Stuff it, weirdo," he said to her in the most affectionate way possible. "What are you looking at?"

"Your STD report," Marty said without looking up. "Has your dick fallen off yet from all of these?"

"I do not have STDs. I got checked once a month when I was—"

"A man whore?" Marty asked as she looked up at him wide-eyed. "Because that's what you were, Derrick. A goddamned man whore."

Derrick rolled his eyes and heaved out a breath, which made him very aware how sore his chest was. "Where is Taylor?"

"I think she said she was going to Paris, or was it Paraguay?" Marty asked looking thoughtful. "These are actually your divorce papers," she said in false sympathetic tones, shaking the stack of papers at him.

Derrick glared at his sister.

"Relax," Marty said, standing up. "She legit just went to get coffee like three minutes ago." Marty made her way over to the bed. "I'm glad you're okay, big brother," Marty said as tears pooled in her eyes and then slid down her cheek.

"I'm so sorry, Marty," Derrick said.

"Are you apologizing for being shot?" Marty asked, laughing through her tears.

"I guess so," Derrick mused, laughing too. "I'm just sorry I scared everyone."

Marty leaned in and kissed her brother's forehead. "Listen shit-head, I will take having the wits scared out of me as long as I don't lose you. I'm just glad you are still here. You're all I've got," she reminded him.

"Me too," he agreed. "Now, what are you really looking at?"

Marty shuffled the papers she was holding. "Some of my sketches. My mentor thinks I should have a fashion show and get my label off the ground."

"You are amazingly talented," Derrick told her. "I mean, the dresses you created for the Gala, they were like art."

"Yeah, and you stained Taylor's with so much of your blood you can't tell its original color," she quipped.

Derrick grimaced. Marty always shot from the hip. "I know."

"You could have died, Derrick, you know that? Somehow, some miraculous way, you didn't. And I am so happy you are okay. But if there hadn't been a way to get you out of there so quickly, who knows what could have happened, you know?" Marty said, looking at Derrick with a little disbelief still on her face.

"Yeah."

"And Taylor, she sat here alone, while you were in surgery, thinking you might die," Marty reminded him with sad eyes. And then her stare became irate, "So can you lay off on the going home shit? We need to make sure you are all healthy and not springing a leak in there. You make it very hard for everyone to be happy you are alive when you annoy the fuck out of them."

She was right. "Well now I feel like an asshole," Derrick said letting his gaze drift back out the window.

"Well if the shoe fits," Marty chided and Derrick gave her a small smile. "Lay off her, okay?"

"I will," Derrick agreed.

"I think that might be the first time you have ever agreed with me," Marty said in surprise.

"You should probably write it down," Derrick remarked.

Marty shook her head, "No, that's lame. Besides, I already shared it on social media. It will come up in my memories."

Derrick laughed and Marty joined him.

"I was totally terrified," Marty said, sitting beside her brother on the bed.

Derrick didn't have the words so instead he held out his arms to his sister.

"Damn, Derrick," Marty said, muffled into his shoulder.

"I know. I'm sorry you guys had to go through all of that," he said in his most sympathetic tone. Feeling Marty move, he assumed she was crying. Then he realized she was trying to get out of his embrace.

"No, not that. Damn, you have really bad B.O.! I brought you deodorant. Use it!"

The sight of Marty holding her nose with tears in her eyes from Derrick's stench was too much for Derrick to take and he burst into laughter holding his painful chest. But still, he couldn't stop no matter how much it hurt. And Marty couldn't keep the disgust on her face for long as she, too, started into a fit of laughter.

"Well you seem to be in a better mood. I hope you only needed a nap," Taylor quipped, walking back in the room with a steaming cup of coffee.

"I'm sorry, babe," Derrick said, "I promise to behave for the rest of the night." He made no promises about tomorrow.

"YOU THINK they will let me go home today?" Derrick asked when he woke up the next morning. Taylor was working on her laptop, trying to keep up with all her work obligations from both Preston Corp and Fletcher Enterprises, in the midst of all the chaos around her.

She smirked and looked up to laugh with him about his comment and realized that he wasn't joking.

"I thought you were going to let it go," Taylor reminded him, a little taken aback.

"I said I wouldn't bring it up again last night," Derrick reminded her. "Today is a new day. You should know to always listen to the language of a deal, Taylor," he chided her.

Taylor slammed down the lid of her laptop. "Derrick, I cannot listen to you ask to go home like I did yesterday. For the love of God," she said hotly.

"No, I won't be annoying, I swear. I will totally rein it in," he assured Taylor.

"Because you think they are going to tell you that you can go home today, don't you?" Taylor asked him incredulously.

"No," Derrick said trying to make a face that said that was a crazy thought but Taylor didn't buy it. "But if they did—"

"Don't get your hopes up, Derrick," Taylor warned him.

"I won't."

But he did. And when the doctor rounded on him in the morning and said that his vitals were stable but they still needed to monitor his lab work and his surgical site, Derrick was pissed.

Whenever someone asked how he was he would grunt back with "I'll be better when I go home." Or if they said, "Can I do anything for you?" he would automatically respond with "Can you get me out of here?"

He was a bigger jerk than he had been the day before, something Taylor had honestly not thought was possible. And Taylor was unable to grit her teeth and let it roll off like she had the day before. Instead, she lost it.

"Derrick Fletcher, that is enough," she said chastising him, feeling totally exasperated.

"What?" he asked, oblivious to his own behavior.

"You are being a spoiled freaking brat and I have had just about enough!" she yelled, suddenly feeling more like a mom than a wife.

Derrick rolled his eyes.

"Don't you roll your eyes at me! Do you understand how scared I was you were going to die and now that you are alive and well all you can do is complain!"

"I just—"

"Want to go home," Taylor finished exasperated. "I get it. We *all* get it. But you don't get to act like a child and have a temper tantrum because you aren't getting your way. These folks all worked very hard to keep you alive and now they are all working very hard to try and not kill you. And frankly I think it's because they like me because I really don't think they can stand you."

Derrick looked insulted. "I don't think that's true."

"They were drawing straws over who had to be your nurse tonight."

"No, they weren't," Derrick huffed and scowled, then looked out the window. He slowly slid his gaze back to her. "Were they really?"

Taylor made her way around the bed and sat next to him, took his hand in hers, and looked at his face as he scowled out the window. "I was so scared," she whispered to him and watched as his face turned to her and concern spread over it. "I was so scared that you were going to die, and that you would never come back to me. I was so scared I would never get to tell you how much I loved you and how stupid I was for not telling you sooner."

"Tay," Derrick said wiping the tears off her face, his own eyes looking shiny. "I would never leave you. I love you so much. It would take way more than a bullet to take me away from the one person I want to be with the most."

Taylor nodded and tucked her chin. "I know, that's actually what kept me going. The only reason that I didn't completely crumble."

"I'm sorry, Tay. I hate that you were so worried."

"I was worried, but I knew you were getting the best care," Taylor said.

"I agree," Derrick said, "as much of a dick as I have been, they have been really good to me. On top of everything."

"And do you know how much I would worry if you came home too soon and something happened and I couldn't help you like they could here?"

Realization spread over Derrick's face. "You totally set me up for that."

"Yes," Taylor said. "Yes, I did."

"You are truly a great businesswoman. You know that."

"I do, actually!" Taylor told him.

He heaved out a disgusted breath. "Fine, I will stop complaining under one condition."

"Okay, name it," Taylor agreed, eager for Derrick to stop being a huge grump.

"You need to go home and get a good night's sleep."

"No way," Taylor stated, completely irritated that she had been scammed herself.

"Taylor, I know for sure that you haven't left this place in days."

"There is a *too rich to be treated like normal people* suite upstairs," she reminded him. "I go there several times a day."

"You have been sleeping with your head on my bed for days, and I am certain you only go there to shower."

"Derrick," she started.

"Tay, if I am going to perk up and be peppy-holly-jolly man, my condition is that you have to go home tonight and get some rest. Otherwise, I am remaining just as irritating and annoying as I have been."

Taylor was silent for a moment and looked over her husband. She looked at the monitor wires still attached to him and the intravenous lines that were tunneled under his skin.

"You totally set me up for that," she said softly and stuck her tongue out.

"Yup," Derrick said flicking a quick glance at the clock. "It's five now. Go home and take a shower and then go to sleep."

"But—"

"Nope, you agreed," Derrick reminded her.

Taylor wrinkled her nose at her husband. "You know you should go into business, right? You drive a damn hard bargain."

"Now give me a kiss with tongue so I can have something to distract me from my current predicament."

"Because I'm such a good kisser?"

"No, because then I'll have blue balls and won't be worried about being in the hospital."

Taylor smiled. "And Marty says you aren't romantic," she mused as she leaned over and kissed her husband on the lips and then slowly deepened the kiss until she was just about breathless. "You need to stay here and get better, because, Derrick Fletcher, I cannot live without you."

Derrick let out a heavy sigh, and tried desperately to hide the pain he had in his chest from it. "Fine, I will stay."

The door burst open and an ashen-faced nurse entered the room, visibly shaken. "Mr. Fletcher, we need to discharge you right now."

Derrick and Taylor looked at the nurse and then at each other. "I thought," Taylor said turning to the nurse, "that the doctor said—"

At that moment, the doctor in question came in the room looking pale and flustered. "Change of plans. You will be discharged immediately," he said signaling for a wheelchair to be brought in. Staff suddenly appeared in the room holding patient belonging bags and stuffing them with all of Derrick and Taylor's things. Four Preston security members entered and closed in around Derrick and Taylor, blockading them as they monitored the frantic work of the hospital staff. The hive of activity around them was hypnotizing.

"What the hell is going on?" Taylor asked in her business voice.

The doctor cleared his throat, "There has been an, um, unforeseen circumstance..."

The doctor was cut off as Henry entered, startling him into silence. "My staff and I will handle this from here, sir," he explained and every hospital staff member looked visibly relieved and left as quickly as they had entered. Henry started pointing at the security team in the room. "Ian, get the bags. Mick, get the wheelchair, and you two," he said, his gaze landing on Derrick and Taylor, "no questions until we get you the fuck out of here."

Quickly, the security team got to work and even if Taylor and Derrick had wanted to say anything there was no time. Henry put his hand to Taylor's back and ushered her from the room as Derrick was helped into a wheelchair, and the two were brought to the hospital helipad. They boarded a Fletcher Enterprises helicopter while police officers stood facing out with guns drawn.

"What the fuck?" was all Taylor could say as she took in the events around her. But her voice was drowned out by the whirring helicopter rotors above.

Henry plopped Taylor into a helicopter seat and buckled her in. Before he could move on, Taylor grabbed tightly onto his coat and she could feel her eyes bugging out of her head. She was pretty sure that was what held Henry in place. "Tell me what the fuck is going on right now!" she shouted over the whir.

Henry reached behind him and grabbed a headset and gave one to Taylor, one to Derrick, put one on himself, and instructed the pilot to change the channel on his headset.

"Well?" Taylor spoke once she saw the pilot change his channel.

"There was an attack at the hospital."

"What kind of attack?"

Henry took a deep sigh and Taylor reached over and grabbed Derrick's hand. "It was an attempted attack on you, Taylor."

Taylor's stomach dropped. She had known it had been her. That she was the real target and the reason her husband had been injured, very nearly killed.

"But the assailant was killed on site."

"Was anyone else hurt?" Derrick asked.

"A hospital security guard was shot, but his injuries are not life-threatening."

"Who?" Taylor asked. "Who was the person, the one attacking me? Do I know him?"

"It was Richard Tappen," Henry replied, eyes locked with Taylor.

"What?" Taylor was, once again, completely floored. "No, no way. He couldn't have—"

"Tappen?" Derrick questioned. "The guy who gave you all that bullshit when you took over?" he asked Taylor.

"Yeah, that's Tappen, but—"

"Well, seems he didn't take to the changes like you had hoped," Derrick said and Taylor turned and glared at her husband.

"The police are going to be at the mansion when we get you there," Henry explained, interrupting Taylor's silent scolding of her husband. "We needed to evacuate the hospital so a full-scale investigation could be performed to ensure Tappen was the only assailant."

"Mansion? My father's mansion?" Derrick asked. "Why the mansion? Why can't we go to our penthouse?"

"It is not secure," Henry informed Derrick.

"No way, you checked it out."

"There is no way I can control access with the number of residents that live there," Henry explained. "I can control it better with you two at the mansion."

"Okay," Derrick said, "I guess that makes sense."

"Wait a minute!" Taylor shrilled into the headphones, making both men wince and look her way. "There is no way that Tappen did this."

Henry looked at Taylor and put a hand on her arm. "Taylor, I responded when I heard there was a situation. I saw him taken down. I reviewed the security footage. He came in with a semi-automatic rifle and demanded access to Derrick's hospital room. It was Tappen."

Taylor shook her head, "I am telling you, Henry, something isn't right. That guy was not the shoot-'em-up type."

"Taylor, he hated you," Derrick said.

"No, he hated the idea of me," Taylor explained. "Seriously," she defended as she met disbelief in Derrick's face, "we have been working together on some projects lately and even he said he felt terrible for how he acted when I took over. I just replied to an email from him today, and he was asking how you were doing," she said looking at Derrick.

"Maybe it was a cover," Derrick said. "A way to get closer to you."

Taylor shook her head. "No, I don't buy it," she said. "My gut tells me no, and I trust my gut." She turned her attention back to Henry, "I want to see the video."

Henry hesitated. "Taylor, I don't think—"

"Tay, you don't want to see that," Derrick said quickly.

"Actually," Taylor said, in a tone that brooked no challenge, "I do. When we get to the mansion, I want to see that video."

"I have it downloaded on my phone," Henry informed Taylor.

Taylor cocked her head, "How? You know what? Don't tell me. Show it to me," she instructed in her business tone. When the towering man made no move, Taylor's irritation ratcheted up a dozen notches. "Now, Henry!" she demanded.

Shaking his head, Henry pulled out his phone and swiped his way to what he needed. He flipped the screen and Taylor watched as a man walked into the main entrance. He was visibly shaky, whipping his head wildly to and fro and pointing a semi-automatic rifle all the while. His movements were jerky, and when he was approached by security officers, Taylor watched as the jerking intensified. He started shouting and suddenly he began firing the weapon.

Henry shut down his phone. "We are here." Sure enough, they were touching down on the Fletcher family helipad.

Taylor climbed out and turned and watched as Derrick gingerly extracted himself from the whirring chopper, bracing his wounded side as he did. Her mind pushed aside what she had just witnessed and instead focused on her husband. She touched the hand he had pressed against his chest when he was out and beside her. "Are you okay?"

"Yeah, just sore," he said, but he didn't stop her from putting her arm around him and helping him make his way to the elevator waiting for them on the roof.

"Mrs. Preston-Fletcher," said a Fletcher Mansion staff member, "I need to take you downstairs to the—"

"No, I need to get Derrick to bed," she told the staff member.

"Taylor, you don't have a choice here," Henry said, crowding into the elevator with them. "The only way I could get you two out of there was to agree they could interview you here."

"Come on, Tay, the sooner we talk to them the sooner we can get answers," Derrick said.

Taylor didn't talk but she silently fumed as she stomped her way into the elevator.

The elevator took them to the first floor of the mansion and Henry led the way toward the drawing room. On the way down the corridor a door opened, stilling Henry and making Taylor tense in apprehension.

Marty exited the open door. "Hey," she said, her voice breaking into a bright smile as she saw Henry, "I thought—" Marty stopped short, her face registering shock as she leaned and took in Taylor and Derrick clustered behind Henry. "Uh, what are you guys doing here?" she asked in a flat voice.

"Someone tried to attack us at the hospital," Derrick said dully.

"No, not us, me," Taylor said. "I am the problem here. And they made us leave."

Marty pointed at Derrick, "Are you even well enough to be home?" she asked.

"I'm fine," Derrick ground out.

Marty rolled her eyes and turned to Taylor, "Did the nurses rebel?"

"No, one of my employees came into the hospital with a gun. He is dead now," Taylor said, still very much disturbed about the latest events around her.

"Oh my God," Marty said in horror. "That's awful. Are you guys okay?" she asked, flitting her eyes around to the three before her.

"Yes," Taylor said, shaking her head. "But now we have to talk to the police," she said waving her hand down the hall to their destination. Taylor was eager to get this night over with.

Marty nodded, now a little dazed herself and then shook her head. "Is this our life now?" she asked in anger. "Like what the fuck is going on?"

"I don't know," Taylor said, hoping that this was not their life, that this was just a run of bad luck.

"Let's go talk to the police, Taylor," Derrick said. "Maybe they have more input."

"Hopefully."

"Well I am going to mark us as safe," Marty said. "I am sure my phone has blown up," she declared shaking her head and making her way down the hall away from the group.

"Mark as safe?" Taylor asked Derrick, her face reflective of her overt confusion.

Derrick shook his head, "I'll explain later."

"This way," Henry commanded as he once again led Derrick and Taylor down the hallway to the drawing room where Detective Watts awaited them.

"Oh for fuck's sake," Taylor muttered under her breath as she entered the room and saw the detective before her.

"What?" Derrick asked, looking at her and following her glare to the detective.

"Hello again, Mrs. Fletcher," the detective said and then turned his attention to Derrick. "Mr. Fletcher, I am Detective Watts" he introduced himself. "How are you guys doing?"

"Well that depends, Detective," Taylor snarked. "Are you going to accuse me of trying to kill my husband again? Maybe of trying to attack myself this time?"

"Mrs. Fletcher, I have to explore every possible angle. Don't worry, your lawyers shut me down quickly."

Derrick's eyes went wide, "You accused my wife of shooting me?"

The detective rolled his eyes. "Haven't you guys seen Law and

Order? It's always the wife," he explained. "Anyway, today Mr. Tappen opened fire on the hospital, and I need to know your history with him."

"Wait," Taylor said, pinching the bridge of her nose, "should I have my lawyer?"

"Something to hide?" the detective asked, eyebrows raised.

Taylor let go of her nose and glared at the detective. She set her teeth and felt her jaw ache from clenching them. "No, but I also—"

"Watts!" a man in a full and heavily starched uniform called to the detective from the doorway of the drawing room, cutting off all conversation.

"Oh for fuck's sake," Detective Watts said low, and it might have made Taylor just a teeny, tiny, bit happy that there was someone there whose presence agitated the detective as much as his presence irritated her.

When the uniformed man crooked his finger at the detective, Watts looked as if he would detonate on the spot. Stiffly he walked to where he had been called.

"That doesn't seem as if it will be a friendly conversation," Derrick quipped as they both watched the detective drag himself to what was most likely his supervisor.

"Good," Taylor spat.

"So he accused you of attacking me?"

"He sure did."

Derrick nodded as he thought that over, "Well, it *is* always the wife."

Taylor whipped her head over to her husband and saw him trying to hide a smirk. "How can you laugh right now? Someone has been shot, another man killed because someone tried to kill me. *And* you were shot and they accused me of it!"

"Tay, I wasn't killed and neither were you," Derrick reminded her. "And you didn't try to shoot me. I was there, I remember. And they said that man was injured and the attacker was killed."

Taylor pointed her finger at her husband, silencing him. "I am telling you, Derrick, Tappen was not coming after me. Something is very off about this whole thing."

"Taylor, they have eyewitnesses and video footage of the man going postal in the hospital."

"I don't care, something is off," Taylor said, shaking her head.

"Taylor, Derrick," Charlie's voice shocked them both out of their conversation, and they turned to find the older man approaching. "I'd like to introduce you to Chief Pompas," he said gesturing to the man who had beckoned the detective away. Chief Pompas was a tall man, his skin coffee-colored and smooth, not a laugh line marring it anywhere.

"Hello Mr. and Mrs. Fletcher," the Chief said eloquently, "It is a pleasure to meet you both."

"You also," Taylor answered politely, "however I wish it was under better circumstances."

"Well I am happy to report that we have confirmed that the suspect taken down at the hospital was in fact the same assailant from the Gala shooting."

Charlie's face lit up at the chief's declaration. "That is wonderful news," he said and directed his attention to Taylor and Derrick. "Taylor, isn't that wonderful?"

Taylor looked at Charlie, and then Todd who had silently joined them. She exchanged looks with Derrick and then she heaved out another breath and turned her attention back to the chief. "Chief Pompas, I'm sorry but I really don't think that Richard Tappen was capable of this."

Taylor saw the irritation flare in the chief's eyes, but he was quick to blink it away before he responded. "Mrs. Fletcher," he said in a very patronizing tone, "a thorough investigation was conducted and we have, in fact, linked Tappen to the scene of the original shooting."

"And how is that? Because the last report I heard, which was a police press conference earlier today, you didn't even have the weapon." Taylor questioned.

Now the chief made no attempt to hide his irritation.

"We do not release all our information for an ongoing investigation to the public, *Mrs. Fletcher*," the chief informed her, saying her name as if it were a curse word.

"Be that as it may—"

"Listen, Mrs. Fletcher, I came here out of courtesy to personally inform you that we have caught the assailant and closed this investigation."

"But what if you have missed something?" Taylor demanded.

"Nothing was missed. The shooter is dead. The case is closed," Chief Pompas spit out. He fit his hat back on his head forcefully. "Good night to you," he said and turned on his heel.

Charlie looked at her completely befuddled. "Taylor, what's going on? I thought you would be thrilled that they had solved this case."

"I just don't believe he could have done this! Richard Tappen is, uh, was—"

"Completely hostile to you when you took over and bucked every decision you made every chance he could," Todd cut in and reminded her.

"Yes I know, but he was coming around—"

"Taylor, they have closed the case," Todd answered bluntly.

"I freaking know that, *Todd*," Taylor said, now enraged, "but that doesn't mean they have the right guy!"

"Taylor, I think you may be too upset that you didn't see this in him, that maybe you thought he was coming over to your side so to speak," Charlie offered gently.

"No, that isn't it. There is no way—"

"Taylor, you have had a long day. I am going to escort you and Derrick upstairs now," Henry cut in.

Taylor was certain her skin was sizzling by this point. They were all talking to her as if she were delusional, and she was about ready to burst.

"Henry, I don't need to be carted away like a child having a tantrum," Taylor said through her teeth.

"No, but Mr. Fletcher looks as though he needs some rest," Henry informed her nonchalantly.

It was then that Taylor turned to find Derrick nearly asleep in his chair. "Oh my God, you're right, Henry," she said. "Derrick, babe, I'm so sorry! Let's get you upstairs."

"Huh? No, I'm okay," he said feigning alertness, but he allowed Taylor to easily lead him away.

SIX

TAYLOR HAD BEEN SO busy trying to prove her point about Tappen that she hadn't noticed that Detective Watts had stopped and spoken with Henry on his way out of the Fletcher Mansion. Nor did she see that he and Henry had exited together. But Derrick had. She also hadn't noticed when Derrick checked his phone to find a text message from Henry that said he needed Derrick to get Taylor to make her way upstairs.

And so he used his recent health issue, as well as what he was sure were superb acting skills, to get Taylor to take him to his childhood bedroom. When they got there, Henry was waiting in the hallway and opened the door quickly for them.

Taylor thanked Henry as she helped Derrick to the bed. Henry shut the door behind him.

"I need to speak with you both," he announced once Taylor seemed to have Derrick settled.

Taylor's shoulders dropped in defeat. "Jesus Christ, what now?" she asked, her voice conveying that she was totally ready for another bomb to drop and that she wasn't looking forward to the boom.

Henry held up his hand. "It's okay, it's nothing like earlier," he promised. "I was just speaking to Detective Watts."

"Ugh, that guy is a douche canoe," Taylor moaned.

"Douche canoe?" Derrick asked.

"Yes, a douche canoe."

Derrick nodded. "Douche canoe," he repeated. "I like it."

"Anyway," Henry interjected, "that douche canoe brought some things to my attention."

Derrick took a little pleasure as Taylor shot Henry a dirty look. "Such as?"

"Well he doesn't believe that Tappen was the Gala night shooter, and neither do I," Henry said. "I also don't think the shooting spree he went on today was evidence of rational behavior."

Taylor gave Henry the stink eye. "But we saw the security footage. We saw him taken down," she reminded him.

Henry nodded, "I know we did. He may have physically done that but I agree with your gut, Taylor, that something is off. I have profiled people for years. I have been around Tappen just like you. This is something else."

Derrick looked at Taylor. "Maybe he isn't a total douche canoe."

"Perhaps," Taylor said doubtfully.

"He also worked the scene at Cedric Preston's death and felt that Cedric's death wasn't a simple overdose."

Derrick's mouth dropped open and he turned to his wife. Taylor had taken on a look of panic at the mention of Cedric's name. "Why does he think that?" Taylor whispered.

"He couldn't get into details. He was trying to get out of here before the chief did," Henry explained. "But he mentioned that he had looked into the other Preston cases. He felt like this was not just a run of bad luck but someone working to take out the Prestons."

Derrick watched Taylor pale and struggled himself up and over to her, even though his whole chest hurt. "It's okay, Tay," he said taking her in his arms.

"What are we going to do?" Taylor asked, looking hysterically up at Derrick. "The freaking police feel like this is a closed case," Taylor said shrilly. Derrick pulled her down and sat her on the bed.

"Taylor, Derrick," Henry said calmly, "I'd like the opportunity to look into this case. The police, as you said, are no help to you now. It's too high profile, they just want it dead and buried. I can investigate and look at things that the police can't look into due to legal issues."

"How?" Taylor asked.

Henry was silent for a beat. "Let's just say I have my ways," he answered carefully. "But I would need you to not question how I get my information. Some of my methods may err on the side of less than ethical."

"Illegal?" Derrick asked.

Henry gave a slight shrug in response.

Taylor was taking it all in with a furrowed brow. "Maybe I can talk to Charlie and Todd and see—"

"No," Henry cut in sharply. He crouched down in front of her. "Taylor, if this is truly someone trying to take you down chances are they have inside information. This needs to be kept between the three of us. When you involve too many people, things get missed. If things get missed it leaves opportunity for someone to try and get at you again."

Taylor was quiet for a moment. "And you would find this out?" she asked hopefully. "You think you can find out if someone is trying to come after me? Who hurt Derrick?"

"I am confident I can," Henry said with a nod. "But I won't do it without your permission."

Taylor looked at Derrick, and she thought about how much she wanted to keep him safe. The police were not taking her seriously, so it seemed like being a law-abiding citizen was out. "Okay, Henry," she agreed, "find whatever you can."

Henry nodded. "Okay, a couple of things I want to make you aware of."

"More?" Taylor whined.

"Safety wise I need to keep you all here. The penthouse had an attempted access while you were hospitalized, Derrick. I can not monitor all entry points like I can here. The security team will stay here in the old staff area."

"Old staff area?" Taylor asked in disgust, turning to her husband. "There are staff quarters here?" she asked him.

Derrick shrugged, "I guess so."

"There are," Henry confirmed. "We will be staying onsite."

"This place is way too big," Taylor muttered. "Yes. Okay, Henry."

"And no one leaves without security."

"Yes, absolutely," Taylor agreed.

"Even your sister, Derrick," Henry said. "I was talking with Rog and we have combined the security teams. She is linked to you guys and with all this craziness there is always a chance someone could target her as well."

Derrick mulled it over. "I agree," he finally said, begrudgingly, "but she is going to hate that."

"I'll talk to her," Taylor said.

"And one last thing. I am going to need access to Preston Corp."

"You always have access to Preston Corp," Derrick reminded him.

"No, I need it uninterrupted."

Taylor looked confused. "What do you mean uninterrupted?"

"I need the building empty."

"You want to close Preston Corp?" Derrick asked, completely taken aback. "There is no way," he balked. "That's an insane idea. The stocks will plummet."

"Yeah Henry," Taylor agreed, "I'm not sure—"

"I know that closing is not a good business call," Henry agreed, "and I am not asking for a long time. But I need to get in there, really check out things, without workers in the way. I want

to look at Tappen's office and see if there are any answers to his actions, something the police may have dismissed. Things in plain sight that they would not have looked at because they found someone to pin it on and didn't need a deeper reason than a business vengeance."

Derrick watched Taylor take it all in as she rubbed a finger over her bottom lip. "You've got it. Preston Corp is closed effective immediately and until you tell me otherwise."

Derrick was astounded. "Taylor, what are you going to tell people?"

"We'll say we need to update the security system," she said thinking quickly.

"But wasn't it just updated when Henry took over?" Derrick asked. "Won't that look suspicious?"

Taylor looked thoughtful for a moment. "Maybe," she said finally, "but I think in light of people trying to kill us, twice, double-checking our security won't be that bizarre."

"You've got a point," Derrick said, "but Charlie and Todd are going to flip."

Taylor shrugged at her husband. "Check it out, Henry," she said. "You have access. But Henry?"

"Yes, Taylor?"

"Don't let anyone catch you, okay?"

Henry smirked. "They never do, Taylor."

AFTER HENRY LEFT, Derrick looked over at Taylor. "You trust him?"

"Yes," Taylor answered, but his query made her question her gut instinct for a split second. "You think that I shouldn't?"

Derrick shrugged, "I just am not sure closing Preston Corp is the right call."

"And what call is better?" Taylor asked. "Sitting around and waiting for another onslaught from the actual attacker?"

"I just think you are putting a lot of trust in him," Derrick defended.

"You're right," Taylor agreed. "I am putting a lot of trust in him. He has earned that trust, Derrick. He is the one who got you out of the gala so quickly that you survived. Who got me to the hospital so I could be with you. Who got Marty out of there and home safely. I think that Henry has the right background to get to the bottom of this," Taylor said. "Closing Preston Corp was my call and it is not going to make the world fall apart."

"Totally your call," Derrick agreed. "I just don't like it."

She tilted her head. "Don't like my decision," Taylor asked, "or don't like Henry?"

"Mostly Henry," Derrick clarified.

She rolled her eyes. "Why?"

"Because he totally has the hots for you," Derrick told her like it was the most obvious thing in the world.

Derrick watched Taylor's jaw drop open, and then close and then open again. Finally she shook her head. "You can not be serious."

"Oh, I am totally serious," Derrick said.

"Derrick, I can one hundred percent assure you that Henry does not have the hots for me."

"See, but you thought that I wasn't into you so you aren't exactly great at reading cues," Derrick reminded her.

"Yeah, well be that as it may you are apparently bad at it, too," Taylor quipped and then held up her hands to stop him. "I need to go and update Todd and Charlie about the closure, so no more of this foolish discussion."

"Okay, make sure you protect your ears," Derrick told her as he relaxed back on his pillow.

"Protect them from what?" Taylor asked with her brow furrowed.

"Todd and Charlie's shrieks of protest."

SEVEN

AND SHRIEK THEY DID.

"Taylor, stocks are already down pretty significantly," Charlie said in a voice that said *I am trying not to panic but the struggle is real*.

"I understand that there has been a downtrend, but this is not the most significant drop in all of Preston Corp history."

"No, that was the Great Depression, and that happened when Preston Corp never even shut its doors," Todd remarked in total snark. "You want to shut down just to *check*?" Todd shook his head. "That's bad business."

"I have to agree, Taylor," Charlie said. "Shutting down Preston Corp—"

"Will give me peace of mind and it is not negotiable," Taylor said flatly. "Besides, I am shutting down the main building. That does not mean all work must cease. We can still work remotely behind the scenes," Taylor reminded them.

"Taylor, as the company's advisors—"

"You advise," Taylor said through her teeth. "The decisions of Preston Corp lie ultimately with me. And my decision is that Preston

Corp will shut down the main office and any other facilities needed so that they can be thoroughly and completely evaluated for any threats."

"Taylor, be reasonable," Todd shot back.

"Taylor," Charlie said more gently. "I understand that current events in your life have left you rattled. But those are in the past. The culprit has been found and killed. It is time for you to move forward, show the world that this will not take us down. That we will work hard to persevere. That *you* will work hard to get this company back on its feet."

Taylor pinched the bridge of her nose in order to not lose her mind on the two men before her and took a few deep breaths. In through the nose, out through the mouth, in through the nose, out through the mouth.

Finally she looked up at the two men who were desperately trying to get her to make the "right" decision, in two completely opposite fashions.

"You two need to listen to me very clearly," Taylor said in a flat tone. "Stocks are going to drop and rise no matter what. Preston Corp will have good days and bad days. This is something that we will be faced with forever and I am willing to give my all to fixing that. But I am not willing to put people at risk. And checking to make sure that the proper security measures are in place and in top working order is not something I am willing to be advised against."

"But, Taylor," Todd implored, "the stocks will continue to drop."

"Dammit, people could die!" Taylor exploded. "Do you realize how many new copycat threats have come down through security since the gala shooting, let alone Tappen's attempt? This world is full of attention seekers who hurt people just to say they have! I am not willing to save us from a few drops in the market just because it may look bad."

"Your grandfather would have never shut the—"

"Stop." Taylor cut Charlie off before he could finish his words.

"You stop what you are saying right now." The men before her were so silent that her voice echoed around the large room.

"Taylor, I just—"

"No, you don't *just* anything," she said softly, shaking with rage. "First of all, I will not be told what my grandfather would or would not have done in this situation because my grandfather was never, ever in this situation. So anything you say would be an assumption.

"And my grandfather, may he rest in peace, is not here, gentlemen," Taylor reminded, looking between them. "I am. I have the ultimate say and my final decision is that Preston Corp will be closed so that security measures may be evaluated."

The two men stood quiet for a moment, unmoving and speechless. For a beat, Taylor wondered if it had been too much.

But then Todd quietly asked, "When do you plan on shutting the building down?"

Taylor glanced up to the large wall clock, "About an hour ago." Before either man could pick their jaws up from the floor, she spoke again. "You two may see yourselves out," she announced and left the drawing room.

Taylor felt a fire within her. And she was certain that soon she might explode. She was working her mind overtime trying to save the company, as well as keep her family safe. With every step, and every action, and every anything that she did, she was questioned, advised, and coerced into a direction that was supposed to make everything better.

But nothing really felt better.

So instead, Taylor followed her gut and went back to take care of her husband. Because if there was one thing she could be grateful for in all this hysteria, it was that he was alive and that she was able to tell him she loved him.

DERRICK WAS WIPED OUT, as much as he hated to admit it.

When Taylor came back from issuing the business close order with Todd and Charlie, he could tell she did not want to talk about it and needed a distraction. And Derrick was all too happy to soak up her attention.

Taylor doted on Derrick, ensuring he was comfortable in bed with ibuprofen for his sore chest and lots of pillows. Now Taylor was getting ready to come to bed, with him.

And she loved him.

It felt damn good to hear her say that. It was like she was making up for lost time. She said it before she left the room, when she came back in the room, and just randomly in conversation. Some may have found it annoying, but Derrick found it soothing.

"Okay, you are all settled in," she remarked, coming back into the bedroom from the bathroom. Taylor made her way to the bed and planted a soft kiss on Derrick's lips. "I love you," she whispered when she pulled away.

"I love you, too."

"Are you comfortable?"

"Yes," he said, smiling at her.

"Okay great, I'm going to head to bed."

Derrick reached out and grabbed her hand as she stood. "What do you mean *head to bed?*"

"I'm gonna let you get rest here so I don't disturb you," she explained, tilting her head towards the door. "I'm going to sleep across the hall."

"No," Derrick answered sternly and Taylor flinched a bit. "Taylor, I don't want you to sleep across the hall. I want you here, in bed with me."

"But I don't want to disturb you, and they said you needed rest," she said, her voice full of concern.

"And I can guarantee that I won't get any of it if you are across the damn hall."

"I just want what's best for you, Derrick," Taylor said in exasperation.

"Tay," Derrick said, softening his voice, "when are you going to learn that *you* are what's best for me?"

Taylor's eyes shone. "I just want you safe," she whispered as a tear fell down her cheek.

"Tay," Derrick said again pulling her down to him, "what is it?"

"I almost lost you," she said as she laid one of her hands on his face and looked up at him from his chest.

"But you didn't," Derrick said. "All I wanted was to come home so that I could lie in the same bed as my wife and have the life I have been waiting for forever. So please," Derrick pleaded softly, "please, will you just lie in bed with me?"

And without a second of hesitation Taylor gently lifted the covers and spooned in close to her husband.

TAYLOR LET OUT her first sigh of relief as she slid into bed, an actual bed, with her husband. When he put his warm arm around her and kissed the top of her head Taylor felt the ton of stress she had been carrying lift off her shoulders.

They laid together, both quiet for a bit, when Taylor noticed the nearly hidden tattoo on his chest again. "Hey," she said softly to him as she traced it with her finger. "How come you never..." Her voice drifted off when she looked up and found Derrick fast asleep. His face was relaxed and Taylor was so glad he had persuaded her to stay with him, because she felt more relaxed, too.

Taylor stayed in place watching Derrick sleep for a while, and then her stomach let out a loud gurgle and she realized she couldn't remember the last time she had eaten. So she eased herself from Derrick's side as quickly as she could without waking him and left the room.

Taylor was starving. She had been rushed out of the hospital and into her house, hounded by officers, thrown a curveball by Henry, dealt with her advisors' temper tantrums, and then doted on Derrick.

Nan had made sure that food was sent to them in their room, but Taylor had only been focused on Derrick and so it was cleared away before she ate it, and she was paying for it now. Checking her phone, she noticed it was nearly eleven, way past when Nan may have still been in the kitchen.

And then Taylor rolled her eyes at herself. She was an adult. She didn't need Nan or anyone else to make her food. She was more than capable of making it herself, no matter how exhausted she was.

"Quite the spoiled brat you've become, Taylor," she quietly chastised as she made her way to the state-of-the-art kitchen. She swung through the doors only to send Marty and Henry springing apart from each other.

Immediately all of Taylor's tension returned, full force. Taylor rolled her eyes and looked up to the ceiling. "Really?" she asked the universe. "Now?"

Marty and Henry looked around, as if there was something in the room that could draw Taylor's attention away from the fact that she had just caught her sister-in-law and the head of her security team in a compromising position.

Finally Marty spoke, "Uh. Taylor..."

Taylor held up a hand. "Save it," she said. "To be honest, I am not surprised by this at all and I don't want to hear your lame excuses," she said truthfully.

"It's not what you think," Henry offered, looking nervous and beet red which was a look Taylor had never seen on him. Angry and fire-engine red, yes. Frustrated and ready-to-pop-a-blood-vessel red, lots of times. But never nervous and that hue of red.

"You guys," Taylor said in complete exasperation, "I have had enough of people treating me like I am an idiot. Whatever you all are doing is none of my business and I honest to God don't care. But," she said as she raised a finger and pointed it between the two bad actors before her, "if this is serious then you need to come clean to Derrick, because I will *not* have him upset by this." Her stern voice echoed in the room as she walked past the two whatever they were and walked over to the fridge, where Nan had left a sandwich with her name on it.

Bless that woman, Taylor thought. She was the only one Taylor really liked treating her like a child.

Especially if it involved food.

EIGHT

DERRICK WOKE THE FOLLOWING MORNING, reached for his wife, and a hot poker of pain seared into his chest. He had to lie back in order to catch his breath. The incision sites were definitely tender still. And then he sulked for a bit because he wanted sympathy from Taylor and she wasn't there.

Derrick shifted himself to the side of the bed and found a note, a glass of juice, and some pills.

Derrick- I went to the main dining room to get some work done. I didn't want to wake you. Please take the ibuprofen I left you, it will help with the soreness. I love you, T.

Derrick didn't want to take the pills. He had popped a lot of pills in his life and had tried really hard since then to not even look at anything in tablet form. He took a drink of the juice instead, ignored the medication, and went to the bathroom. On the back of the toilet was another note. *Please take the pills. It will help you heal faster.*

Derrick smirked and walked over to the sink to wash his hands when he was finished. He jumped back when he saw written on his mirror: *GOD DAMN IT DERRICK TAKE THE PILLS!!!*

"Fine, fine," he muttered and went and took the tablets Taylor had left him, but he wasn't happy about it. Once he had choked them down, he went on the hunt for his persistent wife.

Derrick made his way down to the dining room on the main floor, threw the doors open, and then stood frozen as he looked at not only his wife but Charlie, Todd, and about a dozen other Preston Corp employees. Everyone stared back, eyebrows raised, some with their mouths hanging open.

Because Derrick was in just his boxers.

Taylor looked up and her eyebrows joined everyone else's. "Morning babe, are you hot?"

"Well, yeah," Derrick said doing a little turn. "I mean, look at me."

Taylor nodded. "I am glad to see that being shot had no effect on your self-esteem," Taylor said dryly and made her way over to Derrick. "Did you take the pills?" she asked softly as she came up to him and lightly touched around his incisions.

"Well you really didn't leave me much choice, did you?" he said smiling down at her. "What are you doing?" he asked, reaching out and taking some of her hair between his fingers, smoothing it between them.

"I'm working," Taylor said smiling up at him. "I love you," she said and stood up on her toes and kissed him, "even when you show up at my office in your underwear."

"Office?" he said raising his brow. "See, and here I thought this was the dining room."

"Things change," Taylor said. "Go get some rest," she said, tilting her head to the door.

Derrick shook his head, "I don't want to rest," he said, "I want to work."

"Well you can't," Taylor said.

"I can't?" Derrick asked, baffled. He hated being told no. "Says who?" he challenged a little louder.

Taylor's eyes flared at his tone. She turned back to the people behind her. The ones who were all pretending to work and not stare at the showdown between Derrick and Taylor. "Hey everyone," she called out, "I think the breakfast station should be set up by now. Would you all please go and get yourself something? It should be in the foyer," she announced in a saccharin-sweet tone and people scattered.

When the room was clear, Taylor turned back to Derrick. "Says me, Derrick Fletcher, says me."

Derrick felt his jaw stiffen and he moved it side to side to try and loosen it but it didn't help. "Taylor," he started slowly, "I appreciate—"

"The fuck you say that to me, Derrick Simon Allen Fletcher," Taylor retorted. "You what? Huh? You appreciate me worrying about you? Oh, how sweet," she said, fake smiling at him. "You can save that horse shit for someone else. I am your *wife*. I am the one who is supposed to care and worry and demand that you care for yourself. And I will be damned if you are going to try and pat me on the head and send me away like a well-behaved schnauzer."

Derrick rolled his eyes. "Taylor, I am not pushing you off, but I am a grown damn man," Derrick seethed. "I can take care of—"

"No," Taylor said, her voice becoming thicker. "No, we are a team," she said as a tear slid out of her left eye, "and I am not going to let you push yourself past what is healthy."

"Taylor."

"I almost lost you," she choked out, punching her balled fists into her leg as she said the words to him. "I know I sound like a broken record, but god damn it, Derrick, I almost lost you and I was so fucking scared."

Derrick pulled Taylor to him quickly and inhaled the fragrance of her hair. He hated her being so upset. He wanted nothing for her but sunshine and rainbows and it seemed like all she was getting was gunshots and nightmares. He felt her shake against him for a second before she pulled back, putting her hands on either side of his face. "I almost lost you and I would have never been able to tell you that I loved you. That I do love you. That I have always loved you. That I will love you each day for the rest of my life with every fiber of my being.

"I get it now," she went on, intently staring into his chocolate gaze. "I get all those times you didn't want me to go out or do something. All the times you worked and begged to keep me safe. I get the fear and the pain it caused. The constant worry. I get it because I feel it now," she pleaded with a sob.

"I'm sorry, Taylor," Derrick murmured, as he wiped the tears from her cheeks.

"You can't be sorry, Derrick. You saved my life," she said. "I love you so much," she choked out again as another series of tears came sliding down her cheek. "Now please, let me take care of you."

Derrick felt his heart strings pull as Taylor asked to care for him. He had been yearning for the day when Taylor would tell him these things. He was surprised by how it wasn't as much fun as he thought it would be, mostly since she was telling him no. Again.

But he did accept defeat.

"Okay," he agreed, "I will take it easy."

"Thank you," Taylor said, wiping her eyes. "And I promise that I won't work here all day. I just wanted to get a few things settled," she explained.

"It's okay," he said, "I'm just being a grouch."

"Well, maybe you need some more rest," Taylor said taking his hand. "Let's get you back to bed."

As much as he hated to admit it, Derrick did feel tired. He wasn't used to it. He would have gladly pushed through to do something productive, but right that minute a nap did not sound like such a bad idea. His discomfort had subsided. And so he grumbled his agreement and followed Taylor to their room.

She opened the door and motioned him inside and Derrick could feel the weariness slowing him even more. He was likely more relaxed since taking the Motrin for his discomfort and he could truly rest now. Fatigue set in as he walked towards the bed and climbed in.

But when he turned back to Taylor, he saw she was completely nude.

And suddenly he was wide awake. "Uh, what are you up to?"

"Well, I thought maybe I could put you in a better mood," she offered, sauntering to the bed.

Derrick felt himself instantly harden under the blankets, and he went to move, but Taylor pushed him back down gently from the side of the bed. "No, no," she said, "you need to just relax," she said. "Doctor's orders." Taylor crawled up on the bed, straddled Derrick, and leaned over and kissed him.

Derrick shoved his fingers into Taylor's hair and pulled her face closer to him, sliding his tongue through Taylor's lips and groaning at the contact. It had been way too long since Derrick had been able to kiss her like this. He was starving for her.

Taylor broke the kiss and Derrick made a noise of frustration until he felt her lips on his neck. She slowly skimmed them down his body, laying soft kisses on his wounds, all the way down to the waistband of his boxers. Taylor kissed above it and then she slowly eased the band of his Calvins down with one finger, her lips right behind it.

Derrick moved to pull his shorts out of the way of the path of her amazing mouth and Taylor slapped his hands away. "Just relax," she instructed softly.

"Babe, I can *not* relax with your lips that close to my cock," Derrick groaned out as his breath hastened in anticipation.

Taylor looked at him with a thoughtful expression. "Well then, maybe I should stop," she threatened, moving back slowly, releasing the band of his boxers and allowing them to snap back.

"No!" Derrick shouted, throwing his hands up in defeat and then laying them on the bed and laying stock still. "I'll be good, I promise."

Taylor smiled at her success and then slid her fingers back beneath the waistband and slowly tugged his shorts down over his hips. Derrick did move up slightly only to help them be removed, and she allowed that.

Once his boxers were out of the way Derrick's cock sprung,

firm and ready. Taylor wasted no time, put her lips over him, then took his length in her mouth. Though Taylor's mouth was hot, shivers swept through Derrick's body. His breaths started to come faster as she moved her mouth up and down his hard shaft. The friction she created made Derrick's chest tighten a bit in discomfort, but he could easily ignore that. With the way Taylor was making him feel, he could have ignored a bomb going off beside him.

Derrick thread his fingers into Taylor's hair, desperate to feel her, to touch her. Taylor looked up at him from where she was and the sight of her, looking at him, his cock in her mouth and all the sensations tingling through his limbs was about to set Derrick off. But he didn't want it to be over yet.

When she hollowed out her cheeks and created suction as she moved her mouth over his straining rod, Derrick was sure he saw stars.

"Tay, please," he choked out, "I need you. I need to be inside you." Taylor complied, moving herself up and then positioning her ready core over Derrick's mouth-moistened cock.

As Taylor slid down onto Derrick's hard length, they both groaned. He needed this. He needed her, and apparently she needed him, too. But he needed more, needed to be closer. He sat up, even though it hurt, and slid his hands up her body. He pulled her to his chest as she moved over him, pushing through the burning at his surgical sites because not being closer to her would cause him even more pain. And despite her earlier warning to not move, Taylor didn't stop him and instead slid her arms around him.

He kissed her neck. "I love you, Taylor Preston-Fletcher. No one has ever made me feel the euphoria you make me feel," he whispered in her ear. At his words, he felt Taylor shudder against him.

"I love you, too," she gasped out as she came, her orgasm quaking her core, milking Derrick's cock as it shook through her, and he followed right behind her.

"You know," Derrick said moments later, the two of them still joined, "a shower would really, really help me rest at my optimal rest-ability."

"Oh, yeah?" Taylor asked, smiling at him.

"Mmmhmmm," Derrick assured her, "and I will need assistance because, you know, I am fragile and healing and all."

Taylor raised her brows at him. "Derrick, I have work to do."

"Yeah, but won't you be able to focus better on work knowing that I am cleaned and settled into bed?"

Taylor rolled her eyes, "You are good at this manipulation thing, you know that?"

"It is a skill that has done me well in life," Derrick admitted.

Taylor got herself to her feet, "Okay Mr. Fletcher, come with me, it is time for your sponge bath."

A smile spread wide over Derrick's face. "Anything you say, Mrs. Preston-Fletcher."

NINE

TAYLOR HAD MANAGED to find a sort of routine in the days that followed, and it all helped to keep her mind off of the turmoil that still hung around at the edges of her mind. She worked with the Preston Corp and Fletcher Enterprises staff during the day in the Fletcher mansion's main dining room turned office. Throughout her workday, she would take breaks and check in on Derrick, who was working with physical therapists to stay strong and being evaluated nightly by his surgeon and primary care physician, both of whom were overjoyed with his progress.

Forty-eight hours after agreeing to shut down all Preston Corp facilities for the "emergency security review," Henry came to Taylor in the makeshift Preston and Fletcher command center.

"Mrs. Preston-Fletcher, I have an updated security report for you about Preston Corp," he told her formally.

"Does that mean the security is all set now, Henry?" Todd asked, "because we really need to—"

"The determination of whether or not security is sufficient lies with Mrs. Preston-Fletcher," Henry answered bluntly and Todd glared back at the hulking man.

"Of course, please tell us your findings," Charlie said, sitting back expectantly.

"If you two will excuse us," Taylor said, and was met with shock from both Todd and Charlie at their dismissal. But Taylor just waited, and finally the two men awkwardly excused themselves from the room.

Once the door was shut, Henry took out his phone, swiping and tapping until static white noise came out. Taylor raised an eyebrow at the action, and Henry only shrugged. "You can never be too safe," he remarked. "I think you should have Derrick come here for this, also."

"Why? Is it something that involves Fletcher Enterprises? Or is someone coming after him?"

"No, it's none of those things," Henry said, his tone attempting nonchalance. "I, uh, I need, well I would like if he, uh Derrick, I mean Mr. Fletcher to trust me," he stuttered out.

Taylor furrowed her brow. "Trust you? Henry, I am sure he does. Why are you so—Oh!" she said as realization hit. Henry needed Derrick to like him in some way, somehow, because without that he wouldn't ever trust him with Marty. "I got it," she said nodding, "but let me just say one thing."

"I won't say anything to upset Derrick," Henry promised before Taylor could demand it from him.

"Oh, I know you won't, but this isn't about him. If you break Marty's heart, I will take you out, Henry. Maybe not physically, but you wouldn't believe the things money can make happen," Taylor warned.

Henry nodded slowly, "Understood."

Taylor looked him up and down for a minute and reached for her phone but then stopped her hand in midair. She cocked her head to the side and looked thoughtfully at Henry.

"Tell me Henry, was there really an issue with our penthouse? Was there truly a reason that Derrick and I couldn't be there?"

Henry cleared his throat. "There were attempts to access the building while you were not there," Henry confirmed.

"Something you couldn't handle?" Taylor questioned him.

"Well, I felt that being able to monitor all the access points and having full checks on everyone that could enter and exit was vital to keeping you safe," Henry said stoically.

Taylor pursed her lips. "No other reason?" she asked.

Henry took in and released a big breath. "I need to keep her safe, Taylor," he said quietly. "If I wasn't here, and something happened..." He shook his head, unable to finish his thought.

Taylor nodded, and it made him feel a little warmer. "I got it," she said, and called Derrick to join them.

DERRICK EXITED his room in his pajama pants and a T-shirt this time. He didn't want to be showing off his Calvins again, no matter how good he looked in them.

He made his way down the back stairs and found Charlie and Todd looking completely confused and sitting in some random chairs down the hall from the dining room.

"What are you two up to?" Derrick asked.

"Oh Derrick, how are you feeling, son?" Charlie asked, smiling and standing when he saw Derrick making his way.

"Better every day," Derrick said, shaking the older man's hand, but the son comment burned more than his incisions ever did. "How come you two are out here?"

"Taylor asked us to step out while Henry reviewed his security findings," Todd informed in a tone laced with agitation.

"Oh yeah, and they are in there?" Derrick asked, watching as each man nodded to him.

"Yes, I am not sure how long they will be, Derrick. Would you like us to let Taylor know you were looking for her?" Charlie asked.

"No thanks, Charlie, I'll tell her myself since she asked for me in there," Derrick replied and walked away from the pair before he needed to answer any questions.

He heard a phone chime behind him, and then Charlie said, "Taylor said we are done for the day. She will update us later on Preston Corp's reopening," to Todd in complete astonishment.

"You have got to be fucking kidding me," Todd growled as Derrick opened the door to Taylor's makeshift office.

Derrick closed the advisors' voices out and found Taylor waiting at the table while Henry stood. Derrick made his way over to Taylor and leaned to kiss her. "You rang?" he said dryly, unable to cover his wince as he bent over.

"Are you okay?" Taylor asked him softly as he straightened.

He shrugged. "Tay, I was shot. It's sore," he replied impassively, like getting shot was as common as stubbing one's toe. He turned to Henry, "You wanted to talk to us, I heard?"

"Yes, I wanted to go over what I have been able to find out," Henry told him, his eyes darting back and forth between Derrick and Taylor. "First up, Preston Corp. I went through Tappen's office with a fine-toothed comb but saw nothing out of the ordinary."

"Well, thank God we had a private meeting for that," Derrick said sarcastically and Taylor shot him a glare.

"But I lifted fingerprints and swabbed his desk, checking for anything, for any kind of substances that may have caused his erratic behavior. I'm awaiting those results," Henry explained. "While I was there I ran a comprehensive check of the security system for Preston Corp and it is all in working order."

"Was there a chance that it wouldn't have been?" Derrick asked.

"I had to be sure, Mr. Fletcher," Henry said. "I am having Tappen tracked on the camera footage as well to try and find any pattern in his behavior."

"Okay, sounds like a plan," Taylor said. "Now the million-dollar question, Henry."

"Yes, I am done with Preston Corp. It can be reopened and your advisors can stop breathing down everyone's neck."

"Thank you," Taylor said, relief evident in her tone. She quickly grabbed her phone and sent off a fast text. "Todd and Charlie will be positively giddy to get things back to normal."

"There is one other thing," Henry said. "I have been analyzing the security camera footage from the Gala. I have been looking to see who was at the event or in the crowd the night of the event."

"We had security cameras there that night?"

"No," Henry said, "these are surveillance cameras the city and businesses have installed."

"And how exactly did you get access to private camera footage?" Taylor questioned.

"I am going to refer to our *don't ask, don't tell* clause," Henry reminded her. "Anyway, I was looking at anyone who may have disappeared and reappeared and basically acted shifty." He dropped four photographs onto the table. "This guy is the one that concerned me the most."

Derrick picked up one of the grainy black and whites. He pulled the picture close then he held it out. He dropped the first one and picked up another, repeating the same procedure he had with the first, and shook his head. "He doesn't look familiar—"

Taylor's sharp inhale was loud enough that it stopped Derrick mid sentence. "It's Ben," Taylor said, mouth hanging open. She looked at another picture and nodded her head. "It's totally Ben."

A cold chill went down Derrick's back. How could it be possible that the fucking bearded beatnik was popping back into his life again?

"What?" he asked, shaking his head in disbelief. "No way, he had a beard, and this guy—"

He was silenced by Taylor's look of annoyance.

"Are you really freaking throwing out my judgment that it's him because the guy in the picture doesn't have a beard? For real? Like a completely and totally, easily removable facial hair choice? That is your only rebuttal for it not being him?"

Okay, so it sounded stupid when she said it like that, but he was desperate.

"Who is Ben?" Henry asked, watching the ping-pong match of their conversation with his eyes. He had been so quiet Derrick had forgotten he was in the room.

"He's someone I knew once," Taylor replied quietly.

"Knew in what way?" Henry asked seriously.

"Uh," was all Taylor could say.

"He's nobody," Derrick brushed off, irritated that this guy was still being talked about.

"Derrick, he isn't nobody," Taylor corrected, "and I am positive that this is him." She flapped the picture in his direction.

"How did you know him?" Henry questioned, his tension apparent now as he attempted to get answers.

"I worked with him," Taylor responded, just as tensely, her glare still pinning Derrick.

"At Preston Corp?"

Derrick and Taylor both looked at Henry then back at each other wearing matching *oh shit, what now* expressions. Derrick wondered how she would explain this.

Henry inhaled sharply. "I want to find whoever gunned you down," he snapped out each word, "but it is difficult when you only give me pieces of information."

Taylor heaved out a heavy sigh. "I worked with him at a coffee shop in Maine," she rambled out quickly.

Henry's facial expression didn't change, he just remained stone-faced. And the silence stretched between them.

Derrick knew what Henry was doing. He was trying to let the silence bother Taylor into saying more. But Taylor was the queen of letting silence stretch, and she wouldn't break.

"You worked in a coffee shop," Henry finally stated, disbelief lacing his tone.

"Yes," Taylor replied, nodding.

Henry continued to stare at her, absorbing this information. "Taylor Preston worked in a coffee shop in Maine?" he asked.

Taylor scrunched up her face. "Sort of?" she responded in question form.

Henry's face started to turn red from frustration, and Taylor was worried he would blow. And so, before it was *clean up in aisle seven*, she let it out.

"I-ran-away-from-my-crazy-uncle-and-lived-under-an-alias-with-a-disguise-and-I-worked-in-a-coffee-shop-and-that's-where-I-met-Ben," she rambled out all in one breath.

Henry looked less red, but his expression did not change as he took a second to digest the news that had just been spewed at him machine-gun style.

"Okay, and this Ben, he was a co-worker?"

"Yes," Taylor said easily,

Henry cocked his head, "*Only* a co-worker?"

Taylor flicked a look to Derrick, then looked at the floor. "We were friends, but there was a, uh, a mutual interest."

"Did you two have a relationship?" Henry prodded.

"Nothing serious," Taylor quickly confirmed, and then added, "we did kiss."

"What?!" Derrick exploded, unable to keep his emotions inside any longer.

"What do you mean *what*?" Taylor exploded back.

"You kissed him?" he asked, absolutely flabbergasted. "When?"

"Ten minutes after we got married, Derrick," she shot back with angry sarcasm. "It was before I came back. Before us."

"How long ago was your interaction?" Henry interjected delicately.

"What, like four, five months ago?" Taylor said, trying to do the math.

"Haven't you two been together for two years?"

Whoops.

"Uh," Taylor and Derrick said in unison.

Henry pinched the bridge of his nose, closing his eyes. "Listen—"

"So basically that was all a lie," Taylor admitted before Henry could lose his temper again. "I ran away. After about three years, I found the town in Maine and worked at the coffee shop. I worked there about a year and a half when Ben started there. I was brought back here about four months ago and our "together" story has been fabricated."

"How fabricated?"

"Like *I was abducted after Cedric was found dead, I came back and found out I had to be married to run the company, and so we got instantly engaged* fabricated."

Henry nodded solemnly, as if none of this was friggin bizarre.

"What's Ben's last name?"

"Watson," Taylor answered.

"Okay, I'm going to look into this Ben Watson. I'll start looking for info on him in Chadumor." Henry said, gathering the photos.

"Okay," Taylor said, nodding her head, and then suddenly she shook it as if clearing her thoughts. "Wait a minute! How did you know the name of the town?"

"Because I already knew you had run away and worked at a coffee shop called the Roasted Bean in Chadumor, Maine under the alias Libby Sawyer," Henry said, grabbing all the photos and shuffling them straight. "I just needed you to tell me. I want our communication open."

"How the hell did you—"

"I worked in special ops, Taylor," Henry answered flatly. "I wasn't going to work for someone who suddenly returned unless I knew the back story. I just didn't think it would need to come out."

"You aren't going to tell anyone..."

"Absolutely not. That is your business. Besides, I have signed a legally binding non-disclosure agreement," Henry said and left the room.

Taylor and Derrick watched Henry leave, speechless.

"That guy is crazy sneaky," Taylor said, shaking her head.

"Yeah, I wonder what other kind of secrets he has," Derrick

mused out loud. "So, how did you see him?" Derrick asked once Henry had clicked the door shut behind him.

"What do you mean?" Taylor asked.

"Ben," Derrick said to her, even hating forming the name in his mouth. When Taylor didn't elaborate, he went on. "How did you look at those grainy photos and finger that guy for Ben?"

"I don't know, he just kind of stood out to me," Taylor said, then looked at her husband. "Wait, are you mad?" she asked, completely baffled.

"No, I just don't get it," Derrick said in complete irritation.

"Get what?" Taylor matched his irritated tone.

"How did you see him and never see me?"

Taylor's mouth hung open in confusion as she tried to figure out what it was Derrick was trying to say.

But she couldn't.

"What the hell are you saying?" she demanded stamping her foot for emphasis.

"I went into that damned coffee shop once a month for almost a year, Taylor!" Derrick exploded. "And not once did you have even a flicker of recognition, a moment of *could it be*. But you look for three seconds at this," waving one of the enlarged security shots he still had in his hand with Ben's face on it "and you are like, yup, it's Ben, no doubt."

"So let me just understand," Taylor said calmly. "You are mad because I recognized Ben in this photo?"

"I'm not mad," Derrick said shaking his head, his jawline visibly tight.

"Oh no, of course not, my mistake," Taylor said. "You flip out when you are calm all the damn time!" she shouted.

"Did you love him?"

"Derrick." Taylor said rubbing her face in frustration and hiding her eye rolling all in one action.

"I'm serious, Tay," Derrick said looking at her. "Did you love him?"

"No," Taylor finally bit out. "I didn't love him, okay?"

"But you liked him?"

"Derrick, why are you doing this? He is the past. Henry gave me a picture with one person he was looking at and asked us if we knew who he was, so I looked at this picture and thought about all the people I have ever met and saw him."

"But you never saw me," Derrick said softly.

"I wasn't looking for you, Derrick," Taylor explained in strained tones.

Derrick gave one quick humorless laugh. "Tell me about it."

Taylor felt her blood boil. "Derrick, I am not going to fight with you about this." She spun on her heel to walk from the room but Derrick snaked out his arm and grabbed her.

"How many times?" he asked hoarsely.

Taylor shook her head in confusion. "How many times what?"

"How many times did you kiss him?"

Taylor's face morphed from confusion into anger. "How many other women did you screw before me?" she asked in irritation and yanked her arm from him as she stomped quickly from the room.

SHE WASN'T ENTIRELY sure where she was going, she just knew she had to get as much space away from Derrick as possible. When she stopped, she found herself on the back patio of the mansion. The cool slate under her feet and the chilly air in her nostrils helped calm the burning inferno of rage that had settled within her.

Taylor leaned against the patio's railing, braced herself with her palms against the stone, and looked out over the shrubs and shadows before her.

As Taylor allowed her body to cool down from the heat of her anger, her mind started to clear. And now, standing in the dusk of the California sunset and separated from their heated debate, she understood why Derrick was mad.

He probably went to the coffee shop and stared her down while she worked and Taylor didn't notice a thing. Thinking about it now she wondered how she *had* missed him, but it was true what she said. She honestly had not been looking for him. If there was one person that she had been certain would never attempt to find her, it was Derrick Fletcher.

But if she was really honest with herself, Derrick was the only person she had ever wanted to find her, the only one she ever wanted to see her. But he hadn't. While she had been right in front of him, he had ignored her and toyed with her. She had been brokenhearted. And being rejected made you do stupid things like try to find a replacement for the one your heart wanted.

But Taylor realized that love made you do stupid things, too. Like wonder if your wife, who was abducted after being gone for a long time and then married you under some pretty tense circumstances, really did love you. Or if the guy who was in her life immediately before you suddenly reappeared, would it make her realize that she wanted to be with him and not you? It hit Taylor that her not ever having noticed him when he came to see her in the coffee shop just magnified his fears.

Taylor's life had turned into a chaotic season of a soap opera in just a few months and the worst part was it was all making sense to her. And she realized she needed to make the move to the next scene. The make up scene.

Taylor turned away from the backyard to make her way back into the house only to find her husband leaning on the doorway to the patio.

"I was trying to tell if it was a good time to apologize or if you were still pissed," he said soberly.

"Derrick, you don't—"

"You know how you keep saying you almost lost me?" he interrupted as he made his way to her. "That is exactly how I feel every time I see you. I am so happy you are here and you are mine and I just want to hold you because I almost lost you, Taylor. And sometimes, I am still not sure I am who you want."

"You are, Derrick," Taylor said going over to him. "I am where I want to be." Her voice begged for him to believe her.

"I know that my past is horrific," he said, "but there is no place I wanted to be other than with you, even when I knew I wasn't good for you. And as amazing as I know that I am in a lot of ways, I still need reassurance that you want me." He swallowed back emotions Taylor could see bubbling up. "I need it a lot because I want this to be real for both of us." He gently took a lock of her blonde strands and smoothed them between his fingers.

"I don't want him, Derrick. I wanted you to see me, and you did a great job convincing me that you didn't want me that way. I was trying to hide. I made it a habit my whole life to ignore people staring at me. I especially avoided attention while I was hiding out. I never thought you would be there looking for me, so I didn't see you."

Derrick nodded. "I know," he said coming closer. "But I love you," he whispered, "and I want you to see only me now."

"Well, you're awfully close so I don't really have a choice," Taylor replied with a smirk.

Derrick rolled his eyes, "Hardee-har-har. One other thing, Tay. I need to work," he said seriously. "All this resting and recovering is leaving me with idle time. I need to keep busy."

"You are busy," she defended. "You have physical therapy, and—"

"Please, Tay," he pleaded. "I can still do all of that. I don't want to go back to the office or anything, but I need to do something, anything, to get my life back to normal."

Taylor felt for him. She completely appreciated wanting to bring normalcy back into their life. "Okay, I get it," she agreed, "you have my blessing." Taylor leaned in lightly, putting her lips to his. "I love you, Derrick Fletcher. No one can replace you in my heart, ever," she said closing in and kissing him deeper.

Derrick returned the kiss, but abruptly pulled back with a gleam in his eyes. "Know what I've always wanted to do?" he asked Taylor mischievously.

"I'm not sure I want to know," Taylor remarked, confused about the sudden change in their conversation.

"I want to play strip tag in the hedge garden," he said wickedly, nodding his head to the sculpted shrubbery behind her and wiggling his eyebrows.

Taylor's face scrunched up revealing her thoughts before she could say a word. "You are out of your damn mind," she said.

"Tay, I took a bullet for you," he reminded her with his brow raised.

"I don't care! I am not running around naked in your family's hedge garden," Taylor whisper yelled at him. "It's cold and Henry has freaking cameras everywhere. And besides, this place reminds me of when we were kids and that does not equal sexy to me."

"Well then, can we go back to the bedroom and have sexy time there?" he asked.

Taylor evaluated her husband for a moment. "I feel like you made up the strip tag thing so that I would say yes to sex right now."

Derrick shrugged, "Possibly."

"What purpose did it serve exactly?"

A small smile spread across Derrick's face, his dimple popping out in full force. "You're thinking about sex now," he said pointing a finger at her.

And indeed she was.

"First one naked is on top," she whispered then kissed his lips and took off running, leaving a still-sore Derrick calling behind her as he hobbled forward.

TEN

THE NEXT MORNING Taylor sipped her coffee and smiled as she looked over at her husband peering intently at his laptop, then returned her attention to her own screen. They had moved out of the dining room and were now in the first-floor office in the mansion. It was a much smaller space than the dining room command post she had been working in, but it was infinitely better.

Preston Corp was now open, but Taylor had opted to continue working at home for a few more days. This made for an easier security transition while Todd and Charlie got things up and running at the office, and allowed her to keep an eye on her husband, easing her mind about him overdoing it. She also wanted Derrick to rest up before going back to his office and the only way that was going to happen was if she stayed in the mansion with him and made sure he continued his physical therapy. In order to get Derrick to agree she promised him lots of sex since they were home, but that just seemed like a win-win to Taylor.

Taylor combed through a contract for flooring, ensuring the changes she had requested had been made. She was lost in business jargon when Henry came in and tossed some papers in front of her.

Taylor kept her head bent and flicked her gaze up to Henry as she picked up the papers. "What is this?"

"That is the autopsy of Cedric Preston that was released a couple of months ago."

Taylor stayed frozen, her eyes trained on Henry, and picked up the pages and shook them at him. "Henry, I've read this."

"Aye," he answered, his brogue coming through strong and his eyes lit up like a kid on Christmas morning, "but you haven't read this one." He threw down another stack of papers. The large, normally serious man seemed a little giddy, and, to be honest, a little ridiculous.

Taylor grabbed the new set with her other hand, "And these are?"

"That." Henry said pointing to the newest papers, "is the original report written about the actual autopsy."

Taylor sat back, frowning at Henry, and shot Derrick a confused look before she started shuffling through the new set he had given her. "What do you mean the original autopsy?"

"I mean that this is the report of what actually happened," he explained pointing to the documents in Taylor's hands, "and this was the report that was released to the world." Henry pointed to the opposite stack of papers.

"How is that possible?" Derrick asked, gingerly moving from his chair to come and look at the papers. Taylor knew he was pushing himself in physical therapy so they would discharge him. And watching how slowly he moved did not make her happy with his progress.

"I had someone close to the investigation provide me with these," Henry informed them. "After I read them, I did some investigating. I found out that Dr. Parker, who wrote both of these reports, was hooked up with an offshore account the same day these were written. Soon after, he paid off his two daughters' college education."

Taylor raised her brows, "Uh, Henry, how—"

"Remember when I said there were things you weren't going to want to know how I got? This is one of those things, Taylor."

"Ah, okay," Taylor said and she looked down and started reading the papers. "Wait, this one says blunt trauma. I thought it was an overdose. Doesn't blunt trauma mean he was struck?"

"It says on both of these that the toxicology is the same," Derrick said as he looked over her shoulder at the documents, "and that it is most likely the ultimate cause of death. But in the original it states that the trauma is premortem."

"Premortem? Like before he died," Taylor asked looking up to Henry, who nodded. "So maybe he got high and hit his head?" she murmured.

"Maybe," Henry agreed, "but Cedric was found leaned back on a couch. That much is in both reports. And from what I have read there was no blood on that couch. And, there is this," he said pointing to a paragraph on the original report.

The lower second molar was missing; due to the minimal amount of blood it appears to have been removed postmortem.

"Removed postmortem? Does that mean..." Taylor asked without finishing the question.

"Someone removed his tooth," Henry nodded, "after he was dead. Therefore, he was not alone."

Taylor looked at Henry and then at Derrick. "I feel like the deeper we dig the more questions I have."

"That is generally the way things unfold," Henry assured her, "and then suddenly they all start fitting together."

"If they could start fitting together now that would be great," Taylor muttered.

"Where do we go from here, Henry?" Derrick asked.

"We go talk with Dr. Parker."

ELEVEN

BEING NEARLY eight in the evening, the Los Angeles County Medical Examiner-Coroner's office was quiet, no office chatter or hustle in and out. But Dr. Greg Parker, or Parker as everyone called him, was in his office, as he was every evening until about ten o'clock. Henry had discovered this routine of his through some research.

And that was exactly where Taylor found the good doctor as she peered through the small window in his office door. He was bent forward, looking closely at his computer screen, squinting most likely in order to see the words easier.

Taylor stepped away from the window and knocked. "Come in," Parker called, his tone muffled through the door. Taylor opened it slowly and peeked around the open door hesitantly. The man before her just stared at her, his eyes widening as he seemed to realize who she was.

Or maybe she was in the wrong room.

"Dr. Parker?" she asked as she made her way a little further into the room.

Parker blinked a few times, then he squinted at Taylor, and finally he spoke.

"Taylor Preston," Parker said in bewilderment, rising to his feet to greet his surprise guest. "I've seen you so much in the news lately, I was having a hard time believing I wasn't imagining you," he explained.

"Hello," Taylor said, smiling as she made her way further inside, shutting the door behind her. "It's actually Taylor Preston-Fletcher," she corrected.

"Oh, of course," Parker said, looking flustered and more than a little starstruck. "Please, have a seat," he said gesturing to the seats across from him. "What brings you by here today?" he asked like he was a jewelry store clerk and not a fully accredited doctor.

"Thank you," Taylor said sitting herself in front of Parker's desk. "I was hoping you could help me, Dr. Parker." Taylor explained, giving him a look Derrick had called her damsel-in-distress look. He said when she gave it to people they tripped over themselves to help her, and so she was testing it out now. And it seemed to work.

"I am not sure how, but I certainly will try," Parker answered quickly, seeming very eager to help in any way.

"That would be wonderful, thank you," Taylor said, smiling at him sincerely before she opened her handbag and retrieved some papers. "I was looking at my uncle's autopsy report," she said, taking the report and placing it on the desk, "and I had some questions."

"Cedric Preston," Parker said, nodding, retrieving the papers. "Well, with the amount of drugs that were in his system that was a pretty cut-and-dried autopsy. It just wasn't possible for anyone to survive," he stated and slid the papers back to Taylor.

Taylor nodded, "Yes, I suppose not." Taylor flipped through the report and then slid it back across the desktop to him. "So the trauma to his head was in no way a potential cause?"

Sweat broke out over Parker's brow. "Uh, what...what trauma?"

Taylor reached into her bag again and pulled out another set of papers. "See, I was comparing the report released to the public to this report, which is time stamped before that one. And in this earlier one," she said as she tapped the papers she had slid his way, "you stated there was trauma to the back of Cedric's head. A good deal of trauma, too," Taylor said, turning the pages and running her finger down the words. "It says, and I quote 'a large blunt trauma to the posterior occipital region'," she said looking up calmly. "So Dr. Parker, I wanted to know what the fuck it was all about," she explained and sat back in the chair, awaiting explanation.

Parker swallowed and Taylor watched the pulse bounce quickly in his throat. "I'm not sure—"

"Dr. Parker, let's cut the bullshit," Taylor said, standing and slapping her palms on his desk. "I want to know the truth. I want to know what you found on Cedric Preston's body. I want to know why you wrote two autopsy reports. And I want to know right now," she demanded, enunciating the last two words by slapping her hands on his desk.

Taylor watched as Parker slid a hand down the leg of his khakis.

Taylor leaned forward. "The panic button you are slyly reaching for has been disconnected," she informed him.

Parker leaned back slowly and cleared his throat, "Ms. Preston—"

"Mrs. Preston-Fletcher," she corrected.

"Yes, well I really have no idea where you got this but I assure you the report that was published is the actual one."

"No, it isn't. And I have the Medical Board of California on speed dial and I am sure they would loooove to hear about these," Taylor said, pointing to the papers on his desk. "And lest you think this is the only copy in existence, you'd be dead wrong."

"Y-You can't do that," Parker said, his voice several octaves higher than before, "it's slander."

"I have a lot of lawyers, Dr. Parker," Taylor informed him, "and I have a lot of money. And speaking of money, you were paid a lot of money and it went into an offshore account the day after my uncle died, the day these reports were written, actually. So why don't you start telling me the facts and I won't ruin your entire life."

Parker picked up the original report from his desk and began flipping through its pages, "I thought I had deleted it. I thought this was gone."

"Dr. Parker," Taylor chided, "as a very well-educated man you should already know that nothing is ever truly gone."

He nodded. "This is what I found," he said, sliding the original report back towards Taylor.

"So I assumed," Taylor remarked dryly. "How did he die?"

Parker took several deep breaths and wiped his brow. "He really did have a critical amount of drugs within his body," he said.

"So the trauma, it had no bearing at all?" Taylor asked calmly.

"The trauma definitely would have knocked him out," Parker said confidently, "but it would not have killed him."

"Do you think he could have struck his head after he took all the drugs?" Taylor questioned.

Parker shook his head, then shrugged. "I guess it is possible, but the shape of the trauma to his head seemed to me more likely caused from being struck by an object," he explained, reaching his hand up and behind his own head to demonstrate. "The impact appeared to come down from the top instead of from him falling down onto something." The doctor hesitated for a second. "Also, he wasn't found on the ground or anywhere that would indicate a fall."

"I understand he was found upright per your reports."

"Yes," Parker confirmed, "when I arrived at the scene he was in a seated position on a couch, a needle in his arm."

"So is it possible he struck his head and then overdosed?"

"The amount of trauma to the head, I very much doubt that Mr. Preston was even conscious after he sustained it, therefore injecting a lethal amount of drugs into a vein in his arm would have been out of the question."

"And you are sure that Cedric was alive when he was hit in the head?"

Parker nodded his head, "It was definitely premortem," he said.

"But there was no blood," Taylor said.

"I believe his body was moved from the actual scene."

"Are you telling me that Cedric Preston was murdered?" Taylor asked bluntly.

"Let me just say that I ran tests on Cedric Preston's hair follicles for drugs, which gives me the past three months' drug use prior to his death. You know what I found? Nothing. He was clean. The only drugs that Cedric had taken in the months before his death were the ones in his system when he died. And as I said, based on that head injury, I seriously doubt he would have had the coordination to administer the dose."

Taylor absorbed the information.

"All this evidence of foul play, Dr. Parker. Now tell me, why did you write a new report?"

Parker looked down at his desk and picked up a random paper-clip, flipping it around in his fingers. "I was paid a lot of money to write that report," he told Taylor, his gaze still averted.

"So someone waves money at you and you go against the code of ethics you swore to uphold as a doctor?" she questioned darkly.

"They also asked me to do this to help someone, someone who, if questionable circumstances surrounding Cedric Preston's death were made public, would be at a disadvantage. Someone who would struggle and fail and be publicly strung up because of it."

"And who was that?"

"You, Mrs. Preston-Fletcher," Parker said looking up at her now. "I was asked to change the report for you."

Taylor remained still, and waited.

"See I am not the beast you want to believe me to be. I am offered money a lot. You wouldn't believe how many countries I could buy if I accepted all the bribes that came my way," he said. "But I do this job to be the voice for those whose voice was taken too soon. So I said no when I was asked to change this report. I said it was for the police to sort out. But when your name was brought into it, when they said that you now had to take over this mess and try to salvage it, I felt bad for you," he said, his voice full of pity, something Taylor wasn't expecting. "I have two daughters, just a little younger than you, Mrs.

Preston-Fletcher, and I would do anything to make things easier for them. So I agreed, and I refused the money. But the next day my daughters' tuition and my mortgage were paid in full, and I had an offshore account in my name. I didn't ask for any of that."

Taylor maintained her deadpan expression. "And who would ask you to do that and pay you for it?"

"It was a man. I never met him. There were just phone calls. I could never trace the number. He only identified himself as a Preston Corp representative."

TAYLOR WALKED out of Dr. Parker's office to a side door that led outside and leaned against the side of the brick building to catch her breath.

When Henry had told her she needed to go in and basically threaten Dr. Parker into giving her information, Taylor had felt sick. She had turned to Derrick for support, for him to find this just as crazy an idea as she did, and instead he had agreed with Henry and she was certain she was in a nightmare.

"If we go in with you, Tay, he is going to clam up," Derrick said. "You can do this. You can command an entire company. You for sure can get this knucklehead to 'fess up to why he changed it and what he found."

"I can not go into some office and threaten a perfect stranger," Taylor had insisted.

But she had.

And now that it was done, she still could not believe that she had done it, that she had done it so well, or what she had found out. It all made her feel sick.

"Well, that was informative," Derrick said, coming out from a nearby alley with Henry to where Taylor was propped against the building. "Are you okay?" he asked, cupping her face.

Taylor shook her head, wide eyed. "Someone killed him, Derrick.

Someone really killed him. This was not just a random overdose."
She turned her attention to Henry. "Do you think the same person
who killed him is now coming after me?"

"I think we may need to figure out who killed Cedric first,"
Henry said. "It sounds like Cedric could have been on someone's bad
side."

"Yeah," Taylor agreed, "seems as though he pissed off a someone
considerably. And I really need to find out who requested the
autopsy change. I'm going to call Todd and Charlie."

"No, you cannot mention this to anyone," Henry cut in. "There
are holes in the system, Taylor, and I don't know how far up or down
the chain of command they go or how deep they are."

"Henry, you don't think Cedric's murder is related to Preston
Corp, do you?" Taylor asked. She had assumed something more sinis-
ter, something not so close.

Henry hesitated. "You really can't rule anything out," he finally
said.

His hesitation and answer did not have a good effect on Taylor's
state of mind.

TWELVE

DERRICK COULD FEEL the whirling of the thoughts blowing around in Taylor's mind as they sat in the dining room waiting to eat. Marty usually joined them, but it was later than they usually ate, and tonight she was working on her final sketches to submit. So it was just Taylor and Derrick and silence.

Taylor had barely said a word on the drive from Dr. Parker's office. Once home, she hadn't moved to get out of the car.

"Tay?" Derrick had asked, hoping to make her aware of where they were. Instead, she had jumped and gasped like those horror movie chicks. "Babe," Derrick soothed, a little shaken himself from her response. "It's okay, we are home," he said, talking to her soft and slow, like a wounded animal.

Taylor looked around like she had awakened from a coma, startled and wide eyed, then finally slid across the seat to the door which was promptly opened by Fletcher mansion staff. Once inside Derrick had turned to his wife, still tunneled deep inside her own thoughts.

"Want to talk about it?" he had asked her, but Taylor just smiled a little and shook her head looking away towards the stairs.

They had entered by the kitchen and Derrick's stomach

reminded him of how long it had been since they had eaten as it whined longingly at the delicious scents drifting his way.

"Why don't we get something to eat?" Derrick had suggested.

"I'm really not hungry."

"Where have you two been?" Nan had demanded as the kitchen door swung open and she stood in the doorway, hands on her hips and severe displeasure on her face.

"We, uh..."

"Haven't had a good meal since lunch I am sure of it," she had accused. "You have got to take better care of yourselves. Now get yourselves to the dining room. I am going to fill your bellies."

Taylor had quietly sighed, "Nan, we really—"

"Young lady, I will not have you talking back to me about this matter. You and your husband, whose stomach I heard from the driveway mind you, get going to the dining room so that you can relax and have a proper meal."

Taylor hated being told what to do. She would cut anyone down who even dared tell her what it was she needed to do, something that Derrick thought was incredibly sexy. But when Nan had told Taylor what to do, Taylor didn't even argue.

And so into the main dining room they had gone, which functioned way better as a dining space than an office, and waited as instructed for their food to arrive.

It was silent all around them. Derrick tried to make small talk with Taylor, tried cracking jokes, tried talking business, but she wouldn't engage. She was drawing into herself, Derrick realized. She was letting all her thoughts spin wildly out of control and withdrawing from what made sense. She used to do it all the time as a kid, when their, *okay when one of Derrick's* schemes would fly out of control and her mind would fumigate itself with all the potential for wrong that could, would and was for sure coming their way. Many times Taylor confessed everything they were planning before they'd even started, her conscience ruining their fun and getting Derrick in the shit.

But Derrick wasn't going to let her retreat into herself. The best solution was to find out what had happened to Cedric, find out if those things were connected to the attacks at the Gala and hospital, find the motherfucker responsible, and take him out.

However that was a little out of his realm at the minute.

He didn't particularly care for Henry, but he did know that guy was working his balls off trying to follow up on all these leads and input. And something Henry had said earlier to Derrick had left him with a little relief.

They had been stationed outside the medical examiner's office, in one of the back alleys, waiting for Taylor to come back out. Henry had wired Taylor up so they could both hear everything that was happening, and they were ready and waiting just in case the plan imploded. Yup, super easy for a huge redhead and a poster-child billionaire to just blend in outside the medical examiner's office of all places. It was in the pressure-filled silence that Henry spoke to Derrick.

"Do you trust me, Derrick?" Henry had finally asked softly.

Derrick had looked at him. "Yeah," Derrick had said as if this was the most obvious answer. "Why wouldn't I?"

Henry gave him a doubting glance.

"What?" Derrick said, totally caught off guard by this questioning.

"I just want you to know that this job and making sure you all stay safe is very important to me. I take my job very seriously, but please do not mistake my intensity for interest."

Derrick's face scrunched up in confusion. "I'm not following you."

"I have no other interest in your wife other than what my job entails."

Derrick didn't believe him. "Yeah, I know."

"Because I have someone," Henry went on, "and I know that it would really piss me off if she had to work with someone as closely as I work with Taylor." Henry laughed a small humorless laugh then.

"To be honest sometimes she does have to work with men that close, depend on those men to keep her safe and, well, it bothers me," he admitted.

Derrick looked at Henry from the corner of his eye. "Are you married?" Derrick finally asked.

Henry smiled a small smile and blushed, hanging his head in a shy schoolboy way for a second. "No, but she is my whole world," he said nodding and looking at Derrick. "And yet she drives me bonkers, too."

Derrick laughed slightly, amazed at the relief that he felt at hearing that Henry didn't have a thing for Taylor. "Women will do that to you, especially the ones we're crazy about," he said.

And now Derrick sat across from his silent wife and decided that while Henry took care of catching the guy, he could provide the only alternative—distraction.

At that moment their food was delivered by two kitchen staffers, and Derrick dismissed them quickly. While Taylor stared at her plate, Derrick used the remote tucked away in his chair's armrest to lock the two entry doors and draw the shades. His father used to have business dinners in this room, and he had installed this system in order to allow some privacy. Derrick was going to use it for privacy of a completely different sort now.

Derrick rose from his seat and grabbed his folded cloth napkin on the way up. He walked over to his wife, who had now moved on to pushing her food around on her plate, and pulled her chair back sending her fork clattering with the motion.

Startled she looked up at him, 'What—"

Derrick cut her off with a kiss, which she returned, but it was lackluster to put it mildly. As he kissed her, he loosened and pulled his belt from his pants. Breaking the kiss, he took Taylor's hands and put them palms together and fastened his belt around them.

"Derrick," Taylor struggled to free her hands from his. "I'm not in the mood," she stated stiffly.

"Don't worry," Derrick said, cinching the belt tight to her wrists, "you will be," and then he took the cloth napkin and folded it over itself to tie around her eyes.

"Derrick," Taylor snapped as she moved her head back and forth attempting to thwart his efforts to blindfold her, even moving her legs to try and stand.

But Derrick was faster, putting a knee over her lap to hold her in place and pulling the makeshift blindfold tight with one hand. He leaned down to her ear and growled, "I am going to fuck you so good, Taylor, but you just need to sit there and let me." He punctuated the statement with nipping her earlobe, and then sucking his way down her neck, stopping abruptly and making her groan in disappointment as he finished tying the blindfold on her.

She was no longer tied up in the thoughts terrifying her as she had been a minute ago. Now she was tied up in thoughts of a whole different sort.

"Where should I start, Tay?" Derrick murmured as he slid his fingertips lightly over her cheek and dragged them down her neck. "High?" he asked tugging at the collar of her dress. "Or low?" he growled, sliding his other hand tenderly on her inner thigh under the skirt, using the faintest touch.

Taylor's breath caught and her hips flexed forward just a little. She was definitely not thinking about finding a killer now, Derrick mused.

"I think you have a preference," he said leaning in and kissing her lips softly. "But I need to assess this further and be one hundred percent certain that it is what you want," he smiled at her groan as he removed his hand from her thigh.

Derrick reached back to the dining table, removed an ice cube from a water glass and put it in his mouth for several seconds, while Taylor squirmed in front of him. He took out the ice cube and then kissed Taylor, a hard and demanding kiss. Taylor gasped at the cool sensation as their lips met, but was quick to eagerly return the contact.

Derrick broke the kiss. "Taylor," he remarked, "you're hot. I think

I need to cool you down." He took the ice cube and placed it on her chin, then dragged it down her neck slowly, watching as a chill ran through her. He removed the ice cube and then traced the reverse path with his tongue. Now a shudder ran through Taylor and her breath came out in small huffs as she leaned into his contact.

Derrick broke their connection and looked down and evaluated Taylor's dress. He sent up thanks that her wardrobe choice of a wrap dress with a front tie was perfect for this situation. He reached down, untied the closure of the dress, and pulled the edges apart.

"Derrick," Taylor whimpered as her clothing fell open. She pushed her chest forward and Derrick seriously wanted to reach down, rip off the rest of Taylor's garments that were in the way of his direct access, and get this scene to the good part.

But he also knew, despite the objections of his steel-hard cock pressing uncomfortably against his zipper, that the more he delayed this the more gratifying it would be for the both of them.

Taylor lifted her still-joined hands and reached out to him as he took her in, her hands grazing his cock. The contact, albeit fleeting, was torture. Derrick took a step to the side and closed his eyes to steady himself from the contact.

"No touching, Taylor," he warned as he regained control. Then he lifted her and placed her on the table behind him. Once she was seated, he laid her back and put her hands above her head. "I really want you to stay like this. Can you do that for me?" he whispered in her ear, and then took her earlobe in his mouth and sucked on it, causing Taylor to moan in what sounded like pure frustration. "Can you, Taylor?" he asked again, this time rubbing his straining cock against her core, causing both of them to moan at the contact. "I really want to keep going," Derrick said, moving his pelvis back. "Can you stay like this for me, Tay?"

"Yes," Taylor insisted, her tone pleading. "Yes, please don't stop," she begged, lifting her hips from the table.

Derrick grabbed one of the water glasses from the table and drank it back, sucking an ice cube in as he drank. Then he put his mouth on

Taylor's collarbone and dragged his tongue down to her breast, moving the cup of her lacy bra aside. He watched as Taylor's nipple hardened in the air. He put his mouth over it, drawing it into his heat and then he shifted the ice cube in his mouth to caress the nipple and Taylor cried out at the sudden chill.

Derrick's hand slid slowly up her leg, his fingertips lazily dragging on the inside of her thigh, slowly back and forth all the while he continued his assault on her nipple.

Taylor writhed at the dual sensations and Derrick enjoyed getting her to just feel, all the while keeping her guessing.

But patience had never been his strong suit.

His mouth moved from her nipple straight to her panty-covered core and sucked. The thin fabric was already damp from Taylor's arousal, and Derrick drenched it suckling her.

"Oh God, Derrick," Taylor called out, lifting her hips to get herself closer to his mouth. Derrick used the opportunity to rid her of her panties allowing him deeper access to her. When he put his mouth back over Taylor's bare core, she began trembling at the direct contact. When he used the tip of his tongue to massage her clit, Taylor twisted and thrashed beneath his mouth. She moaned and panted, calling out his name as she came on his tongue, and then was limp.

Derrick rose up, removed her blindfold, and kissed her, their tongues tangling together. Derrick opened his pants, and removed his painfully stiff cock from its encasement. Pulling Taylor's hips to the edge of the table, without breaking their kiss, Derrick sheathed himself with her. The filling caused both of them to halt the kiss, their eyes connecting and moaning contentedly as they joined.

Derrick lifted Taylor and sat back in the dining chair they had abandoned. Taylor put her still bound hands behind his neck and Derrick pushed her blonde locks from her face.

"I love you, Taylor Fletcher," he said over her lips.

"I love you, Derrick Fletcher," she whispered back and she started to move over him.

Derrick had restrained himself for so long that he was holding back, enjoying the sensation of Taylor sliding over him as best he could. But then Taylor threaded her hands in his hair and yanked his head back, forcing him to look at her. "Derrick, I want to feel you come inside me," she demanded.

Those wicked words from her sweet mouth were no match for his willpower.

Derrick did as he was told, came inside Taylor, and called out something garbled as he did.

Moments later when they had caught their breath Taylor looked at her husband. "What was that you just said?" she asked, a bemused expression on her face.

Derrick shrugged. "I have no idea," he admitted, amnesia quickly setting in.

"It sounded like 'guacamole mashed potatoes' to me," Taylor said, her brow furrowed in amusement.

"Well that sounds almost as good as what just happened here," he said.

Taylor laughed and kissed him. "Thank you for helping to clear my mind."

"Anytime," Derrick assured her. "Especially if this is how I get to do it."

"It was definitely a method I have never utilized before," Taylor agreed, "and it got the job done."

Derrick reached up and tucked a lock of Taylor's hair behind her ear. "Will you talk to me now?" he asked gently.

Taylor sighed, "I don't want this to be so close to home," she said.

Derrick furrowed his brow, "How do you mean?"

Taylor sighed again, this time heavier. "I feel like this is going to sound stupid," she confessed.

"Try me," Derrick offered.

"Okay well, when you got shot, in my head this was a random act of violence to a point. I assumed someone was targeting us, well me, but that it was someone. A stranger. A whack job with a crazy agenda. Then when Tappen attempted to attack me, even though he worked for Preston Corp, he was definitely not acting of his own accord. You saw that footage. So again, I felt someone, in no way connected to us, was responsible.

"When Dr. Parker confirmed that Cedric's head was bashed in, when he pretty much verified that someone had killed Cedric, my first instinct was that a drug dealer had had enough with his shit, or he had borrowed money from some shady characters," Taylor explained and then paused.

"What about now?" Derrick prodded.

Taylor looked to the side for a moment, seemingly collecting her thoughts. "Now," she said looking back at Derrick, "well, when Henry said I couldn't ask Todd and Charlie, when he said this could be something that went through Preston Corp, it's just too close." As she spoke Taylor's eyes brimmed with tears. "How can something so close, something potentially in my day-to-day be responsible for hurting us? For killing Cedric?" Taylor rolled her eyes, which caused some of the tears to tip over the edge of her lids. "I mean, not that the crazy bastard didn't have that coming."

Derrick kissed Taylor's forehead and pulled her all the way into him, glad she was still on his lap and he could comfort her so easily. "Tay," he said softly into her ear, "we don't know anything, and Henry is being careful. You know how cautious he is with everything, and so far that has been to our advantage."

"What if the company I am trying to save is responsible for hurting you?" she asked, her voice wavering.

"No," Derrick said, pulling her back a little and looking at her, "this is why we need to talk things out and neither of us should be allowed to tornado in our thoughts. When I do it, I think you are leaving me for a guy in a coffee shop. When you do it, a 150-year-old family legacy company pulled the trigger on me.

"Taylor, even if someone who is linked to Preston Corp was behind us being attacked, and I hate to break it to you, but with access to Tappen they probably are, it is still some whacko with a hidden agenda."

Taylor searched Derrick's eyes, quiet. "You're right."

"And that has nothing to do with what your family created so long ago that is so important and wonderful to so many people worldwide."

Taylor smiled at Derrick. "I love you. Do you know that?"

Derrick nodded. "I do, but it is still good to hear you say it," he said smiling back at her. "And I love you, too, Taylor. Always."

Taylor's eyes widened a bit. "That reminds me," she said, a grin spreading over her face.

"Oh God, what?" Derrick asked because whatever she was reminded of looked devious.

"Remember how you said your tattoo was all gone? Except for those leftover lines?"

Derrick stayed quiet. He hated talking about that stupid tattoo. It was a time in his life that was very bad, very dark, and it still shook him to his core.

"How come you didn't mention the lines you left that made words?" she asked, squinting at him.

"You mean these?" he asked lifting up his shirt over his pec cautiously.

"Uh, yeah! How come you never mentioned those?" she asked in irritation.

"It was the original reason I went to the stupid tattoo place," Derrick said, "and then I kept drinking, among other things, and I had them put the freaking ugly tribal shit on my side. But I wouldn't let them cover that."

"Why did you get it?" she asked quietly.

Now Derrick sighed heavily. "Well, in my sober teenaged brain it was a declaration to you. I was going to get it and show you that I was sorry and that I loved you. As I partied a little harder, it became a *screw you* to my dad. And when I was obliterated, I did the rest of it as the ultimate *fuck you* to my dad," he explained. "I was pissed, in so many ways," he said.

"I love it," Taylor whispered.

"Good," Derrick said, kissing her lightly on the lips. "Will you still love it if I tell you I screamed like a little bitch when the needle touched me?"

Taylor laughed. "Oh yes, always," she said winking.

THIRTEEN

TAYLOR RUBBED her forehead as she reread the email from the marketing department. She had tried to make her wishes for the latest campaigns clear and still, after dozens of emails and phone calls and video chats, still there were errors.

Taylor groaned loudly, and punched at her keys as she replied in frustration.

"Problem?" Derrick asked sarcastically across from her in their home office.

Taylor rolled her gaze up to him over the screen and kept typing. "More marketing issues," she ground out.

"More issues, or the same issues over and over again?"

Taylor fired off her latest clarifications and slammed her laptop closed. "The same ones," she whined and leaned back in her chair, throwing her head back and staring at the ceiling.

"It's because you need a face to face," Derrick said. "You need to go back to the office, Taylor."

Taylor lifted her head to look at her husband, but left herself leaning back in the chair. "I don't think that is the answer."

"Really?" Derrick questioned. "Because you have laid it out for them every way possible and it still isn't right. You've been working on this thing for weeks. It should be farther along."

"I know," Taylor gritted out through her teeth.

"Taylor, you don't have to babysit me," Derrick said gently.

"I'm not," Taylor defended.

"Yes, you are," he said smiling. "And it's fine, I get it, I really do. But you can not stop your billion-dollar company any longer to take care of me."

"I haven't stopped it," she argued. When Derrick pegged her with a 'come on now' look she rolled her eyes. "Okay, I took some time away but you are more important than anything, Derrick."

"I know," he said. "But you have to go back."

"And what are you going to do while I am not here?"

"I will work, do my therapy, and hopefully head back to the office soon after you do," he said casually.

"Exactly," Taylor said, defeated. "You are going to rush yourself."

"Tay, I am doing fine," Derrick said, exasperated. "Yes, I am sore, but it is so much better than it was. You have to stop treating me like a china doll."

"You were shot," Taylor reminded him.

"I know that," Derrick fired back. "I am very, very aware of that—you won't let me forget."

Taylor was quiet for a minute. "I don't want to fight," she said.

"Me either," Derrick agreed, "but you have to release control on me and take it back at the office."

Taylor chewed on her lower lip. He was right, but it was hard to leave him. What if he needed her? What if something happened?

"Let me get you some coffee," Derrick said, getting up. "It will cheer you up and make the fact that you are not my mom clearer."

"Ha ha ha," Taylor said as her husband left. He was moving easier every day, she didn't see him wince ever, so either he had become aware he was doing it or he was feeling better.

It was time to cut the cord.

There was a knock on the office door. "Come in," Taylor beckoned, and Henry slid through the doorway. "Hey, Henry," Taylor greeted.

"Taylor," Henry said giving her a nod, "where is Derrick?"

"Coffee run," Taylor said smiling.

Henry nodded, "I have some reading material for you."

"Do tell," Taylor said dryly. "The last time you brought me reading material it was an autopsy report."

"Well, I do hate to be predictable," Henry said, handing a stapled document over to Taylor, "but it's another autopsy."

"Whose this time?" Taylor asked looking at the documents.

"Tappen's."

Taylor looked over the document quickly. "Well, no shock here, cause of death was a bullet wound," she murmured. "Was this released to the public?"

"Nope," Henry said and Taylor knew better than to ask any more questions. "It wasn't the cause of death that drew my attention, as much as the toxicology report."

Taylor was skimming the long and hard to pronounce words on the report when Derrick returned to the room with nectar of the gods —coffee.

"Henry," Derrick nodded to the other man. "Whatcha reading?"

"Tappen's autopsy," Taylor said without looking up.

"We have got to get you a subscription to Vogue," Derrick said, resuming his seat.

Taylor's eyes landed on a word that looked familiar. "What's this here, this Datura stramonium?"

"It's a drug that can be used as a mind control drug," Henry answered.

"Mind control?" Derrick asked.

Henry nodded.

"Have you seen it used before?" Taylor asked Henry.

"Aye," he said, "its mechanism of action is not a precise thing. I have seen it used where it makes the victims pliable, they just do whatever they are told. That's a mild response."

"What does a severe response look like?" Derrick asked.

"Delirium, violent behavior, paralysis, and even death. It has gotten recent exposure by being used in Mexico on tourists—thieves slip it in their drinks and coerce them to empty their bank accounts."

Taylor's mouth fell open. "This explains things. This explains Tappen's behavior," she said stunned.

Henry nodded, "Someone got to Tappen and fed him a pretty hearty helping of this plant the day he came to the hospital."

Taylor looked at the name on the page before her again. "The name is familiar to me, though. I feel like I've seen it recently," Taylor remarked.

"You have. It was on Cedric's toxicology report," Henry said.

Taylor whipped her head up and looked at Henry. "Cedric took this?" Henry nodded. "Well, what does that mean?"

"I have no idea, but I am going to start digging into his life. What his day-to-day looked like. I need to find who he interacted with and if they would still have reason to come after Preston Corp."

"Perfect," Derrick said, "you can see if you can gather more information with Taylor tomorrow, because she is going back to Preston Corp."

"Derrick," Taylor said in her warning tone.

"Well, that is perfect timing," Henry said. "It would look weird if I was suddenly poking around if you were not there. Now I can use you as an excuse."

Taylor glowered at her husband who pretended like there was breaking news on his laptop. She looked at Henry who looked relieved that trying to figure the next part out just got a little easier. Taylor closed her eyes and fumed.

"Heigh-ho, heigh-ho."

FOURTEEN

THAT EVENING, Taylor left Derrick in bed and went back down to the office of Fletcher Mansion. It made sense for her to head back into the real office, she knew that it was time, but the thought of leaving Derrick here scared her.

And to be honest, the thought of leaving the cocoon of Fletcher Mansion when someone wanted her dead was not all that appealing, either.

So here she sat at the desk trying to get something accomplished and get her mind occupied for a little bit. She needed to make sure business was on track. She needed to make sure Derrick had plenty of rest and time to heal. She needed to make sure Henry got to the bottom of all of this. But most importantly she needed to keep everyone safe.

Taylor rubbed her temples to try and alleviate the pressure that was inside her head. When it didn't work she threw her head down onto the desk and groaned.

Surely even billionaire CEOs were allowed a temper tantrum from time to time.

When Taylor's phone chirped next to her head she groaned even louder and picked up her head thudding it onto the table, an action she immediately regretted. She gave a few seconds for the new ache to lessen and then she snaked her arm out and picked up her phone, pulling it to her and opening the screen.

It was a text from an unknown number.

Libby?

Just seeing the name on her screen made her bolt straight upright, any headache completely forgotten.

Who is This? She texted back, afraid she already knew the answer.

Ben.

Goosebumps broke out all over Taylor's body.

You are in danger Libby.

Taylor looked at the screen and watched as her hand shook.

Are you there? Please Libby you are in danger.

Finally she answered. *In danger how?*

I need to meet with you and explain.

Taylor processed all the problems around her and all the unanswered questions and suddenly the answer was clear.

Standing, she grabbed her phone and texted, *Where can I meet you?*

TAYLOR PUSHED her body against the door frame she was hiding behind in the alley. This was a shitastic neighborhood, and there were people shouting just down the street and bottles smashing. It was like something out of a sketchy B movie and Taylor was the stupid starlet in the leading role. This was such a crazy idea, yet here she was.

A singsong whistling alerted Taylor to Ben's arrival, and she peeked out around the doorway to see a figure coming through the shadows. The figure whistled again and then the figure spoke, "Libby?"

"Ben?" Taylor called, ensuring it was, in fact, who she was there to meet.

"The one and only," he replied and Taylor was surprised by how she could still recognize the sound of his voice.

She stepped out of the shadows and cleared her throat, which signaled Henry to come in and tackle Ben.

"What the fuck!" Ben shouted as he hit the ground with a thud because there was really no other way to hit the ground if Henry came flying at you than with a thud. He struggled, but his lithe figure was absolutely no match for Henry's ginormous frame.

Taylor jumped back as Ben was taken down, and watched as Henry zip-tied his hands together effortlessly.

Ben moved and wriggled the entire time that Henry restrained him. He flipped his head back and forth and finally turned his face to Taylor. "What happened to meeting alone, Taylor?" Ben asked.

Irritation crept all over Taylor. "Oh, so now I'm Taylor? Okay, *Jeff*," she threw at him. On the way to the meeting, Henry had revealed some of the information he had found on Ben, the first being his name was not Ben Watson, but Jeff Benson.

"You lied to me, too," he said.

Taylor threw her hands up in the air. "Then why did you trust me to come here alone? Did you think I would just come here unprotected? Huh? You yourself said I was in danger, how fucking stupid would that have been?" she demanded in exasperation.

Henry pulled Ben or Jeff or whoever he was to his feet. "Yeah well, not everything between us was always a lie, now was it, Taylor?" he asked crassly, the innuendo not lost on her.

It also wasn't missed by Derrick who came out from the shadows and punched him across the face, knocking him out.

Taylor rubbed her face with her hands, "Really, Derrick?" she asked all muffled through her hands. "Was that necessary?"

"Yes," he answered blankly, shaking his hand out.

Taylor felt her face redden with anger as she glared at her husband.

"Taylor, the way he was shooting his mouth off, he is lucky I didn't snap his neck," Derrick sneered.

Taylor rolled her eyes. "Yes, but now he is unconscious and useless to us finding anything out," Taylor pointed out.

Derrick shrugged, emotionless. "He'll wake up," he said flatly.

Henry hefted Benson's limp frame from the ground and passed him off to Mick and Ian. "Truly, he was asking for it, Taylor," Henry remarked.

Taylor took in the faces of Henry and Derrick and then finally shook her head. She had liked it better when Henry hadn't been trying to get on Derrick's good side. Taylor stalked over to the car wondering how long it would be before Benson would be able to talk to them. He claimed he had something to explain and Taylor was eager to hear it.

THE FORMERLY BEARDED DOUCHE, or Ben or Jeff, as anyone but Derrick may have referred to him, was in the back of an SUV that Taylor and Derrick's SUV was following.

"Are you going to stay mad long?" Derrick finally asked Taylor. She had been looking out the window and had not acknowledged his presence the entire ride.

Taylor turned and opened her mouth to answer him when their vehicle pulled over to the side of the road. Derrick looked around, as did Taylor. "What's going on?" she asked. "Is it paparazzi?"

"No," Henry said, turning back to look at them in the back seat. "Mick just messaged me, said Benson woke up, says he is willing to talk," he explained. "I figured you two would want to talk to him."

"Yes," Taylor said eagerly, a little too eagerly for Derrick's liking. "If he has answers then we need to talk to him."

"Okay, so do you want to bring him to the mansion?"

"Hell freaking no," Derrick said. "I am not letting that beatnik near my house."

Taylor turned to her husband. "Well, where are we supposed to take him?"

"Oh, I have some ideas on where I would like to take him," Derrick admitted. He was sure he could find some dumpster to drop him in between here and home.

"I think I have something," said Henry, who had been busy texting away. Henry put the SUV in drive and made a sudden U-turn, then a few other quick turns in some very dark areas.

"Where are we going?" Taylor asked Henry.

"Well, we need to take him to a low traffic place to question him," Henry said, "so that's what we're going to do." Henry drove in silence through more darkened streets. The landscape became more and more run-down around them. Many of the businesses they passed had boarded windows, and the ones that were open looked less than desirable. Finally, Henry pulled into a darkened parking spot. In front of them was a house that sagged, resembling the defeat within the neighborhood around it.

Derrick looked to Taylor who had leaned forward and was taking the building in through the front window. "What is this place?" Taylor asked.

"An old crack den," Henry answered.

Taylor jerked her head away from the window and back to Henry. "I'm sorry, what?"

"The cops raided this place last week, arrested a bunch of people. They generally watch places like this for a set amount of time and then it's empty until the users come back."

"And this is a good place for us because?" Taylor asked letting the last word hang so Henry could fill in the blanks.

"Because the cops are no longer watching it, they have moved on, it has zero chance of having any wiretap devices, and no one around here is going to talk because they don't want the cops back here at all."

"If you say so, Henry," Taylor said, her hand on the door handle.

But Derrick wasn't nearly as trusting of Henry as Taylor was.

"I'm sorry, but maybe we should wait until daylight to talk to this idiot. Don't you think that would be safer?" Derrick argued.

"What are you saying?" Taylor asked.

"You know, that maybe you can wait and talk to him in the morning? After you've gotten some rest?"

The way Taylor looked back at Derrick, with her eyes bulging and her mouth hanging open, sort of made him feel like he had said something wrong. "Sleep? I can't *sleep*, Derrick. I can't sleep knowing someone is trying to hurt the people I love. I have to get to the bottom of this and he may have pieces to the puzzle that has become my life." Without further interruption she wrenched the door open and slid out.

Derrick scrambled out after his wife, who was apparently not able to listen to reason.

"Where do we go?" Taylor asked Henry quietly, although if Henry was right, she could have shouted and no one would have cared or paid any attention to them.

Henry pointed towards where the front door used to be, where there was now a piece of plywood. Before it was a set of dilapidated stairs that led to a porch. The porch floor resembled a slice of Swiss cheese, boards broken off in multiple spots. The three of them approached the front porch and Henry grabbed a long plank of wood from the ground, laying it over the brittle steps.

"After you," Henry motioned for Taylor.

"Gee, what a gentleman," Taylor muttered. She turned her phone flashlight on as she placed her foot carefully onto the plank, grateful she had worn flats. The board held firm and Taylor teetered her way up, followed by Derrick and finally Henry. Once on the porch surface they moved across it carefully, avoiding broken boards and holes as they went. Henry slid his hand in a gap in the plywood and easily pulled the freshly screwed piece out of the house's old rotted wood frame.

Taylor slid through the opening and found a space that was more sad to her than frightening. The walls, what was left of them, appeared to have been a light color at one point, but were now discolored dark gray and covered in places with spray paint. Mattresses were everywhere, some against walls, some right next to each other and some in the middle of the room, like stained islands. All of the mattresses were free from sheets and most had the springs coming through them. The saddest part of all was the various dolls and teddy bears that took up residence near the mattresses. Taylor briefly thought of what horrors their owners' little eyes had seen.

Mick hustled Benson in behind them and brought him to a room in the back of the dwelling. Mick forced him onto a chair that looked as war-torn as the rest of the place, and the fact that it was still standing was incredible. Benson rubbed his wrists where the zip ties had chafed. When Mick saw Taylor, he looked back at Benson. "Remember what I said," Mick threatened, pointing a finger close to his face.

"Yup, yup, no touching or slit throat," Benson said nodding, never taking his eyes from Taylor.

Derrick leaned against the wall to the side of the opening, and just watched.

It was dark in the building, but with the meager light from her phone she was able to see the man she'd known as Ben clearly for the first time. He was clean-shaven now, and his hair was shorter, but his eyes were, of course, the same. She had thought those eyes were so amazing once upon a time. Thought nothing could compare to their slight hazel-green edge. But now as she looked at them, she found them extremely dull. They held no flame to the milk chocolate stare of her husband.

"So," Taylor started but Ben interrupted her.

"First let me just say I am sorry for the snark I was throwing at you before."

Taylor raised her brow. "Who told you to apologize?" she asked smirking and looking at Mick out the corner of her eye.

"No one," Ben said. "I was pissed off you didn't trust me enough to meet me alone, but you were right when you said you were in danger, so I don't blame you for coming with protection." And then he shifted his attention to Derrick, "And I deserved that punch, so sorry again."

"Apology accepted, but let's just get to it, shall we?" Taylor said sternly trying to rein in some control. She wanted answers but she also wanted to get the hell out of there.

"Sure, so tell me what you know about me so far."

"That your real name isn't even Ben, it's Jeffrey Benson and you were in the army before you went AWOL and seemingly dropped off the planet."

"Okay, well, most of that is true. My name is Jeffrey Benson, but I've always also answered to Ben because of my last name. But I didn't go AWOL. I was in a special forces unit but they made it appear I went AWOL so I wasn't traceable, and apparently it worked. Once I 'disappeared' I worked to gather intelligence on enemies, or those the government suspected of being enemies. A sort of spy because I could blend in easily."

"Were you on some kind of assignment when I met you?" Taylor asked.

"I was but not for the government. I was given the boot from my post when they suspected I might have been figured out. They just sort of gave me my walking papers. Left me for dead in a way because if any of the people I have gotten crap on find out who I am, I'm dead. So I stayed off the radar and moved a lot, changed my look a lot, and took the occasional job that came my way."

"What sort of jobs?" Derrick asked.

"Surveillance, or detective jobs. Private investigating stuff, but large cash amounts so I only had to take them here and there."

"So you were hiding out in Chadumor, at the coffee shop?" Henry asked.

"No, I was on a job."

"What was your job?" Taylor asked.

"I was hired to find you."

Taylor knit her brows together. "Find me? By whom?"

"Your uncle."

Taylor's throat closed up, and she felt cold run through her veins. "Why?" she croaked out.

"He wanted—"

"Did he want to kill me?" Taylor blurted out. She couldn't keep the question from bubbling out of her. It had been what she had always feared. "Or were you supposed to kill me?"

He recoiled at the question. "What? No!" he replied vehemently, moving his hands in a no way signal. "No, Taylor, he never asked me that. God, he never even wanted to know your location."

Taylor absorbed that odd tidbit before she spoke. "He didn't want to know where I was?" Taylor asked, confusion now replacing her fear. "Then why did he send you?"

Benson heaved out a big breath. "So here is how it goes. I was contacted by Cedric via a courier with a handwritten letter. All it said was a place to meet and a price to be given to find someone. It was a good deal of cash, so I went.

"I met him in an alley, the same alley where I had you meet me, in fact. At the time I had no idea who he was."

"How was his demeanor?" Henry asked. "Was there anything about him that stood out, any behaviors or characteristics you thought were off?"

"Yeah, he was antsy."

"Antsy how?" Henry asked.

"He was paranoid," he said. "Lots of jumping, and looking over his shoulder."

"Did he seem to be on any substances that might cause his paranoia?" Henry cross-examined.

"He didn't seem high, no. More like panicked someone was behind him the entire time. The way he was acting freaked me out, and I have been in war. He was like some of the shell-shocked guys. Just totally trying to act like he had it together but he did not have it all together.

"Anyway, he handed me your photo, Taylor," he said, breaking eye contact with Henry and turning his gaze to her, "and said he needed to find you. I recognized who you were in the photo instantly and I got real suspicious real fast. I started to try and say without spooking him that I didn't stalk people. He said you two were related but again I thought it was a big red *he is a stalker* flag. But then I really looked at him, and I asked him for his ID. When I realized he was who he claimed to be I asked why and he said he needed to make sure you were alive."

"When was this? When did he ask you to look?" Derrick asked.

"It was about fifteen months before the last time I saw you, before you disappeared from the Roasted Bean," Ben said to Taylor.

"How did you find me?" Taylor asked quietly. It was of little importance but she wanted to know, needed to see where she had messed up for some reason.

Ben smiled a humorless smile, and shook his head. "It wasn't easy. Cedric had absolutely nothing to go on. Just said you most likely were in disguise and probably as far away as you could get. And you were. You had totally disappeared. I've tracked down drug lords easier than I was able to track you down. But then I had a lucky light bulb one day in the grocery line."

"Do tell?" Taylor said dryly, now annoyed with the way he was dragging it out.

"I followed him," he said motioning his head to Derrick.

"How the fuck did you pull that off?" Derrick asked with irritation.

"It was right after you punched that photographer. I saw the photos of you going after him and I watched the video footage online. I noticed how fired up you got when they mentioned Taylor. It was more than *you had a bad day at the office* fired up, it was personal. So I got in contact with your office."

"How?" Derrick demanded.

"Because I'm smooth," he replied to Derrick sarcastically, "and when I spoke to your secretary, she said you were out of town for a meeting. And I called a week later and it was another meeting and then another. So I followed you to the airport and watched you get on your flight. I hacked into the system and figured out what your fake name was and the next time you got on the same flight, I got on, too, and I followed you to your next flight, and the next until you got off in Maine and I saw you in complete disguise go into Roasted Bean and stare at the counter girl.

"And then I looked at the counter girl, and noticed how she never really looked up for long, and let her hair hide most of her face. So I went there more often on a hunch. I started playing the open mike, asked the counter girl questions to get her to look up, and I could line up the similarities. And it paid off."

There was a shifty silence around them for a beat while everyone took that in and then it started to stifle Taylor.

"Okay, so you told Cedric where I was, and then he told you to just watch me?" Taylor asked in disbelief.

"I never told him where you were."

"I feel like you are talking in fucking riddles so if you could just go ahead and tell me what the hell happened that would be great," Taylor said with an edge.

Ben gave a curt nod and picked up the pace. "I couriered that I had information. I could have given him the information then but I wanted to be paid. He couriered back a check with a lot of zeros on it, and told me to never, ever tell him where you were. But that if I stayed and made sure you were safe, he would keep sending checks with lots of zeros on them."

"Why?" Taylor asked, completely baffled.

"I have no idea," Ben answered, bewilderment at the whole thing in his tone. "I would send courier info every two weeks confirming you were safe and he would send back payment."

"And that was it?"

"Yes."

"And he never told you why he wanted to find me?"

"Not the whole time I was there. I didn't even speak to him again once I located you. But the night before you left, that night he called me. A courier met me as usual and gave me the envelope but this one was thicker. It had a burner phone in it and a note to call Cedric. I talked to him and he sounded really jumpy and asked where you were and when had I seen you last and were you okay. He just kept rambling out questions. I reassured him I had just left you and you were fine and he said something was going to happen. That something bad was coming and if I didn't hear from him, I had to tell you to talk to Mellon."

"Melon?" Taylor asked slowly, her face screwed up in confusion and aggravation. "Like the fruit?"

"I asked him what that meant and he said go to Mellon and he could tell you what was happening, said you wouldn't be safe. I tried to ask more questions and he hung up. I tried to call back but it went directly to an automated message. The next thing I knew you were gone and he was reported dead. But I am telling you he was panicked. He knew something bad was going to happen and he was constantly worried something was going to happen to you."

Derrick looked back to Taylor, "Do you think he was planning to overdose?"

Taylor shrugged, "I cannot even pretend to imagine what was going through Cedric's pathological mind just before he died." Taylor turned her attention to Henry. "Where do we go from here?" Taylor asked.

"We start looking into connections between Cedric and anyone named Mellon."

"Good luck," Ben said coolly, "I tried, but the number of people with that last name in LA alone is crazy. And I really didn't know anything about Cedric. I tried to look into him but he was locked down pretty tight."

Taylor dropped her face into her hands and then pulled them slowly down it. This meeting was supposed to answer her questions but now she just had more.

"Well, fuck."

FIFTEEN

DERRICK WAS IN BED, ready for sleep, but it was not an option currently as his wife paced the length of the room replaying and over-thinking the events of the last several days.

"Taylor, you need to get some rest," Derrick whined, because now he was cranky. He hadn't gotten sex, as he had been promised earlier, and now he wasn't getting sleep. On top of all of that, Henry had just let that stupid, previously bearded freak beatnik go.

Derrick hadn't bought his apology one bit. He knew what he had been doing when he had said those things in the alley to Taylor. When they were done talking to him, they had gotten out of that horror movie house and headed to the SUVs. Taylor loaded in and Derrick watched as Henry had given the asshole his card and told him to let him know if he thought of anything.

"You're letting him go?" Derrick had asked Henry as he made his way to his own side of the SUV.

"Mr. Fletcher, I am not the police. I can't arrest him," Henry had said, seemingly apologetic.

Derrick silently fumed for a beat. "I just don't trust that guy."

"Don't worry, I will be keeping tabs on him," Henry assured him.

But Derrick didn't want tabs kept on that guy. He wanted him to be locked in a cell, and he didn't doubt that there may be one on the Fletcher Mansion property—the place was pretty old.

"Are you even listening to me?" Taylor exclaimed, stamping her foot and dragging Derrick's thoughts back to the here and now.

"Yeah," he lied, but Taylor just rolled her eyes.

"I just feel like I need to get this all organized in my head before I go back to the office," she said, still pacing.

"What is there to organize?"

Taylor flailed her arms. "Everything!" she exclaimed again.

Derrick flopped his head back on the pillow and then looked over at the bedside clock. It was nearly one in the morning. He was obviously not getting any rest until Taylor felt like she had some sort of system to deal with this. So he heaved out a heavy breath, which he was glad to notice did not hurt all that much, and rolled out of bed. Time to hash this shit out.

Derrick intercepted Taylor on one of her passes and pulled her to sit on the foot of the bed beside him.

"Where do you want to start?" he asked her, and when he saw the relief in her eyes, he knew this was what she needed.

"It just all seems so messed up," she said, a little quiver to her voice.

Derrick nodded. "Yeah, you're right," he agreed, "and it's a lot all at once. So let's look at it piece by piece."

"Okay, so Dr. Parker said the head trauma may not have killed Cedric, but that the drugs for sure did. But," Taylor said holding up a finger, "he also said Cedric wouldn't have been able to administer the drugs because of the head trauma. So who gave him the drugs?"

Derrick shrugged. "We don't know, Tay, but it sounds like Cedric hooked up with some pretty shady characters. I mean they took his tooth out when he died," Derrick reminded her. "That almost seems like it was a trophy of some kind."

"Yeah, but if this was someone who was looking for vengeance, why the drugs? Why not just bash his head in until he died?"

"Maybe he was shooting up when they bashed?" Derrick said shrugging.

"Yeah maybe," Taylor said, mulling the idea over. "I wonder if Cedric had some crooked deals. Like maybe when he couldn't get money from Preston Corp anymore he turned to, um, alternative incomes. Something very illegal."

"That seems like a good possibility," Derrick agreed, "considering the trauma."

"Maybe Mellon is the killer," Taylor said.

"That could be possible, or Mellon could be someone with more information," Derrick said, not wanting Taylor to be panicked or hopeful that this Mellon person could be the answer. "Let Henry look more—we can't do anything until we have more pieces."

Taylor nodded but looked uncertain. There was still more that bothered her.

"What is it, Tay?" Derrick soothed.

"Why did he send him to watch me?" Taylor whispered.

Derrick tried not to sneer at the mention of the previously bearded beatnik. "Who knows if what that guy says is even legit, Taylor."

"But what if it is," she pushed. "What if he wanted to find me but then that was it, just watch me?"

"What bothers you about that?"

Taylor pondered for a minute. "It doesn't match what I know about Cedric," she said finally. Taylor licked her lips then chewed her bottom one as she held deliberations in her mind. "He was a monster," she told Derrick, "so him just sending someone to watch me, to not tell him, well, it makes him sound like he was trying to protect me, and," she swallowed, "and—"

"And that was not Cedric," Derrick finished for her, and Taylor looked at him and nodded. This was what she didn't get, and probably what bothered her the most. Cedric doing anything even remotely humane to Taylor threw her world into question.

"We don't know everything now, Taylor, but Henry will find the missing pieces," he said. "Don't stress about what may or may not be true, please."

"I just feel like I can't do anything to get the answers and I need them," she said in distress.

"You can try and coyly ask about Cedric's business dealings tomorrow," Derrick said. "That's why you need to rest," he encouraged gently.

Taylor smiled at him and rolled her eyes. "Subtle," she said.

"You know what," Derrick said rising, "I am going to give you something to help you sleep."

"No, you're not," Taylor said.

"Oh yeah, I am," he said looking down at Taylor.

"What exactly are you going to give me?"

He bent and quickly scooped her up, causing a slight stretching sensation in his chest. "An orgasm."

Taylor protested, "Derrick put me down, I am too heavy!"

"Please," Derrick scoffed, and threw Taylor down on the bed. "Now be quiet, I have work to do," he said and crushed his mouth to Taylor's, hearing her contented sigh. Maybe this night hadn't turned out so bad after all.

SIXTEEN

TAYLOR GROANED as her alarm wailed loudly.

"Make it stop," Derrick whined as he hid his head under his pillow.

Taylor opened one eye and reached out an arm, slapping wildly until she finally made contact with her phone and stopped the noise. She dragged her body up and rolled her head trying to wake up some part of herself. Finally she took a deep breath and bit the bullet, forcing herself to the shower.

Once she was showered, dressed, and had some makeup on, Taylor felt sort of like a normal human. She did a final check of herself in the full-length bedroom mirror. She felt confident but butterflies still filled her stomach. She was eager to get back to the office, but leaving Derrick behind didn't feel right.

"You look gorgeous," Derrick said from the bed behind her, and Taylor looked back at him. She licked her lips at the sight—her devastatingly handsome husband with perfect bedhead, shirtless amongst the stark white sheets.

Taylor suddenly needed a nap.

Derrick wagged a finger at her, "Oh no you don't. You stop looking at me like that right now or you are not going to work."

"Staying home with you seems like a wonderful idea," Taylor admitted, taking an unconscious step towards the bed.

Derrick popped quickly out of bed. "No way, Mrs. Fletcher," he said, "this shop is closed until you bring home some bacon."

"I can not believe you are turning me down," Taylor scoffed with mock hurt.

"It's what you get for keeping me up so late," Derrick sassed.

A knock at the door had them both turning in the same direction. "Mrs. Preston-Fletcher, your security team is ready when you are."

Taylor looked back at Derrick. "I think that's a sign," she said.

Derrick sauntered over to his wife, kissing her on the lips. "Have a great day. I can't wait to see you later and reward your hard work," he said giving her another kiss.

Taylor wrapped her arms around her husband and gave him a squeeze. "Take it easy today, okay?"

"You got it. Now go," he said, giving her backside a healthy swat.

"Ow," she exclaimed as she jumped, "that hurt."

"Hope it's sore all day," he said, winking at her.

She rolled her eyes. "I love you, you pervert."

"I love you, too, Mrs. Preston-Fletcher," Derrick said, his wide grin displaying his dimples.

And with that Taylor left, because those dimples, well they had just incinerated her panties.

MICK AND IAN were waiting by the Range Rover to take Taylor to the office. "Where's Henry?" Taylor asked as she climbed in.

"He had some behind the scenes work to do, Taylor," Mick said cryptically.

"Ah," Taylor said nodding. "Gotcha. Okay, well let's head out then."

They drove in silence and Taylor watched as they turned and exited, and she realized she had never actually driven to Preston Corp. In fact, she had not driven in years, and back then it had only been in the large Preston Manor driveway. She promised herself that when all this hysteria was behind them she would drive again, because maybe there would be a time she could leave her home without a security team.

A girl could dream at least.

As they arrived at Preston Corp, Taylor spied a small cluster of paparazzi who went insane at the sight of their tinted-windowed SUV. She watched as they bumped into each other and dropped their drinks trying to get out their cameras and phones.

"Looks like you will be world news tonight, Taylor," Mick joked.

Taylor laughed, both because he was right and because she noticed the guys were much more relaxed without Henry nearby. "It would seem that way," she agreed with a smile.

They pulled into the underground garage of Preston Corp and over to the private parking area for Taylor. She waited in the back, as she had been trained, until the two men surrounded her door and opened it for her.

Taylor exited the vehicle and was walking behind it when a loud bang echoed around the garage. Taylor was shoved behind the two huge men and pressed against the back of the SUV. Mick and Ian had guns drawn and pointed at the sound.

"It's just me, just me!" a familiar voice shrieked and Taylor realized it was Charlie who had burst through the door to the garage area, effectively scaring the shit out of everyone. "I'm sorry, I wasn't expecting Taylor today."

"It's okay, guys," Taylor said, and released a breath. She became rapidly aware of how scared she had been, and could feel herself shaking as the adrenaline waned from her body. She swallowed hard and took a calming breath. "Hello, Charlie," she said in a voice that was steadier than she currently felt.

Charlie smiled broadly at her. "Hello Taylor, so good to have you back," he said, embracing Taylor.

"I thought it was time," Taylor lied as she led the way into the building.

Charlie rambled constantly the entire way up the elevator to the floor where Taylor's office was housed. "The financial meeting we were going to Skype you in for is happening in twenty minutes, Taylor," he announced as they arrived at Taylor's office door, "so I will leave you to catch up." Charlie opened the door for her.

"Thanks, Charlie," she said as she made her way through.

"Taylor," Charlie called in after her, and Taylor turned to look at the older man. "So good to have you back home," he smiled and shut the door.

This was home, she realized, and Derrick was right. It did feel good to be back in a routine.

Taylor sat at her enormous and ornate desk, the one that used to be her grandfather's, and heaved out a breath. She had just booted up her desktop and pulled up the financial reports for a final refresher when her door blew open, and Todd barreled through.

"What are you doing here?" he demanded.

The ease Taylor felt at having any sense of normalcy disappeared and her jaw tensed at Todd's words. "Close the door," she ordered, narrowing her eyes.

Todd did as instructed but irritation at being told what to do radiated off of him. "What—"

Taylor shot to her feet. "Do not come into this office and try to boss me around," Taylor stated sharply to the stone-faced man before her.

Todd huffed a breath, "I didn't mean to—"

"I work here," Taylor said. "I own this fucking place. I am in charge of hundreds of thousands of people's livelihoods, including yours," she informed him, looking him up and down. "That, Todd, is what I am doing here," she said.

Todd was silent for a moment. "We just didn't know you were arriving today," he offered as an explanation.

"Well I'm here, don't bother with a welcome back party now," she said. "Let's go to the meeting," she ordered, grabbing her iPad and pushing past Todd.

TWO HOURS LATER, Taylor left the meeting and felt infinitely better than she had going in. Numbers were good. Really good. Better than they had been in years. And Todd had not uttered a word.

It was going right. Finally something good was coming from all the mess that Cedric had left Preston Corp in. All the effort and changes were finally making a difference, despite all the madness that had been happening. Derrick had been right to push her to come here, as it was a great distraction.

When Taylor left the meeting she walked back to her office with the marketing department VP—a little to discuss the next campaign, a lot to further avoid Todd. She walked with the man until she got to her office door, Mick behind them the entire time, and then went inside and collapsed in her chair.

She felt like she finally had something under control.

She decided she should check in with Fletcher Enterprises, also. Derrick had not yet taken over completely, though the Fletcher business structure allowed for more autonomy in the departments so things were still forging ahead well. But Taylor was still in charge there, so she called Arthur.

"Hello, Mrs. Preston-Fletcher," Arthur answered after half a ring.

"Hey Arthur, just checking in for the day," Taylor said as she made a coffee at her office Keurig.

"Uh, yeah, everything is great," Arthur said, sounding a little perplexed.

Taylor took a sip of her coffee. "That didn't sound reassuring,"

Taylor said to the man, laughing a little. Usually he would give her a daily rundown of calendar events at the company.

"Well, I am just surprised you are still checking in with Mr. Fletcher back at work."

That made sense to Taylor. "Oh, well, I know he is doing some stuff from home but until he comes into the office—"

"He did," Arthur interrupted. "He came in about an hour ago."

Coffee spewed from Taylor's mouth as she spit it out. "He what?"

"Um, well, see, he came—"

"Arthur, are you telling me my husband is in that building with you, right now?" she asked, biting out every word.

"Yes?" Arthur answered apprehensively, seeming to be unsure where his loyalty lay at the moment.

"Damn it!" Taylor shouted and slammed her desk phone down. She saw red and didn't even think twice about what she did next.

Taylor wrenched her office door open and exploded through it, sending Mick and Ian jumping, and stomped down the hallway. She ignored people who called her name and walked into an open elevator, as her security detail hurried to catch up.

"Taylor, where are you going?"

Taylor turned her heated stare on Mick, silencing him. "Get me to Fletcher Enterprises. Now."

And they did. They took her down into the connected tunnels, and moments later she was making her madwoman march down the halls of Fletcher Enterprises. The workers parted like something biblical as Taylor stared straight ahead at her destination—Derrick's office door.

"Mrs. Preston-Fletcher, uh, Mr. Fletcher is in a meeting," Arthur said as he saw her and ran to catch up with her from down the hall. When Taylor didn't stop, Arthur reached out a hand to try and grab Taylor's arm, and Ian had the man against a wall.

If Taylor had been in her right mind, she would have been appalled. Instead she was grateful Arthur was out of the way, and she continued on.

Taylor pushed Derrick's office door open and walked past Claire, his wonderful secretary. The woman didn't even look up from her computer screen. "Hello Mrs. Preston-Fletcher, I've been expecting you," she said in a singsong tone.

Taylor continued through to Derrick's inner office, and flung the door open, sending it slamming against the wall and creating a loud BOOM in its wake.

Panic covered Derrick's face, but he quickly covered it with a smile. "Hey babe! I was just—"

Taylor looked at the two men sitting opposite Derrick. Both looked like they had soiled themselves. "You two, out," she instructed and they wasted no time honoring her request.

"Taylor," Derrick said, having the audacity to sound irritated, "we are in a meeting."

"Oh, I'm sorry," Taylor sympathetically mocked. She turned to one of the men as he was escaping the office. "Darius, are the plans done? Are they signed? Have they even been evaluated?"

"Uh, no Miss, um, Mrs. Preston-Fletcher, I mean ma'am."

Taylor nodded. "Thanks, meeting's over, buh-bye." And the man quickly exited through the door, which Mick pulled closed.

Taylor turned to her husband, crossing her arms over her chest. She could feel her nostrils flare as she glared.

Derrick tried to speak first, "So—"

"What the actual fuck, Derrick?" Taylor shouted.

"Calm down," Derrick said gently, and it had the same effect on Taylor as a flame to a stick of dynamite.

"Did you just tell me to calm down? What, like I caught you having a snack before dinner? You told me you were going to stay home. You promised me you would not come to work if I did," she reminded him.

"Well, I didn't come when you did," Derrick said, "I came hours later."

So this is what a stroke feels like, Taylor mused as she felt her pulse tick up and her face flush with heat.

"I did not do this to piss you off," Derrick said.

"Do. Fucking. Tell."

Derrick sat down and heaved out a sigh, "You left and I got up and did my therapy and made some work calls. Then I met with the doc and he said I could come back to work."

Taylor waited. There was more to this story and Derrick would spill the truth. She just had to be patient, and that was difficult—very, very difficult. Because really all Taylor wanted to do was shout at her husband until she was hoarse.

Slowly Derrick shifted under Taylor's stare. "Okay, maybe he didn't say I could come back to work."

"Tell me."

Derrick huffed out a breath. "I don't want to be home alone in that huge mausoleum," he whined. "I did my therapy and the therapist said I was doing great and she said she was cutting her visits down. Then the doc came in and I asked when I could come back to work. He said everything was healing well and that if I wanted to come back here he could check in with me in the office.

"So I was going to talk to you when you got home," he continued. "Really I was. I went and I showered, and I shaved, and I thought *hey, if I am going to work let me dress the part* and so I got a suit on and then I went to that office and tried to work and I just, I don't know, I couldn't. I like being at work, I like moving with everyone here. I like being involved." He shook his head. "At the mansion, without you, I was just lost."

Taylor closed her eyes and took several deep breaths. She breathed in for four counts and out for five counts. She opened her eyes and saw her husband waiting for her to speak, his face screwed up as if the next time her mouth opened it could be extremely painful.

"I understand," Taylor said slowly, working very hard to maintain composure. "But why didn't you call me? Talk to me?"

"I was afraid you would freak," Derrick said. "I realize now that was a mistake."

Taylor looked Derrick over. He looked happy. Well, he actually looked scared, but he looked more content here at the office, more at ease than he had locked up at home. Derrick had always thrived on being in the thick of things, and it was how their businesses were so successful. Those who ran them had always been in the center of the chaos. In this way Preston Corp and Fletcher Enterprises had always been very similar.

"I know that you are healthy and that you were eager to come back to work, but the reality is that someone is trying to kill me, Derrick. They have already gotten to you once. What if that had happened again?"

"I left with security," Derrick said. "I wouldn't be that stupid. I let Henry know and had a couple of the guys bring me here. They are outside the door, didn't you see them?"

"No, in my rage I was just a touch blind," Taylor said.

Derrick got up. "I'm very sorry to upset you, it was never my intent."

Taylor looked at him. "I know I can't control you, Derrick, but there is a lot happening all around us. I really can not handle extra surprises right now."

"Yeah, this was not my most shining moment, huh?"

Taylor shook her head.

"I'm sorry." He slid his arms around her and tried to win her over with a dimpled grin. "If it makes you feel any better, Claire yelled at me as soon as I walked through the door."

"Give her a raise," Taylor said.

"Please don't be mad," Derrick whispered to Taylor, still looking a little nervous.

"I'm still mad," Taylor admitted, "but if this works for you, we will get through it." She kissed Derrick lightly on the lips. "I have to get back to work now."

"Okay," he said and gave her another soft kiss.

Taylor turned and made her way to the door. "Hey," Derrick

called after her as she opened the door, "do you want to catch me up on what you worked on while I was out?" he asked.

Taylor looked over her shoulder as she opened the door. "You wanted to come back to work," she reminded him. "Figure it out yourself," she said and shut Derrick in his office. She walked calmly back out of the outer office, and knocked on Claire's desk as she went by. "You're getting a raise, don't let him forget," Taylor told her.

"Thank you, Mrs. Preston-Fletcher, always good to see you."

SEVENTEEN

DERRICK WAS glad to be back to work, to be in the grind, to actually feel useful again.

But he was tired as fuck as the afternoon went on. At four he decided he had put in enough time for his first day back.

Calling it a day, he texted to Taylor.

Okay, heading into one last meeting, I will meet you back home.

Derrick made a face at her response. He really wanted her to drive home with him, like they used to, but he had figured she wouldn't jump to leave just yet. He was sure she had a lot to get done, and he was sure she was also still a little pissed at him for his spontaneous return to work.

Maybe he should stop for tulips.

His phone chimed and he checked it to find a selfie of Taylor blowing him a kiss. She had captioned it *I love you, you giant pain in the ass.*

Derrick smiled at the picture. *I love you too, you are my whole world,* he replied and made his way out. He said goodnight to Claire and picked up his security detail of Rog and Sam on the way out. It was annoying to be followed around, but he really had not enjoyed being shot, so he would put up with it for now.

Once Derrick climbed into the SUV he sank into the leather and rested his head back. Next thing he knew the car was stopped and he was home. Derrick felt ridiculous at how much just being in an office for a few hours had exhausted him, but it also fired him up to get back to full strength.

Derrick made his way inside the mansion and headed toward his bedroom. His incision sites were pulling, and he knew a shower would help them ease a little. He climbed the stairs and was making his way down the hall toward the wing where his room was when he heard loud voices. He turned the corner and found Marty and Henry talking in the hallway near his room. And from what he could see and hear it didn't seem like a pleasant conversation.

"I don't care, I am not going out with all these guys following me," he heard Marty hiss.

"Marty," he heard Henry's thick brogue growl back at her, "it isn't safe right now for you to be out without—"

"Tough. Shit." Marty growled. "I am not a child, and I—"

Both figures froze as Derrick came closer to them. He looked between the two. "What's going on?" he asked.

"I want to go out," Marty said hotly, "and he," she added, throwing her thumb in Henry's direction, "says I can't without two guards, a police detail and a helicopter flyover."

"Miss Fletcher, that is not what I said," Henry said tensely, his restraint palpable. He turned to Derrick. "I told Miss Fletcher that it is best if she has a security detail with her when she leaves to ensure—"

"I don't want an entourage to go to the store!" Marty shouted.

"Marty, he's right," Derrick said, "it isn't safe."

"Why not? They shot the guy who shot you, didn't they?" she asked Derrick.

Derrick mulled over how to sidestep around Marty to keep her in the dark about them still trying to find the *real* shooter. "Yes they did," Derrick started carefully, "but sometimes these acts have copy-cats looking for any way to get to Taylor and they wouldn't hesitate to hurt you. You need a detail."

Marty's eyes went wide. "You are siding with him?" she demanded of her brother.

"Yes," Derrick said, as if it was the most obvious thing in the world.

Marty looked dazed for a minute. "You can't stand him, why the fuck would you side with him?" she challenged.

"Because he is right," Derrick pushed back. "I have been shot and it fucking sucks, okay? So you can stay here and have a temper tantrum, or go out with proper security like our head of security is asking you."

Now Marty's face turned red. "I am a grown woman—"

"Well, you aren't acting like it. I don't like being followed around either but I did it!" he shouted at his sister. He heaved out a breath, "Look Marty, it's just until things are safer."

But Marty didn't stick around to listen. She turned, went back to her room, slammed the door, and sent the wall art and chandeliers rattling in her wake.

Derrick turned to Henry who was looking down the hall where Hurricane Marty had just whooshed by. "I don't know what has gotten into her," Derrick said to Henry. "She has gone out with security before."

Henry turned to Derrick. "She wanted to drive herself alone. I just don't think it's wise right now," he said quietly.

Derrick actually felt bad for the guy, he looked so upset. "Don't worry about making her mad, Henry," Derrick said, trying to soothe the hulking man. "She gets like this when she doesn't have a boyfriend. She is between a couple right now." Derrick laughed but no humor crossed Henry's stony face. "Thanks for keeping her safe, Henry."

"Nothing else I would rather do, sir," Henry said, then walked away.

Derrick felt like he was missing something about what he had just encountered. He looked down the hall to Marty's door, and debated whether or not he should go and talk to her. But Derrick shook his head to himself. Dealing with Marty was not a storm he wanted to weather right now. Instead he went to his room and followed through on his shower.

———

TAYLOR GOT HOME MUCH LATER than she had intended to, or wanted to. It was nearly seven-thirty by the time she came out of the elevator into the Fletcher Mansion, and she was starving. Her stomach wanted her to go straight to the kitchen, but she wanted to find Derrick first. She was still pissed he went to work without telling her, but she wanted to know how his day had gone, and to eat with him.

Taylor's big plan of discovering some dirty secret about Cedric's dealings never got underway, something she didn't even realize until the ride home. Things were running fine at Preston Corp, but once she was in the building she was pulled in about a thousand different directions and she forgot all about her mission.

Taylor made her way to the bedroom she and Derrick shared, and found her husband fast asleep on top of the covers, wrapped in a towel.

She smiled. It seemed that his first day back took more out of him than he thought. Taylor took a few minutes and ogled her husband, enjoying the beautiful view, then made her way to the closet. On her way out of the closet, now in comfortable clothes, Taylor heard the sound of Derrick's stomach growling and it made her realize they both needed food.

Silently, Taylor escaped to forage and bumped right into her sister-in-law on the way.

"Hey," Marty said somberly after they regained themselves.

Taylor furrowed her brow at the usually joyous and quick-witted

Marty. "What's wrong?"

Marty took a deep breath and Taylor watched as she internally wrestled with herself, finally saying, "Nothing."

"Well, thank God you went into fashion because that was the worst acting job I have ever seen," Taylor said. She grabbed her sister-in-law by the arm and ducked into her room just down the hall, shutting them inside. "Spill," Taylor demanded.

"He doesn't trust me, Taylor," she finally said as she sat on the edge of the bed, and the whoosh of relief that Marty felt was palpable to Taylor.

"Who?" Taylor asked, and then rolled her eyes at herself. The only *him* Marty would worry about trusting her was Henry. "Ignore me. Why do you say that?"

"He won't let me go out alone. I have armed guards everywhere. And when I ask if there is something going on, he tells me no," Marty complained. "I am not stupid. Obviously, there is more going on than everyone being worried about copycats."

"Marty—"

"Or he doesn't trust me, and he is keeping me under lock and key," she continued on, plowing over whatever Taylor was going to say. "Either way it's crappy, either way he doesn't trust me."

"Or perhaps he feels the less you know the safer you will be?" Taylor implored Marty.

Marty took a deep breath. "I know more is going on, but I don't want you to tell me," she told Taylor. "I want him to tell me. I want him to know he can confide in me about things that are happening. Especially if it directly involves the people I love."

Taylor looked at Marty and could feel her angst. It wasn't being left in the dark that bothered her as much as Henry keeping her chained in that room, and not telling her what was happening on the other side.

"Can I ask you something?" Taylor asked gently, sitting next to Marty on the bed. "Whose idea was it to not tell Derrick about your relationship?"

Guilt pooled in Marty's eyes before she looked down. "I just... well when it... I wasn't sure." Marty swallowed hard and took a breath. "When it all started, I wasn't sure how it would go," she admitted, shrugging. "So why get everyone involved, you know?" Taylor nodded. "And then Derrick just hated him, so I was hoping he would warm up to him first and then he went and got shot and now I don't want to upset him. I want Derrick to accept him. I don't want to tell Derrick about us and then he flips out and Henry gets hurt."

"So turn it around, Marty, and apply the same reasoning to what Henry is doing with you," Taylor encouraged. "Maybe Henry doesn't want you to know because he is afraid it will get you hurt the more you know."

Marty groaned as she flopped herself backwards on top of the bed with a small bounce. "I know you're right," she admitted, "but it still sucks."

"I know," Taylor agreed.

"And he is never around. I hardly get to see him while he is doing all this secret stuff," Marty whined.

"Well that's my fault," Taylor said.

"It's his job, Taylor, but to not know, to just be told he is taking care of it and not to worry—"

"It makes you worry more?" Taylor guessed.

"Yes," Marty said in relieved agitation, like she was so grateful someone else finally got it.

"You have to show him you believe in him, too, Marty," Taylor said. "It's give and take. You want him to divulge something important, but you aren't willing to share your relationship, something important to *him,* with Derrick. Hell, I wouldn't even know officially if I hadn't walked in on you two going at it in the kitchen," she reminded Marty.

"So I should tell Derrick?"

Taylor was silent for a minute, thinking about all the happenings and changes around her.

"I'll take that as a no," Marty said interrupting Taylor's thoughts.

"I think you should slowly tell him you are in a relationship," Taylor stated finally. "Let him warm up to that idea, let him see how happy that makes you before you drop the H-bomb."

"H-bomb?" Marty laughed. "Oh my God, that is our new code name for him, H-bomb," Marty said excitedly.

"Maybe just bomb," Taylor reconsidered. "The H could be too specific."

Marty laughed her full belly-and-snort laugh, then took a breather. "Thanks Taylor," she said. "Talking it out helped me, and I haven't had anyone to talk it out with."

"Yes, talking helps for sure," Taylor agreed. "We should probably all see a therapist."

"Yeah, we should get on that," Marty acknowledged.

Taylor's ring tone for Derrick suddenly filled the room. She smiled, "Hello?"

"When are you coming home? I am starving," he whined.

"Well I am home, but you were napping," she informed him.

"Oh," he says, "well, where are you? I have looked everywhere."

"Clearly not. I am in Marty's room, talking," she answered.

"Well Jesus Jehoshaphat, I have been all over this place. It's bigger than the Louvre—it's too much," he complained.

"You sound hangry. Meet you in the kitchen?" Taylor asked.

"Uh huh," Derrick mumbled.

"You are already there and are eating something, aren't you?" Taylor guessed. "I can hear you talking with food in your mouth."

"Love you," Derrick said over another mouthful and hung up.

Taylor rolled her eyes. "You coming to eat?" she asked Marty.

But Marty shook her head. "I have thinking to do," she said. "But don't forget movie night tomorrow night," she reminded Taylor.

"Course not," she replied and hugged Marty close. "I love you, Marty."

"I love you too, Sis," Marty said, squeezing her back.

And Taylor loved the full heart feeling she had at the sound of that.

EIGHTEEN

THE NEXT EVENING, Taylor was escorted out of work by Mick and Ian. It had been another busy day filled with meetings and phones calls, and it left Taylor zero time to even think about snooping, never mind actually doing it.

Now, even on her trek to the car, Taylor had her head buried in her phone. She had just received four text messages from Charlie about contract details, and her email chime was going crazy in the background. All the chaos would drive anyone else crazy, but Taylor was actually enjoying it. She never felt so free and alive as when she was wheeling and dealing. But she knew to tell anyone this would have them questioning her sanity.

Taylor slid into the SUV after Ian opened the door, and once she was seated, turned back to him. "Thanks, Ian," she smiled and went back to her phone. *Be kind to everyone* had been a credo in her home growing up. Her mother said that was one of the greatest things she had ever learned from Taylor's father—that it mattered just as much to be kind to the janitor as it did to be kind to the guy you needed to make a million-dollar deal with.

Taylor glanced up when she noticed her security detail did not get in the car and saw Henry in the driver's seat.

"Long time no see, Henry," Taylor said to him, as she tapped out instructions in a text and then flipped into her emails, skimming through them to find the one which needed her attention the most.

"So I've been doing some research on Cedric's habits before he died," Henry announced to Taylor.

"How come?" Taylor asked absentmindedly. She was engrossed in her emails that she was still behind on and only half listening.

"I'm hoping to shed light onto why he was bludgeoned to death," Henry said dryly.

"Ah, yes," Taylor said, now completely focused on Henry. "What did you find?"

"Glad to see I have your attention now," Henry quipped. "So he didn't use any phone correspondence starting two months before he died. It just abruptly stopped."

"Well that doesn't shock me, to be honest, Henry."

"Why is that?"

"Because he was batshit crazy. You should see what he did to the mansion where we used to live."

"I have."

"You've been to my house?" Taylor asked in horror.

Henry gave her a curt nod and met her eyes briefly in the rearview mirror. "It was when I was checking the security status before you officially hired me."

Taylor took that in. She felt like a coward having not been back there, for feeling unable to go back. "Is it still in shambles?" Taylor asked quietly.

"It closely resembles a demolition job gone bad if that is what you are asking," he confirmed as he pulled into the underground garage of Fletcher Enterprises.

The door to the car opened and Derrick slid in as Rog closed the door behind him. "Hi," he said leaning over to kiss Taylor. He winced just slightly and Taylor noticed he was doing that less and less. It made her feel so relieved to know that he was starting to feel better. "Henry," Derrick greeted, nodding to the other man as he settled in his seat.

"Mr. Fletcher," Henry returned with a nod, "I was just telling Taylor how I was looking into Cedric's routines before he died."

"Oh yeah? To see if we can find out who knocked him into the bucket?"

"Tactful, Derrick," Taylor reprimanded, as Henry started to fill him in on their conversation from moments before. She was totally trying to take the attention away from the fact that her husband caught Henry's drift way sooner than she had.

"So while he didn't make phone calls, he was all over email. He did many work and business transactions with his Preston Corp email. He buried it pretty well, but it was still easy to dig up the information. I could tell I was not the only person who had attempted hacking it."

"Okay, well could you get any information from there?"

"No," Henry stated as he pulled out of the parking garage, "but on a secret account that he had hidden under an alias I was able to find the name of his psychiatrist."

"Wow, I really enjoyed the setup there, Henry," Taylor said.

"It was sort of like a roller coaster ride," Derrick agreed. "First he set it up that he found something and then there wasn't anything on it, but on the *other* one—"

"Okay, Laurel and Hardy," Henry interjected bluntly.

"You made him mad," Taylor whisper-yelled at Derrick, smiling at him. She had missed their back and forth talks before and after work. It almost felt normal again, except for the fact that Henry was trying to discuss a potential murder with them.

"Anyway," Henry said sternly, trying to regain control of the situation, "I'm taking you to meet with this psychiatrist." Silence filled the vehicle. After several seconds, Henry heaved out a disgusted sigh. "Don't you want to know his name?" he finally asked.

"Are we allowed to talk now?" Taylor asked, perplexed, trying to hide a smile.

"It's Mellon, the psychiatrist's name is Dr. Xander Mellon."

"A psychiatrist? Cedric is sending me to a psychiatrist?" Taylor asked in confusion and disgust. "Well that is fucking ironic."

"What a terrible name," was Derrick's response. "Xander Mellon sounds like some weird mutated fruit," he said incredulously, earning an irritated glare from Taylor in return. "Come on, I know it's weird it's a psychiatrist, but you can not tell me his name didn't have you puzzled, too."

"Yeah, you know, I didn't give it a second thought," Taylor said to her husband.

"Anyway," Henry interjected again, "I located him in Pismo Beach, and we are going there now."

"Is he expecting us?" Taylor asked.

"I think he will make time for you," Henry said dryly.

CLOSE TO TWO hours later Henry pulled into the driveway of a Spanish style, two-story home. Its cream-colored stucco stood out starkly against the darkening sky of the evening.

Taylor and Derrick looked at each other as they took in their surroundings. Derrick finally shrugged in confusion.

"Henry, this is not an office," Taylor finally informed the larger man.

"Aye," Henry said, meeting Taylor's eyes in the rearview mirror. "Dr. Mellon retired last year. This is his home."

"Henry, I can't just go into someone's home," Taylor announced.

"You are correct," Henry agreed. "I would ring the doorbell and see if he invites you in."

Taylor glowered at her head of security, then looked at her husband and found him trying to mask a smile.

Taylor turned her attention back to Henry's stare in the rearview mirror. "You know, Henry, I don't know what it is about this wild crusade that has turned you into a comedian, but I feel it is really, really ill-timed," she said as she jerked the SUV door open and headed to the front door.

"Suppose we should follow her," Derrick said after a moment of silence.

"Aye," Henry agreed.

And with that, the two men trailed after Taylor who was already ringing the doorbell. After several seconds, Taylor turned to Henry. "Maybe he isn't home," she said softly. But as the words left her lips a figure came into view behind the patterned glass door in front of her.

The door opened and an older man with a snow-white beard and half-moon glasses appeared before them. His face transformed from blissful ignorance to full realization when his gray eyes met Taylor's blue stare.

"Taylor Preston," he said, a bemused smile gracing his lips. "I have been waiting for you to turn up."

"Have you?" Taylor asked apprehensively.

The man nodded sadly. "Yes, Cedric said you would need answers," he said, turning abruptly. He was about five paces away when he looked over his shoulder and shouted, "Come in! Come in!" and beckoned them to follow him further into the house.

"Um... are you Dr., uh, Xander Mellon then?" Taylor asked as she took a step forward, pausing at his first name, and Derrick knew she was thinking what a crazy name it was, too.

"Yes, an unfortunate name, isn't it? My parents had an odd sense of humor," the doctor pointed out.

Taylor flicked a glance to Derrick, who gave her his best *see, I told you* look.

"Uh, may I talk to you about Cedric?" Taylor asked, trying to rein the conversation back in as they moved.

"Of course," Dr. Mellon said, coming to a round table in the kitchen at the back of the home. He pulled out one of the wrought iron chairs, making a god-awful screech against the clay tile floor, and took a seat, motioning for Taylor to do the same.

"Uh, well," Taylor fumbled as she took a seat across from the doctor. She had wanted to find this man so he could help her fill in the gaps, and now she wasn't sure where to start.

"When did Cedric first start seeing you?" Derrick asked, and Taylor nodded like *yup, of course that was the most fabulous and best question ever.*

A sad smile ghosted over Dr. Mellon's face. "I met Cedric for the first time about thirty years ago," he said, looking at the wall as he remembered. "He had entered a rehab program I was training in as a new psychiatrist."

"Did he show signs of mental disturbance then?" Taylor blurted out. She was really curious to find out when the crazy had started, when the downward trend had begun.

"No," Dr. Mellon answered calmly. "At that time, his drinking and drug use was the reason for seeking help. His major depressive break happened years later."

Major depression? "Okay, but what about his, uh, I don't know, his mental illness?" Taylor asked.

Dr. Mellon had a very practiced and effective poker face. "Cedric suffered from addiction, depression, and anxiety."

There was a long pause from everyone else in the room.

"And?" Taylor asked finally.

Dr. Mellon laughed, "And nothing, that was it."

"There has to be more," Taylor demanded. "Was there schizo-phrenia or bipolar or something more?"

Mellon slowly shook his head, "No."

"When exactly was the last time you spoke with Cedric?" Taylor asked, her voice now holding a slight edge to it.

"A few days before he died I—"

"So recently? Because the man I knew was not sad or nervous, okay. He was a raving lunatic," Taylor said, her face and tone becoming hot.

"Mrs. Fletcher, I—"

"Don't. Don't talk to me in that *you are crazy, he was fine* voice. It wasn't fine, he wasn't fine. If he was under your care while he was ripping down walls, taking out electronics from my home, and then threatening to kill me then I think it is you who needs to be committed!"

"Tay, sit down, it's okay," Derrick said at her side as he held her hand. Taylor hadn't even been aware that she had stood during her rant. "It's okay, sit."

Taylor nodded, shaking with the emotions that ran through her.

"Taylor," Dr. Mellon said, his tone no longer laced with pity, "let me explain my relationship with Cedric. I met him when he went to rehab. He did really well. He was able to figure out a lot of things about himself. Cedric was a success story. He had freed himself from the tight hold addiction takes on so many. And when he left that program, I didn't see him for, gosh, maybe four or five years."

"What changed? Why did you see him again?" Derrick asked. Taylor was glad he was able to be on the ball with the questions because she was absolutely lost.

"Mr. Preston requested I take him on again as a patient," Dr. Mellon answered.

"Cedric did?" Taylor asked in confusion.

"No, Taylor, your father. He wrote to me and asked me if I would take Cedric on as a patient."

"My dad?" Taylor asked. She could feel her face tense up in all sorts of emotions, which she was way past being able to mask. "Why?"

Now Dr. Mellon seemed to struggle with his response. "What do you know about Cedric, Taylor?"

"I know he was the craziest person I have ever encountered in my life," Taylor replied flatly.

Dr. Mellon ghosted another sad smile and nodded, "It seems his years with you were not his best."

Derrick could see Taylor getting fired up at the man's words.

"Were you seeing him then? After Grant contacted you, did you and Cedric reconnect?" Derrick asked.

Mellon nodded. "He and I began sessions after Grant reached out. And things were going well. He came regularly for a long time, for years and then he just stopped. He contacted me again about six months before his death. We spoke on the phone, then he would send emails, but we never met in person."

"Do you have copies of those emails?" Henry asked, speaking up for the first time.

Mellon looked thoughtful. "Perhaps," he mused. "Cedric, and his whole family really, were very private. I take patients' privacy very seriously and I safeguard their conversations with me through several layers of security. I will have to look."

Henry gave a nod, "That would be helpful."

"Okay, so let's back up for just a second," Taylor said, holding up a hand. "What was he like when my dad asked you to see him again? His demeanor?" she asked in irritation. She got the feeling that the good doctor was holding on to information about Cedric and was not in a hurry to give it away. And it was really starting to annoy the shit out of her.

Dr. Mellon hesitated before he spoke again, "Have you looked at Cedric's journals?"

"Journals?" Taylor asked in annoyance.

Mellon shook his head. "No? I suspect they might help you understand more about him."

"What are you talking about?" Taylor bit out.

"Cedric found during his time at the rehab facility that he felt better journaling—more drawing than writing but they did evolve to a graphic novel of sorts. He was extremely talented with drawing. I think that is why it worked so well for him to get his feelings out. He put everything in them."

"How would his doodles from rehab help me?"

Mellon shook his head. "No, he kept up with it. When I started to see him again he said he still did it. And then when we spoke again he said he had probably filled dozens of books over the years."

"Why can't you just tell me what I'm asking you?"

Dr. Mellon sobered. "Because your family has secrets, Taylor, and they are not mine to tell."

———————

TAYLOR WAS beyond frustrated when they left the office and Derrick could feel it radiating off of her as they drove back to the Fletcher mansion.

After Dr. Mellon had dropped the clouded Preston family secret bomb, Taylor looked like she was ready to burst. So he had taken over.

"So we will find the journals, and then we are coming back," Derrick had informed Dr. Mellon.

"I look forward to it," he had said, looking almost relieved.

Taylor had reached in her Birkin bag and slapped one of her business cards down on the desk. "If you can think of anything in the meantime that you are willing to tell me, contact me," she instructed the man.

Mellon had calmly picked up the card and nodded. "I will," he had assured her. Mellon reached into his own wallet and grabbed his card. "In case you need me," he said as he handed the card to Taylor. Taylor had looked like fire was going to spew out of her eyes as she accepted his card, but she bit her tongue.

But now Taylor simmered as the landscape passed by them.

"Why couldn't he just spit it out?" she finally said to the window.

Derrick smirked. He had been waiting for her to finally say something. "Sounds like there are things that he wants you to find out for yourself," Derrick said.

"Yeah I get that," Taylor spat at him and then heaved a sigh. "I'm sorry, I just want to figure all this shit out and keep our family safe. I hated being trapped before and now I am scared to go out! I'm still trapped!"

Taylor closed her eyes and heaved out a tense breath.

"Hey," Derrick said, bumping her with his shoulder.

Taylor looked at him out the corner of her eye, "What?"

"What do you call a guy with a rubber toe?" he asked.

"What?" Taylor asked, completely irritated.

"Roberto," Derrick said, wiggling his eyebrows.

Taylor closed her eyes and turned back to the window in aggravation, both at his inopportune comedic timing and the fact that she really wanted to laugh at his stupid joke.

"How much does a pirate pay for corn?" he asked, but Taylor ignored him. "A buccaneer!"

Taylor rolled her lips in and bit down to keep a smile from breaking through. She had serious issues here and her husband was apparently trying out for a comedy club. She would not give in to him.

"Why did the lifeguards kick the elephants out of the pool?" Taylor shook her head. "Because they kept dropping their trunks!"

Henry coughed in the front of the SUV, but Taylor was positive that he was covering a laugh and now she was mad at him, too.

"How do chickens cheer for their favorite team? Come on, they egg them on. That one was foul but easy, Taylor," Derrick said.

She couldn't hold it back anymore. She shook her head and smiled, turning to him. "Is there a point to these horrible jokes?" she asked, rolling her eyes at him.

"Yes, it got you to laugh and to relax. And when you relax you can think better than when you are tense and frustrated," he reminded her. He put a hand on the back of her head and pulled her to him, planting his lips on hers. "Relax, Tay, we will get this all figured out."

Taylor closed her eyes, heaved out a breath, and leaned her forehead into Derrick's. "It's hard," she whispered to him.

"I know," he nodded.

"I want my happily ever after," she said looking at him. "I have the happily, but the ever after keeps getting interrupted by bullets and secrets."

The bing of her email alerted her, and she slid her phone out of the bag at her feet. She opened the home screen and clicked into her email app to check it. She was still behind in work from when Derrick had been in the hospital, so she was quick to check any email, text, or phone call, day or night.

The subject line was 'About our visit', and was from none other than Dr. Mellon.

Taylor clicked without saying a word, curious what the good doctor had to say just a little over an hour since their departure.

MRS. PRESTON-FLETCHER,

I have been here musing over our meeting and do feel badly that I have sent you on what could possibly be a blind search. I wish that things had been different in so many ways

for your family.

I do have something of a peace offering, if you will. I have attached the letter your father sent me years ago when he asked me to help your uncle. I found it within the files I had secured regarding Cedric. I feel that this is more about Cedric's care than about your family's past, and therefore I feel comfortable sharing this with you now.

I look forward to speaking with you once you have some pieces to the puzzle.

Best,

Xander Mellon

TAYLOR OPENED the attached file that Dr. Mellon had titled *Grant Preston,* and her heart stammered a bit as her father's hand-writing appeared on the small screen. She had memories of her father, but she could not remember ever seeing his handwriting. It wasn't beautiful, but it wasn't illegible, either. Instead it was something in between. And to Taylor, it was perfect. She took a minute to just take in the scrawling penmanship before she actually read what was on the page.

DR. MELLON,

My name is Grant Preston. I am not sure if you recall but I met you several years ago when my brother Cedric was under your care for his drug addiction issues.

I am writing to you now because I am once again concerned about Cedric. He has fallen into a downward spiral in the last year and he won't let anyone in. He spoke so highly of you during and after his program. I am hoping that you would be willing to take him on as a patient.

I would like to speak with you further on this matter in person if you are available.

Thank you and I look forward to hearing from you,
Grant Preston

"WHAT ARE YOU LOOKING AT?" Derrick asked as he peered over her shoulder.

"He sent me the letter my dad sent him."

"Who did?"

"Mellon. He just emailed it to me," Taylor said rereading the letter.

"Is it helpful?" Derrick asked her.

Taylor looked at the script on her phone again and smiled up to Derrick sadly. "Not to figuring out Cedric," she said and looked back at her phone, "but it does help me to remember I came from some pretty fabulous people."

Derrick kissed the side of Taylor's hair and pulled her to him. They stayed that way the rest of the way home.

NINETEEN

IT WAS movie night in the Fletcher Mansion.

Taylor had totally forgotten about their weekly date after the drive to Pismo, and Marty was pissed.

It was something Taylor, Derrick, and Marty had started when they all began living together again and Taylor actually loved it. Derrick claimed to only look forward to it when he picked the movie but she had for sure seen him glued to the screen for her pick of *The Fault in Our Stars* during their last movie night.

But Taylor was totally not feeling it tonight, so she tried to tell Marty they could move it to another night that week. It didn't go well.

"You want to move movie night," Marty asked, horrified. "How can you want to move movie night?" she questioned.

"It's just been a long day, Marty. I had a meeting pretty far away and—"

"It's our tradition, every week this is movie night," she reminded them. "You can't just break a tradition."

"Jeez Louise, Marty, she just wants to do it another night. She isn't canceling Christmas," Derrick said, his irritation clear. "Besides we have only been doing it a few weeks. I would hardly call it a tradition."

"That's how traditions start, Derrick," Marty informed him in a condescending tone, "and so what, just because it's only been a few weeks we should just treat it like it doesn't matter? Huh?"

"Marty—"

Marty held a hand up in her brother's face. "No, Derrick, don't say anything else. We are having movie night, damn it. I clear this night every week especially so we can be together. As a family," she said, now looking at Taylor. "And you two are not canceling on me, because you don't cancel on family."

And didn't that just hit Taylor right in the feels.

"You're right," Taylor said, and then looked at Derrick. "She's right—it's our thing. We will change and meet you in the living room."

"Tay," Derrick started.

"Go change," Marty said through her teeth at her brother. "The pizza will be here in ten minutes," she said and turned off to the living room, already in her pajamas with her blanket in her arms.

IT WAS Marty's week to pick the movie and she had picked *Spaceballs* because a.) she wanted to infuriate her brother b.) it was one of her favorite movies and c.) because she felt the ridiculousness of the movie might help ease the tension that had been surrounding all of them.

As the credits began, the Fletcher siblings bickered about the movie choice while they ate pizza as if they had never seen food. One of Taylor's favorite things to do was to watch Marty and Derrick interact. She had always wanted a sibling, wanted inside jokes and someone who would take the worst insults you could hurl and then hug you the next minute. This was as close as she got to it, and she loved every second of it.

About thirty minutes into the movie, Marty, who had been working day and night on a final collection for her last semester of design school, drifted off to sleep. Fifteen minutes later, Derrick, who had just been making fun of his sister who "couldn't hang" was right behind her, snoring.

Taylor was honestly not paying attention to the movie. Her mind was instead in every direction besides wherever the *Spaceballs* cast was headed. She closed her eyes and tried to settle her mind. She had, at one point, practiced meditation every day, and had found it really relaxing. It had been especially helpful when she was trying to control thoughts about a crazed uncle potentially coming after her or fears associated with being abducted and forced to take over a billion-dollar industry.

But as crazy as those two things were, life had become much more complex than even that. So Taylor sat and focused on her breath. Slowly she returned to a rhythm that soothed her. But as with all meditation, her mind wandered, and it kept getting wrapped in work stuff, investigation stuff, and then, finally, her father's letter. She came out of the meditation, shut off the movie, covered up the sleeping Fletchers, and went in search of her phone to read the letter again.

It was the rule that phones were in other rooms during the movie. Another Marty rule, but it was a good one—it switched the focus. If anyone needed them badly enough, they could call the house, Marty always claimed.

Taylor went to their bedroom and found her phone, which of course had several text messages and a missed call from Todd. Taylor ignored all of the notifications and went to her email. Opening the app she started to scroll past all the new messages to the previously opened one, when one of the new emails caught her eye. It was a new one from Dr. Mellon, this one titled *More on CP*. It was time stamped just thirty minutes earlier.

. . .

MRS. PRESTON-FLETCHER,

I apologize for this late email.

After we met earlier, I started to look at my files on Cedric as I promised I would. It was how I came across the letter from your father. And now I have found the last email that Cedric sent me. He told me you might be coming to me for answers. I had not noticed it at the time, but he attached something entitled "For Taylor." It would seem he would have wanted you to have this. I have not opened this file, as I assume it was for your eyes only. I admit I was blindsided by your visit, otherwise I would have looked at these things before we met, perhaps have made your visit more worthwhile.

-Xander Mellon

THE FILE ATTACHED WAS a large one, so Taylor grabbed her iPad, allowing her a bigger screen to see what Cedric had bequeathed her. Taylor opened the document and found a scanned-in book cover. Her heart raced. Could this be one of the journals that Dr. Mellon had spoken of?

Sliding to the next page, Taylor confirmed that this was probably the first book he had started at rehab, since the inside page was labeled *Healing Winds Recovery Center.*

What a stupid name, Taylor mused in irritation. When had winds ever been healing? She thought about the destruction it caused with hurricanes and tornadoes and figured the name was something picked by throwing darts at a board.

She also noticed the date scribbled in the corner *August '85.* Doing a little bit of math, Taylor figured that would be about the time when Cedric was headed into rehab.

Taylor slid her finger across the screen again and was brought to another page with really nice penmanship. At the top of the lined page was *Cedric Preston*, and a paragraph followed below it. Taylor reflected on how different his penmanship was from her father's. It seemed they were different in a lot of ways.

Taylor refocused on the words written and started to read.

THEY SAY this will help and that it's part of the healing process, and so here I am writing in this ridiculous cheap ass book. I am required to write at least 200 words per day. They will count and it may be read if they think it will help my treatment. They said it didn't matter what I wrote in here, so I'm going to fill up these pages by complaining about doing this.

But I can't just complain because I also need to focus on the question posed for the week: Why do I think I am here?

Okay, well that won't take 200 words. I am here because my father asked me to come. And I will do anything for my father. He and my mother are great people and they didn't cause me to do drugs. I was never abused or under stress to get to this point. And I don't believe that I got to this point, the point where I needed to get high every day, because I am some spoiled rich kid either. My parents worked really hard to keep me grounded. They made my brother and me work for things, and earn our way. Yes, we had the best of everything, but outside of food and clothing we had to earn things.

I tried drugs and got hooked. I am what they warn you about. I was at a party and fell into the peer pressure thing because social settings aren't really my thing and I tried some coke, on top of the booze and the pot and then found a feeling of invincibility I could never recreate with anything else. Without it I am not a fun person.

So my Dad asked me to come here to clean up, because he doesn't want me to be a statistic.

There is my first 200 words, probably more. And I still hate writing in this fucking book.

TAYLOR SWIPED when she got to the end of the passage and on the next page was a beautiful sketched picture of Taylor's grandfather and grandmother. Taylor zoomed in, examining it. She couldn't believe how good the drawing was. It could have been a photograph it was so perfect. In the bottom corner of the page was Cedric's neat signature.

"He was so talented," Taylor whispered, and she felt a little embarrassed of being in awe of his work. It was like thinking a serial killer was handsome—it just felt so wrong. This was certainly something she never knew about him, but how would she really have ever known anything when she could never talk to him.

She swiped to the next page, skipping the paragraph and focusing on the drawings in it. After each journal entry there was a drawing, and Taylor swiped quickly through, briefly looking at each one. There was a leaf on a branch, one of a younger Dr. Mellon, her father, also younger than she remembered, and a young woman.

Taylor paused. There was something about the woman.

She had been swiping so quickly that the screens kept flipping in front of her without her swiping.

She was a very familiar looking woman.

Taylor swiped back through the pictures seeing bird, butterfly, and needle drawings before she reached it. Taylor pulled the tablet close to her face and zoomed in, trying to look closely and see that the person wasn't who she thought it was.

But the closer it was, the more obvious it became to her that it was, in fact, a drawing of her mother.

Taylor sat and stared at the screen before her, unable to look away. Of all the crazy things that had been thrown at her in her life, and lately that number was astronomical, this may be the one that had her head spinning the most.

Taylor got up from her frozen position on the chair and walked to the closet. She found the jacket she had worn earlier and ripped the stiff slip of paper from her pocket. And from inside the closet she dropped to the floor and dialed the number she found on the business card.

A sleep-laden voice answered her call.

"Dr. Mellon."

"Why is my mother in Cedric's stupid book thing?"

There was a pause, "Taylor?"

"Yes."

"I'm sorry—"

"I got your email and opened the attachment and it was a journal. It appears to be his first one from rehab," she said rattling out her explanation. "So I looked at Cedric's book and I found a drawing of my mother. Why is my mother in this stupid book? You said this book was from his time in rehab that was way before he met my mother."

"Taylor, your mother was a patient with Cedric."

"No, she wasn't," Taylor dismissed immediately. "My mother grew up in southern Arizona and met my father at a music festival in Baja."

"I'm sorry, Taylor, but—"

"No, she—"

"Taylor, you need to listen to me," Dr. Mellon said sternly, finally silencing her. He didn't shout. Perhaps if he had shouted she would have shouted back or if he had said nothing she would have just rambled on. But it was his no-nonsense fatherly "listen to me" that got through to her. "Cedric met your mother while they were both in rehab. They were friends."

Taylor shook with the sobs that she was working very hard to keep silent. "What was she in rehab for?" Taylor finally got out, her voice raw and broken.

"Your mother was addicted to drugs, Taylor," Dr. Mellon explained gently.

"She never told me," Taylor whispered. "Why wouldn't she tell me?"

"I am sure she wanted to protect you, Taylor. It's what parents do. Perhaps we can set up a meeting," Dr. Mellon said. "I can try to fill you in on what I know."

"Why didn't you just tell me?" she whispered.

"Because I thought someone in your family should tell you those secrets."

DERRICK WOKE up on the couch with Taylor glued to his side, and though he was having some pain at his incision site he smiled and tilted his head so that he could lay a kiss on the top of hers.

"My mother was a drug addict," Taylor said as his lips touched her hair and Derrick froze.

"I'm sorry, what?"

Taylor leaned her head back and met Derrick's eyes. "Mellon sent me Cedric's journal thing, and there was a drawing of my mother in it."

Derrick was working his barely awake mind really hard to try and take in what Taylor was saying. He wondered if he was still asleep, but as he blinked his eyes he knew he was awake. "Tay, that doesn't mean she was a drug addict."

"I called Dr. Mellon."

"Wait, when the hell did that happen?" Derrick asked, completely confused.

"After you fell asleep," Taylor said.

"Okay," Derrick said trying to catch up, "so you called Dr. Mellon."

"Yup."

"And what did he say?"

"That my mother was a drug addict."

Derrick looked at his wife for a second. "I feel like there is more information that you are not giving me."

"My mom lied to me, Derrick," Taylor said. "She never told me this and I feel like everything I did know about her was a lie." Taylor bit her lip, but still tears fell and she fought to not sob.

"Tay," Derrick said embracing her, feeling her shake against him. He couldn't fix this. The one thing he could not make better for Taylor was the past, especially this kind of past. He let her cry and when she seemed to slow down, he leaned back to look at her. "What can I do, Tay?" he asked, almost begging. Nothing was worse, he decided, than watching the person you love be so devastated.

"I would just feel so much better if I could talk to someone about what happened, about any of this shit, and finally get some answers," Taylor said as she hung her head. "But they are all gone."

Derrick nodded his head, feeling helpless. Suddenly it came to him, and he started to shake his head. "Not everyone, Tay," he said, smiling at her befuddled look because he may have come up with the best solution.

TWENTY

TAYLOR LEFT Derrick immediately after he announced his perfect idea and made her way to the kitchen.

She needed to talk to Nan.

When Nan came into the kitchen and saw Taylor, she looked a little startled but it quickly morphed into delight. "Hello, my darling!" she exclaimed. "Are you needin' a little nighttime snack?"

Taylor shook her head, "Not tonight, Nan," she said. In fact Taylor felt like she might be sick. "I wanted to ask you something."

"Of course, dear."

"I need you to tell me about my mom."

"Oh my dear, that is a subject I could never tire of," Nan said joyfully. "Your mother was—"

"My mom and Cedric," Taylor clarified.

The jolliness fell from Nan's face and she began to slowly shake her head as she sat herself on a stool beside the large kitchen island. "That, my dear, is a tale without a happy ending," she said, her expression pained.

Taylor heaved out a sigh and pulled a stool up next to Nan's. "Nan, things are happening around me," she said with exasperation, "and I am trying to make sense of it all. There are secrets. Damn it, everywhere I turn there are secrets, and I need to know about them. And Nan," she implored, "you are my only family left from the time those secrets originated."

Nan sat stone-faced for a time, probably hoping Taylor would renege on her request. When that didn't happen, she sighed resoundingly and spoke. "I dinna want to be the one telling you this tale," she said to Taylor, leaning forward and patting her leg.

"I know, Nan," Taylor said sympathetically, leaning herself forward and touching the older woman's forehead with her own, "but please."

Nan looked into Taylor's eyes and then closed her own and took a small breath. "Cedric was such a happy young man, such a free spirit," Nan reminisced, smiling a little. "He was so kind and artistic. He had this amazing talent of drawing. Did you know that?" she asked Taylor.

"I have been recently introduced to that information," Taylor said dryly.

"He really struggled," Nan went on, "because he knew his father wanted him in the business world. But that boy," she said shaking her head, "that was just never going to be for him.

"However," Nan said, leaning back emphasizing her next point, "he never would have wanted to upset his father, so he went along with it. He never wanted to upset anyone and that was his problem. He would just go along with what everyone else wanted. And as every story like his goes, he got in with a crowd he couldn't say no to." Taylor watched in awe as Nan reminisced about this stranger who bore no resemblance to the Cedric that she knew.

"What made him go to rehab?"

"It was Cedric's third car accident in a year, but this one sent two people to the hospital. That was the final straw for your grandparents, and so off he went to rehab."

"Was he angry when he went?"

"Oh no," Nan said, smiling a sad smile, "Cedric was never angry."

"You're kidding? Every time I ever saw him, he was mad," Taylor said bewildered.

"That was, well, it was a different time," Nan answered, looking at Taylor with pity. "He wasn't always that way. In fact, in my heart, the man you knew was not Cedric at all."

Taylor was having a hard time believing that someone could just go off the rails so far, but instead of voicing that she pressed on. "So what happened?"

"Well, he came back six months or so after he, well, left. And when he returned, he brought with him this vision, your mother, dear," Nan clarified and then paused looking out into space, a small smile gracing her lips. "Elizabeth was just a natural beauty." Nan reached one of her weathered hands out and cupped Taylor's chin. Her touch was warm, with just a little scratchy dryness, but it was all a comfort to Taylor. "A beauty just like you. And she came in so very timid and polite. She was quiet and tried to stay out of the way but you had no choice but to be entranced by her.

"Cedric spoke to me and said she was a friend and that she needed a job. That he was hoping we could take her on as staff at Preston Manor. It was clear that Cedric wanted to help her. He told me enough to know she'd had a rough go of it and she needed a fresh start. But it was also clear that he did not think of her as just a friend."

"What did he tell you about her?" Taylor questioned Nan, eager to get even a scrap of information on her mother.

"Not the information you're looking for, Taylor dear," she said gently. "Just that she had been tossed aside by those she trusted and had nowhere to go."

Taylor nodded, accepting that Nan did not have the answers she so craved, and so instead kept her on the topic she did have answers for. "Why did you think Cedric didn't think of her as a friend?"

Nan struggled for a moment, as if trying to find the best way to say what she was thinking. "Have you ever seen how plants bend themselves toward sunlight, move in whatever direction they can in order to get closer to the sun's rays?" she asked Taylor. When Taylor nodded, she went on, "That was how Cedric looked at Elizabeth—like she was his food source. If she was in the room his eyes tracked her like prey.

"I agreed to take her on under the condition that if there was any funny business, or she didn't pull her own, she was gone and Cedric agreed. I needn't have ever worried though, because your mother was a fabulous worker. That day, she started with me in the kitchen and whatever I asked of her she did without question. I won't lie, I was testing her. For two weeks I made your mother work like a dog and not once did she scoff or eye roll or back talk. Always please and thank you."

Taylor bit her lip. It all sounded like her mom—hardworking, polite. She had drilled these two things into Taylor growing up, telling her constantly how vital it was to not just depend on her Preston name.

"And Cedric, he was just so happy," Nan said. "He would come and check on her, smiling and his eyes brightening each time he caught a glimpse. He was completely and totally under a spell. Always making sure Elizabeth was okay, getting along fine, had everything she needed. He was completely and totally head over heels in love with Elizabeth, there was absolutely no doubt," Nan said, and she shook her head slowly. "But Elizabeth, that girl did not feel the same."

Taylor was ashamed, but she actually breathed a sigh of relief when Nan said that, one she hadn't been aware she was holding. She thought of her mother and her gentle face, and great manners and soothing ways. The thought of her with beastly and erratic Cedric made her sick.

"Now do not misunderstand, Elizabeth cared about Cedric but it was definitely not the way he cared about her. He watched her, worshipped her with his eyes, but you never saw him lay so much as a finger on her. Elizabeth treated Cedric like a brother. She teased him, stuck her tongue out at him, rolled her eyes at his jokes. She touched him, but never in an intimate way. It was always like a sister—

straightening a tie, picking off lint. Her fingers never lingered, the way a lover's do. She had a great friend in Cedric and she looked out for him. She was there, I suspect, to make sure he stayed on track, that he stayed without the drugs. And he looked out for her, too," Nan looked thoughtful. "He always hoped it would turn into more."

"Did he tell you that?" Taylor asked. Nan sounded so sure of it she wondered if he had told her something.

"No," she said with a small smile, "but you could tell. I think, no, no wait, I *know* he was always hoping and waiting for it to turn into more. When she would pick lint off his suit jackets, he would stop breathing. You could see him absorbing, memorizing the contact.

"A few months went by, and Elizabeth stayed in the kitchen with me and she slowly met the family, your family. She was just as kind and polite with all of them."

"Did she, I mean, when did she meet my dad?"

"Oh, well not for a while. He was away at this time, learning the business, going to meetings, working long hours. He had an apartment close to the city and he didn't come home as often. So Elizabeth was here for about four months I would say before..." Nan faltered then. She left the words hanging and suddenly looked hesitant to go on.

"Before what?" Taylor pressed.

Nan wavered, finally swallowing and taking a big breath before she began again. "It was before Simon and Delia's wedding. Simon had asked Cedric and Grant to be in it. Those three were thick as thieves, for years. And now they would all be in the wedding. So Elizabeth was in the kitchen working one evening a couple of days before the big event, and your father walked in.

"Grant's head was down looking at something, and your mother was walking across the room, bringing this rather large tray of dishes over to the sink to be washed and they ran right into each other, literally right into one another.

"It got everyone's attention because she dropped the pans she was carrying and his papers went flying and we all came to see and it was like something out of a movie. In the midst of all of that chaos was your mother and your father completely captivated with each other, just staring into each other's eyes. People ran around getting the papers and grabbing the pans and the two of them just stood there staring at each other.

"So I introduced them and they shook hands but still the two never broke eye contact. And then Cedric came in, completely unaware of anything off and said he was so glad to finally introduce two of his favorite people." Nan's eyes focused on Taylor's. "I felt my heart shatter for him, Taylor, I really did. There was an instant connection, a chemistry between Grant and Elizabeth. Cedric dinna see it, or maybe he just dinna want to see it. There is no doubt about it, Cedric wanted Elizabeth. He was in love with her. He was possessed by her. But Elizabeth never felt that way about him. And I know that before your father ever came into the picture, she made it clear they were just friends. She said as much, treated him as such, but Cedric just loved to be around her."

The pair sat in silence for a moment, and finally Taylor spoke. "I remember seeing a picture of Cedric in Simon and Delia's wedding and he just looked so happy," Taylor remarked.

"Aye, he was. He had begged your mom to go just as friends. He was on cloud nine that day. I am sure being at a wedding with the woman that you love gives you all kinds of thoughts and probably blinds you. That is the only explanation I have for him not seeing what everyone, and I mean everyone, could plainly see.

"After their first meeting, your father kept making trips to the kitchen. Grant always found his way down when he was home—that boy could eat. But his trips to the kitchen were far more frequent and far less about food when Elizabeth was there. And Elizabeth, bless her soul, tried to ignore him, truly she did. She always sought out a task to do, busied herself. But it was no use. Slowly they started speaking to each other, and I think they stole time to themselves, eventually.

"Grant actually decided to start staying at home, sold his apartment. And still Cedric was going along, checking in on Elizabeth, making sure she was okay. Loving her with his eyes. And then, well, then he found out."

"How?" Taylor asked, caught up in the romance of her mother and father.

"Well, Cedric caught them red-handed I'm afraid," Nan said, and when Taylor opened her mouth to ask for more, Nan stopped her. "And that is all I will say about that.

"It was a huge blowup. The whole family was rattled for days. The boys were screaming and Cedric, well, his heart was broken. He had just been blindsided by the whole thing. So blinded by his own feelings that this was a giant shock. He said things, horrible things, to your mother."

Taylor's jaw tightened.

"But your mother was not going to let him get away with that. He accused her of chasing money, and I remember she said to him, 'If that was the case, Cedric, I would have gotten on my knees when you told me who you were, don't you think? I love you, Cedric, I do, but like a brother. Not like how I feel about Grant. I am in love with Grant. I am sorry I never had feelings for you, but I told you I didn't. I was trying to figure out how not to hurt you, but hiding how I feel about Grant has only made it worse. Look what I have done! I have divided you and your family!'

"And then she left."

"Wait, what?" Taylor asked, "She left?"

Nan nodded. "Yes. She left, and that broke both Cedric and Grant. She told them they needed to work this out because she wouldn't break up a family. Grant begged her to stay, but she said she couldn't come between them anymore. Weeks went by, and the two brothers wouldn't even look at each other. Grant stopped coming to the house almost all together, and if he did stop by one would leave if the other walked in."

"And then your grandmother had enough," Nan proclaimed, laughing at the recollection. "Oh, I miss that woman, Taylor, she ran this ship so well. It was rocky seas after she was gone," Nan said. "Anyway, your grandmother sent them both away, had them dropped off in the middle of nowhere one night, alone together in the woods. Just camping supplies and an order to work it out like men.

"So Grant and Cedric went away, camped and hiked, spent time together. And when they came home, Cedric apologized to your mother. I thought at first it was him being the peacemaker, relenting and giving in to his brother. And I am sure that was part of it, but mostly I believe he was trying to make Elizabeth happy. I don't think he could live with the idea of her not being in his life at all. And he knew Grant made her happy. And that is what Cedric always did—whatever it took to make people happy."

"But it changed Cedric," Nan explained. "He was never the same after that. That light was gone from his eyes, from his face. He brightened really only in Elizabeth's presence, and it was awful to watch the mix of emotions in his eyes. Soon after her return, your mother and father got engaged. Cedric said he was happy, told them all the right words, but he didn't mean it. When your parents married, he was miserable. To his credit, though, he stayed sober."

Taylor now thought of the other picture displayed on the Fletcher walls, the one of a sour-looking Cedric. It all became clear.

"Do you know when he went back to using?"

"Well, his personality was so different after the fallout with your mum and dad happened, it really is hard to say," Nan said, hesitating. Taylor could tell there was more, and had it been anyone else she would have gone into her no-nonsense business approach, laying down the hammer and making them talk. But she was never going to do that to Nan. "But," Nan finally said, nodding a bit, "when your Mum announced she was pregnant, well, he did not take it well."

Taylor thought back to how harsh Cedric was to her, how crazy he was. "So he started using because of me," Taylor said flatly. "Great, he despised me from the womb."

"No, Taylor," Nan said sweetly, "he despised the fact that your parents had the life he wanted, and your father had the woman he wanted. But when you were born, Taylor, he was overjoyed. He came alive again, it was like a small bit of the old Cedric had come back," Nan said, smiling.

Taylor felt an odd rush of relief at that news.

"He tried to ignore you at first, but it was your father who handed you to him, and I swear he fell in love with you," Nan said. "I had the pleasure of watching it all happen. It was beautiful. You were their olive branch," Nan said.

"Then what happened," Taylor asked, "because he didn't stay that way." Her eyes welled a bit in frustration.

Nan looked out of answers. "I really don't know, Taylor. He was here and happy and bright. And then, well, then he just wasn't. I don't..." Nan stopped herself and held up a finger. "Wait here," she said and then took off.

Taylor wished someone else was there with her so that she could try and talk out what the hell had just happened. Instead, she pushed her palms into her eyes and sat there alone. Two minutes passed, five minutes passed, it was approaching on the ten-minute mark and she was about to go and find Nan herself when she returned with a large manila envelope.

Nan was winded. "This was hard to find," she announced shaking the envelope at Taylor.

"What is it?" Taylor asked, taking the envelope from Nan.

"Cedric mailed this to me. I got it about a week before he went to be with the Lord," Nan said as she gave the envelope to Taylor. "There is another envelope inside and it has a note to give it to you, Taylor. I was so confused as I had not seen you in years. Then when you came back, things were in such disarray for you, I honestly forgot I had it," Nan explained, and then shrugged. "And maybe a little bit of me thought it wasn't the time for you to see it," Nan confessed.

Taylor peeked inside the envelope, sure enough finding another, very well-taped envelope inside. Taylor looked up and gave Nan a smile, and then closed the space and hugged the older woman tightly.

"This life has been much too hard for a sweet woman like you," Nan muttered over Taylor's head.

Taylor nodded, but she was hopeful she was getting closer to what would make it easier.

DERRICK WAITED in his room for Taylor to come back from talking to Nan. He looked around his childhood bedroom and heaved out a sigh. He missed his space, he missed having a place that was his own, but he was glad that, in this instance, living at Fletcher Mansion was helpful for Taylor.

The door suddenly swung open and took his attention away from his floating thoughts.

"He left me this envelope," Taylor stated as she walked into the room. She opened the envelope she held and pulled out another. The second one was wrapped in wide, clear tape, wrapped multiple times over. Taylor turned the rectangle around looking for an entry point. "Got scissors?" she asked.

Derrick had no idea, but he went to the desk in the room, rifled through the drawers, and lo and behold, found a pair.

Taylor cut the tape, reached in, and removed yet another envelope, this one white and letter-sized. She opened this one with ease, since it was sans tape and she just had to lift the flap, removing a single sheet of paper.

"What is that? Derrick asked, as Taylor's eyes scanned it.

She shook her head, frowning as she met his eyes. "I have no idea. It's an address with some numbers after it," she explained as she turned the paper to him.

Derrick took the paper and looked at it. The font looked like it had been typed out on a typewriter: 56 Shell Street, Los Angeles, CA.

2000-03-05-09-13

81

07-06-09-03

Derrick grabbed his phone and punched the address in. "It's a self-storage place," he said, "and its Yelp reviews are shitastic," he relayed, showing Taylor the Google results on his phone.

Taylor's eyes went wide. "What do you think is in there?" she questioned Derrick softly.

"No idea," Derrick said looking the letter back over again. "When did he send this to you?" Derrick asked.

"Nan said she got the envelope about a week before I came, well, back."

"It's almost like, like he knew..." Derrick trailed off.

"Like he knew something was going to happen to him?" Taylor asked. "I get that feeling too."

"He must have been caught up with some messed up people."

"We need to get Henry," Taylor snatched the letter back. "We need to go there."

"Tonight?" Derrick asked. He wanted to know who was behind all this shit, too, but he was tired. And, apparently, an old man.

"Yes," Taylor stated, grabbing her iPad and walking out the door, leaving Derrick to follow reluctantly.

TOGETHER THEY MADE their way to the basement, where staff quarters were housed. On the way down Taylor filled Derrick in on what Nan had told her, and they still had time left over to walk in silence.

"This place is so huge," Taylor murmured as they went down the old stone staircase.

"Yeah," Derrick said. "It still feels just as huge as it did when we were kids."

"We really need to look at our housing needs when this is said and done," Taylor said as they came upon the door to Henry's room and knocked.

As they waited, Derrick swiped through the journal on Taylor's tablet. "He was a really good artist," he said.

"Where the hell is he?" Taylor growled in frustration, ready to go in search of another security team member when Henry opened the door about two inches and peeked out. "Henry, we need—"

"Taylor, this isn't a good time," he said quickly and quietly.

Taylor ignored Henry. "Yeah, okay. Listen, I think I found some stuff about Cedric but I need your input."

"Taylor, I am not decent," he said, widening his eyes.

"Henry, I don't need you to be in a damn suit, but I need to talk to you."

"Tay," Derrick said slowly, turning her to him, "give the guy some space." Derrick looked back up at Henry over Taylor's shoulder. "Give us a call when you're, uh, decent," Derrick said and pulled Taylor by the arm away from Henry's door.

"What are you doing?" Taylor demanded, wrenching her arm out of Derrick's grasp. "I need to talk to him."

"Tay, he has a chick in there," Derrick said.

This stunned Taylor into silence, and she was then able to be led away.

"How do you know?" she finally snapped at her husband.

"It was totally guy code," Derrick said, putting his arm around Taylor and walking her back up the stairs, "and he told me the other day that he has a girlfriend."

That news had Taylor tripping on her feet as she tried to stop but Derrick kept her moving forward. "He did?" she asked. "Wh-when did he tell you that?"

"The other day at the Medical Examiner's office," Derrick said, "He told me he wasn't into you and that he had someone he cared about as much as I care about you," Derrick said. He shrugged. "Maybe he isn't such a bad guy," he said as they made their way up the second-story stairs.

"No, he isn't."

"I mean I wouldn't want him dating my sister or anything but he isn't a bad guy."

Taylor suddenly became overcome with a coughing fit, however it sounded very similar to laughter.

"You okay, Tay?"

Taylor nodded and continued to cough all the way to their room.

TAYLOR PACED at the foot of their bed checking her phone every time she turned to pace the other direction. After repeating this about fifty times she stopped and threw her hands up in the air. "I can't wait any longer, I'm going back down," she announced and turned to the door, only to be pulled into a bear hug by Derrick.

"Oh no, you're not," he said.

"Derrick, I need to check this place out," she whined as she struggled to extricate herself from his strong arms.

"You are going to have to wait," he whispered in her ear. "I have some suggestions on how to keep you occupied while we wait for Henry."

"Derrick, I..." Taylor stopped herself as an idea came to her. She spun around and wrapped her arms around Derrick's neck. "I have an idea," she said softly, biting her lip.

"Yeah?" Derrick asked, touching his lips to Taylor's. "Tell me," he whispered.

"Let's sneak out and go ourselves," she whispered against her husband's lips.

Derrick jerked his head back, "What?"

"Come on, babe, it'll be fun," she coaxed.

"No way," Derrick said stone-faced. "Someone is out there trying to kill you, Taylor."

"But if we sneak, they won't know how to get to me," she said. "Think about it. I usually leave with hordes of security. If it's just a single car leaving, no one will think it's us."

"No, Tay, it's a bad idea," Derrick said firmly.

"Derrick, I need to check this," Taylor said just as firm.

"Well, I am not helping you," Derrick declared, crossing his arms across his chest.

"Fine, I will just go myself," Taylor said, unfazed that her attempt to seduce Derrick into her plan had failed.

"No, no you're not," Derrick said putting himself between Taylor and the door. He shook his head at her. "Taylor, have you lost your mind?"

"Yes, as a matter of fact I have," Taylor said with wide eyes. "I am in the middle of this wild goose chase from Cedric that I am hoping can lead us to answers and some damn closure. And I am not waiting for Henry to finish getting his groove on to find out!"

Taylor watched as Derrick took a deep breath and waited for his calm speech about patience. She could feel a fire light inside of her at the thought of what he would say.

Instead Derrick heaved out a sigh and walked past Taylor. She spun and watched Derrick disappear into the closet.

"What are you doing?" she called.

Derrick reappeared holding two black sweatshirts. "It's cold out," he said tossing one of the sweatshirts to Taylor, "we need to bundle up a little and dress in dark colors if we are going to sneak out."

Taylor smiled brightly at her husband. "I love you," she said as she pulled the hoodie over her head.

Derrick shook his head, trying to suppress his own grin. "Coercing me into bad ideas. My, how the tables have turned."

They left the room and crept their way to the garage. Taylor clutched the letter from Cedric in her grasp. She was eager to see if the place on the note was actually a storage area and what answers lay there.

Once the doors opened to the garage, Taylor and Derrick scurried their way over to his car collection, only to stop short when Henry appeared from the side of one of the SUVs.

"And just where are you two headed?" he asked, his arms folded across his chest.

Taylor panicked, and did the only rational thing. "It was his idea," she said pointing at Derrick.

Derrick loudly scoffed at his wife. "You liar, I told you it was a bad idea!" he defended, turning himself to Henry. "I told her it was a bad idea," he told the large man before them.

Henry closed his eyes and shook his head. "You know your safety is in question," he began.

"I know, I know, but I need to check this out," she said shaking the letter at him, "and I couldn't wait for you to finish whatever it was you were doing."

Henry turned a dark red. "And what exactly is that?" he asked, pointing at the letter.

Taylor heaved out a breath and rattled off all the information she had obtained from Nan. "And then he sent me this, and I need to go here."

"I googled the address and it came up as a self-storage area," Derrick explained.

Henry took the paper from Taylor. "Taylor, I think maybe I should have this checked out before we go. There could be—"

"No, I want to go," Taylor insisted, "and I want to go now."

Aggravation crept onto Henry's face. "Taylor, I am working on something tonight."

"Is it a lead?" Derrick asked.

"No," Henry answered slowly. Taylor could tell by the conflict in his eyes it was his relationship with Marty that was his top priority. And she saw her in.

"What is it? Is it because you know something I don't? Are you not telling me something? Because if there is something you are keeping from me, then I could have *trust* issues with you, Henry. It would be like if Derrick was keeping stuff from me and telling me not to worry about it," Taylor said, watching Henry's eyes light up with what Taylor was trying to say. "If he kept something important from me and wouldn't let me in then I think that maybe I would feel like he didn't trust me and without trust what can we have? Can we even have anything without trust?" she pushed.

"I do trust you," Henry said, conveying to Taylor his understanding. "Is that what it, I mean this, this is about?"

"Uh, yes," Taylor said as Derrick furrowed his brow in confusion. "But for now I really need to go there," she said pointing to the letter. "Which car are we taking?" she asked him.

Henry sighed. "This one," he said patting the back of the one he stood near.

"Okay," Taylor said going around to get in the back seat on the driver's side, Henry close at her side.

"I do trust her," he whispered to Taylor as Derrick opened and shut his door on the opposite side.

"Then show her," Taylor hissed back, climbing in and shutting the door behind her and grabbing her husband's hand as they went off after answers, yet again.

THE ADDRESS TOOK them to a self-storage unit located just on the fringe of Skid Row. Out front of the business was a sign, once lit up by neon it appeared, but the glow had since faded out to nothing. As they got closer, Taylor saw that the sign said *Frank's Self Storage, Est 1973*. She swept her gaze around the outside and saw sturdy-looking fencing, several times reinforced, with barbed wire wrapped around the top, giving the structure a prison feel. It looked practically abandoned, most of the lights on its perimeter no longer shining, either having been broken or the lightbulbs not replaced.

They pulled up to the keypad and Henry punched in the first set of numbers under the address on the now crumpled paper that Cedric had sent to Taylor. The gate before them slid open with a heavy whine, its reluctance to function clear as it jerked open to allow their car through.

As they pulled into the lot Derrick looked around. "I thought I would feel safer behind these gates, but I actually feel like I am part of a horror movie."

Taylor rolled her eyes at her husband. "You are being so dramatic —" she started but was cut off by the sound of the gate whining loudly closed behind them, making her jump. She looked back to Derrick, and he just gave her a look that said *see, I told you.*

Henry was silent the entire time, creeping forward slowly to the back of the gated facility. He turned, following a rusted-out sign that signaled him to continue further inward, where he finally stopped outside a garage-type, roll-up door with the number 81 painted on it.

"Stay here," Henry said, taking his gun out and getting out of the vehicle. He went over to the door and punched numbers into another keypad, and then pulled up the rolling door enough to crouch into the space. After about a minute he came back and opened the car door.

"I don't want to attract too much attention," he said, "so we will have to crawl through the space like it is." Taylor and Derrick followed him out and all crouched inside the space. Henry used his phone to provide a sliver of light, closed the door behind them, and then searched the walls and found a switch. Taylor was certain it wouldn't do anything, but after it was flicked up the fluorescent hum sounded and the space illuminated.

"Ho-ly fuck," Derrick said as Taylor blinked her eyes to adjust to the lights.

She gasped as she took in the space. The entire storage unit was filled from floor to ceiling, just packed with furniture. And Taylor recognized the pieces before her from Preston Manor. Her eyes went wide as she scanned over the relics. So this was what he had for her— old furniture, the furniture he took out of her home as he had destroyed it in his craze?

Fury flashed through Taylor like a flame shooting up and out. "Goddammit!" she shouted, kicking and shoving the large antique pieces before her. She grabbed a glass tray on top of one of the pieces before her and slammed it against the wall, shattering it into countless pieces.

She was stopped as arms wrapped around her from behind. "Tay, Tay, relax," Derrick tried to soothe, but Taylor kicked out her legs and sent the bureau before her rocking and then crashing to the ground joining the remnants of the glass tray.

Derrick spun Taylor in his arms. "Taylor!" he shouted and finally Taylor stilled, but then she just fell forward into her husband and wept.

She cried, moaned, and sobbed into her husband's chest. It was the definition of an ugly cry. "I, I just, I..." she tried to hiccup out.

"Shhhh," Derrick soothed, rubbing her back.

"I just want answers," she bawled out. "Even from the grave he is torturing me."

"We will find answers, Taylor, I promise you."

Behind them Henry cleared his throat. "Taylor, Derrick," he called and they turned to find him crouched down among the pieces of the furniture on the floor.

And plucking notebooks from the carnage.

TWENTY-ONE

TAYLOR SAT in her office the next day and clicked through the financial files that had been sent to her. She hadn't wanted to come in today. She had wanted to stay in that storage container all night and find every book in there, but Henry had convinced her otherwise.

"Taylor, let me get this place cleared out," Henry had argued the night before. "If I can get everything out of here, and back to the mansion, you will be able to go through all of it."

"We can do it now," she had argued back, "we can—"

"Tay, it is packed in so tight, there is no way we can get to everything without taking it out and we can't do that now," Derrick had reasoned.

Reluctantly, Taylor had known they were right. So here she sat, focused on the thing she had been trying to get to all week—looking into Cedric's finances.

The financial situation during Cedric's tenure as CEO was like watching a thermometer reading drop when placed into ice. The decline started about two years before Taylor came back and continued at a rapid rate. Taylor marveled at it, wondered how and why divisions were not closed. How had they even been able to function at this capacity?

There was a knock at Taylor's door and she called out a welcome, only to regret it when Todd entered. She had been pretty adeptly avoiding him since the day she returned, but she had known it was only a matter of time.

Taylor sat silently at her desk as Todd came and stood behind the chairs across from her.

"Can we talk?" he asked.

Taylor waved a hand at the chairs, as she didn't trust herself to open her mouth. Her patience meter was low.

Todd took a seat and focused his attention on his fingers. "I want to apologize for the other day," he said.

"Huh?" It was the only thing she was able to get out that resembled a word. Of all the things she expected him to be coming in here for, this was not it.

Todd sat up and looked at Taylor. "I was wrong for coming on like a crazy man when you returned the other day. I was a jerk," he held up his hands before Taylor could say anything, "and I know that is my baseline but you should not have been on the receiving end of it."

Taylor looked at Todd, and as much as she wanted to keep him in the time-out corner, she knew this apologizing stuff was probably hard for him. "I surprised a lot of people, I get it. Apology accepted," she said.

Todd sat back and nodded, glanced around the room and then back to Taylor. "Your Dad would have loved seeing you running this place," he said finally.

His comment jarred Taylor. This was a side of Todd she had never seen before, him talking about people in an affectionate way. All she ever remembered was how gruff and rude he was, even when she was a child. He tolerated nothing, and it made Taylor fear and even resent him. She recalled him at events for Preston Corp over the years just as sullen and sour as he was in business meetings. Then

Taylor recalled how kind he was to her at the hospital, how his demeanor had softened toward her just a bit. She had thought she would never see that side of him again, but here it was.

"How so?" Taylor finally responded, but warily. She wasn't sure if she should continue it, but she was fascinated with anything about her parents, especially her father. Her memories of him were not as vivid as those of her mother.

A ghost of a smile came and quickly left Todd's face, but his overall countenance was softer. "He was just so proud of you. He loved talking to you about stocks and business," Todd reminisced, his eyes once again bouncing all over the room. It was almost as if it would be too personal for him if he looked directly at Taylor. "This was his dream, for you to work here beside him."

"It was my dream, too," she admitted as her eyes burned with unshed tears. As her family members died so had those dreams. This company didn't feel the same without them, but she wanted to keep it alive for them, to remember them, to honor them.

"How did you meet him?" Taylor asked, eager to see if Todd would close up again.

"Through Cedric," Todd said then shook his head. "God, it seems so long ago," he said, seemingly baffled.

"So you knew Cedric first?" Taylor pressed.

Todd nodded, leaning forward and bracing his elbows on his knees, "Yup, we met in college."

"Cedric went to college?" Taylor asked.

Todd let a small laugh escape and then cleared his throat. "For a very brief time he did. I met him in an economics class. He was so kind, but he paid no attention at all and he was going to flunk. I offered to tutor him for a job at Preston Corp."

"Wow, that's—"

"Unexpected?" Todd asked. "It really was. But I was in a tough place. I had school loans and a family and no job."

"A family?" Taylor exclaimed before she could stop herself, and then watched as some of the clouds returned to Todd's face.

"Yes, um, my wife was pregnant and I needed to support us, so I found out who Cedric was and threw myself at his mercy.

"And he was kind. I expected a stuck-up jerk with a rich-kid attitude but he was none of those things. So I came on here as a janitor at night, became friends with Grant as I worked through college, and got moved up along the way, eventually working beside him."

"I can't believe you were the janitor," Taylor said, trying to process this verbal confession as quickly as it was being delivered.

Todd scoffed then. "Me either. But you do what you have to," he said looking at Taylor. "You do whatever you have to for your family."

"What, um, where is your family?"

"My wife died in childbirth. My daughter, too," Todd said, his face completely stony. I threw myself into work after that, which is probably why I moved up so quickly. This place became my world. Just like it is for Charlie. This filled the void."

"I'm so sorry, Todd," Taylor said softly. She wanted to say more, to hug him, but she knew that would be too much for him.

The softness that had covered his face just a few minutes before disappeared. The expressionless facade was back up and in full force. Todd just nodded and then got up suddenly. "Well, I just wanted to apologize."

Taylor nodded as she saw the man she never realized was so broken stride away. "Todd," she called after him, "what happened with you and Cedric? You didn't seem to be his biggest fan towards the end," she said.

"He changed," Todd bit out. "He started with drugs and he was never the same. And then when Grant, well, when he died, Cedric accused me of horrible things," Todd remembered. "He tried to have me fired, tried to fight me physically," he shook his head. "And then he nearly killed this company, like he was trying to get it shut down."

"I was just looking at his finances," Taylor said, "trying to see where it all went so wrong."

"About the time your grandfather died, I would say that was the start of the spiral," Todd explained, "and then when the board was gone it was just a free-for-all."

"Do you think he had something illegal going on?" Taylor asked. "I mean his purchases and the money he used just don't match up," she said gesturing to the screen before her.

"Well, drugs don't come with receipts, Taylor," Todd reminded her with his trademark snarky tone back in full force. "It was his downfall for sure, those drugs. I wouldn't have put it past him to be paying a crazy amount to some cartel member. I'm sad to say that Cedric became a monster. It's awful because the man he could have been was amazing and it was such a loss."

Taylor nodded, "I'm sure." Todd turned to leave again. "Thanks for talking to me about my dad," she said as Todd opened the door.

He stopped at the door. "One of my favorite topics ever," he said without looking back, and then he closed the door behind himself.

Taylor fell back into her office chair and tried to process what the hell had just happened. She was still just as in the dark about Cedric's finances, but now she had insight into who Todd was, not that it helped her situation at all. But it did make her feel a little more at ease about his attitude.

Taylor spun her chair to the window behind her and looked out over the smog-infested city. She watched the people on the streets going about their day, and once again envy of their simple lives washed over her.

When a knock came again on her office door Taylor groaned and spun back. "Come in," she called out and was relieved when it was Henry. She hoped he had answers and not more emotional baggage to hand her.

"I got the storage units emptied. The contents of them are currently being moved to the mansion."

"Them?" Taylor questioned.

Henry nodded. "Yes, the entire row we drove down last evening? Cedric owned all of it. Everyone single one was filled to the brim with furniture."

"From where?" Taylor asked.

"No idea," Henry said. "I had a conversation with Frank."

"The owner?" Taylor asked, remembering the burned-out sign from the night before.

"He was the owner, now he only manages the place. Cedric was the last owner," Henry said.

"He bought that place?" Taylor asked, disgusted.

"He did indeed. Cedric wanted so many storage areas Frank told him he would be better off buying the whole place, and he did."

"Wow," Taylor said shaking her head slowly as she took that in, "so Cedric owned Frank's Self Storage."

Henry nodded, "And guess whose it is now?"

Taylor rolled her eyes. "Let me guess, I am now the proud owner of Frank's Self Storage?" Taylor mused sourly.

"You got it."

Taylor shook her head and looked at the clock. "Well, I am going to call it a day. I need to look at those freaking journals," she said, picking up her phone and calling her husband.

"Yo," he said as a greeting.

"Yo? Really?" Taylor asked.

"What up, dawg?" he pressed and Taylor laughed.

"I am heading out. The storage place is now housed in the Fletcher basement," she said.

"I just finished my last conference call. I can check out, too," Derrick said.

"Perfect, I can't wait to tell you what I just found out I own," Taylor said, smirking at Henry.

"God, I hope it's a restaurant because I am so hungry."

Taylor huffed, "See you soon."

TWENTY-TWO

WHEN DERRICK SAW the inventory of furniture in his basement he wondered where the hell it had all come from.

"This is not all from Preston Manor, is it?" he questioned Taylor who looked as appalled as he felt.

Taylor walked forward surveying a bureau. "Some of this looks too new," she said. "Like he bought it and immediately filled the storage units with it."

"Totally odd," Derrick said. He turned to Henry, "How did you get all this stuff here, anyway?"

"I asked Benson," he said.

Derrick sneered. "The beatnik?" he asked in a growl.

Henry nodded, "I figured this would help me keep tabs on him, some manual labor."

Derrick liked the idea of that loser having to lug heavy furniture around. "Just him?"

Henry shook his head. "I had him hire out a crew, kept us out of the loop. Fletcher staff emptied it here. It lets him think I trust him, giving him a task," he explained to Derrick.

"Do you trust him?"

"Not yet, maybe not ever," Henry said.

"Same," Derrick said.

"Aha!" Taylor called from an aisle of furniture in the back, and suddenly her hand appeared over the top and threw notebooks towards Derrick. "Help me," she said as she opened and closed more drawers.

"Yes, dear," Derrick said and off he went to help his wife find notebooks from her dead uncle whose head was bashed in by potentially the same person who had shot him and drugged her employee.

Sometimes life was complicated.

———————————

TWO HOURS LATER, Taylor, Derrick, and Henry had opened every drawer and cabinet that had been brought in from the storage facility and had come up with one hundred two books of varying shapes and sizes. There had been no rhyme or reason to where the books were stashed in the furniture. Some of the furniture had none, and some pieces held five. They were scattered in the cabinets and drawers of the new and old furniture. It took a long time, and Taylor could only guess it had been Cedric's way of keeping the wrong person from finding them all. A few together may not have made any sense, but all together she hoped and prayed they told a story. Once the journals were collected, they loaded them into boxes and carried them upstairs to the office.

"Now we have to get them in order," Taylor muttered as she plucked the first book from the box before her and started flipping quickly through it.

"What are you doing?" Derrick asked, noticing that Taylor wasn't even stopping to read anything in the books as she picked them up, flipped through them, and then set them down.

"I'm trying to figure out a time order for these," she said like it was obvious.

"Without reading them?" he asked.

Taylor threw a book at Derrick, "Flip through it. I don't need to read the words, I can tell by the pictures."

Derrick flipped through the journal that had been flung at him. "Holy Christ," he muttered as he gazed upon beautiful sketches of Taylor as a baby. "Look at these, Tay," he said, pulling her attention to the book. He stopped on one picture of Baby Taylor holding a leaf and he read the neat penmanship on the back. It read:

Her beautiful blues,
Are so full of life,
They make me believe,
I'm not dead inside.

That's deep, Derrick thought. He looked up to Taylor perplexed.

Taylor shrugged, "Apparently he was crazy about me when I was a baby, then I guess he was just crazy." Taylor reached out and grabbed a stack with one hand and slowly flipped through them. "This one looks like it was drawn by a kid using a pencil for the first time," Taylor said.

Derrick came over and shook his head. These pictures were not the near photographic quality of the others. "Are they even by him?" he asked, but Taylor just pointed to the signature in the corner, which was the only thing that semi-resembled the other works. "What happened to him?" Derrick muttered.

Henry's phone chimed, booming around the office walls. "Taylor, Dr. Mellon is here to speak with you," he told her after checking the message.

"Oh yeah," Taylor said. She had forgotten all about her appointment with him when she was on her book hunt. "He can come here," she said gesturing to the room.

"He might even be able to help us with organizing these," Derrick offered. Seeing his wife become instantly tense at the mention of Mellon, he was trying to ease her.

"Maybe," she said, nodding, but he knew she hadn't really heard him.

Mellon came in followed by Mick and surveyed the books and boxes around them. "You found them," he said in awe. "Well, that didn't take long."

"Tell me about my mother," Taylor blurted out. It came out in one long word, like she had been holding it in and it just flew out when her mouth opened.

Dr. Mellon took a seat in one of the chairs and motioned for Taylor to do the same. She shot a quick glance at Derrick who nodded to her and pulled a chair next to her, both of them sitting at the same time.

"Where would you like to start?" Dr. Mellon asked her in a soft tone that reminded Derrick of beach waves. Damn, this guy was good.

Taylor heaved out a breath, "Can you tell me what she was addicted to?"

"Cocaine and heroin," Mellon said somberly.

Taylor nodded, "And her family, did she ever talk about her family?"

"Her mother and father were drug addicts as well," Mellon answered. "They overdosed at different points when she was growing up and your mother went to live with an aunt, who was her only living relative. Elizabeth became an addict soon after high school when her aunt was diagnosed with terminal cancer. She admittedly didn't know how to cope with the illness, and that was what brought her to that world. It was her aunt's dying wish that she get clean, and she left her the money to go to Healing Winds."

Taylor nodded.

"Do you want to ask me more about her?" Dr. Mellon asked Taylor gently.

Taylor shook her head. "I, um, I'm not sure how much more I can process," she explained.

"I understand," he acknowledged. "I wouldn't know how much more to add. I only knew her for a brief time early in her life and what Cedric told me later."

"Can we talk about him? Cedric, I mean?"

Mellon nodded. "You have found the journals. I will hold up my end of the bargain and we can discuss Cedric."

Mellon explained how Cedric had been kind but very irritated that he had to be at the rehab center. He corroborated Nan's story of Elizabeth and Cedric being just friends, but that Cedric spoke about her with such "intensity" in their private sessions he knew he had deeper feelings.

"I tried to persuade him to not enter into any kind of relationship until he was fully healed from his addiction," Mellon said sadly, "but he was insistent that they were just friends. It was almost like he wanted to believe it, too."

Mellon went on to tell Taylor that he saw in the news that Elizabeth had married Grant and he immediately thought of Cedric. It was years later, after he had seen more stories of Cedric's issues in the tabloids, that Grant had reached out to him.

"He said he had still been journaling," Dr. Mellon said with a small smile, "and I was glad at least some of my therapy plans had been successful."

"Was he using then, when he saw you again?" Derrick asked.

Mellon nodded. "He was severely depressed. He said the drugs made him forget about it for a little while. When your mother announced her pregnancy, he went on a bender. I didn't hear from him for months, and then he called one day out of the blue, and said he needed my help. He wanted to be clean again."

"What changed then?" Taylor asked.

Dr. Mellon's whole face lit up as a smile crossed his face. "He fell in love again," he explained.

"He did?" Taylor asked befuddled. "With whom?"

Mellon barked out a laugh. "With you, Taylor, with you!" he said. "He wanted to be there for you, be a great uncle to you, watch you grow," Mellon said. "And so he got clean," he continued, sounding pretty shocked, "quickest I have ever seen anyone. I changed our visits to every other month, and then, well, and then there was another big change."

"What do you mean?" Derrick asked. "Another change how?"

"We had our visit and he was acting, well, strange. Eyes darting, twitching, cringing," Mellon said. "He would talk but it wasn't to me. I asked if he heard voices and at first he said yes and then he said no. I thought maybe he was using again, made him do a drug test and it was clean. I asked to see him the next week and he agreed, but when he came back, he lashed out. He said the voices got worse when he saw me. Told me he was on to me, that I was just trying to get him," Mellon shook his head. "That was the last time I saw Cedric, that day, years ago."

"Do you think he had a psychotic break?" Taylor asked.

"It would appear to have some sort of mental component but, well..." Mellon paused, gathering his thoughts. "I have trained in countless facilities. I have treated mania, depression, bipolar, and schizophrenia of all different sorts. His behavior was nothing I have ever seen. I contacted other specialists, other heroes in the field of psychiatry. None of them could help me pinpoint a cause for Cedric's behavior."

"Come on, Dr. Mellon," Taylor said, standing and grabbing for one of the journals. "Look at these. Do these look like something from someone mentally well?" she asked handing him the book. The journal held drawings that were not to the caliber of Cedric's beginning works, but instead looked like rough drafts drawn with the wrong hand of a middle schooler.

Mellon took the book from Taylor, and shook his head. "I wish I could explain it, but I was never able to evaluate him again."

"Did he ever act like he wanted to seek revenge?" Derrick asked hesitantly, trying to both change the subject as well as get the answers they needed.

"Revenge? On whom?" Dr. Mellon asked puzzled.

"On his family, on me?" Taylor asked.

"No," Mellon said shaking his head. "No, he never spoke of hate towards his family. Cedric loved his family. Even when he spoke of Grant and Elizabeth, he was upset but conflicted. He loved his brother and Elizabeth, he wanted them to be happy, wanted the best for them. He just hated they were together."

Taylor leaned forward dropping her face in her hands. "I don't get it," she muttered into her palms then pulled them down her face. "Cedric told us to find you, said you would have the answers, but you don't seem to."

"I'm sorry, Taylor," Dr. Mellon said, his sympathies clear on his face. "Perhaps I can help with trying to timeline the journals?" he offered, as almost a peace offering. "Maybe something will come up I can help decipher."

"That would be great," Taylor said.

"May I use the bathroom?" the older man asked. "I presume a place this large has at least one," he joked.

Derrick smiled and nodded, "Sure, down the hall."

"Mick will accompany you," Henry told the doctor, opening the door and directing his subordinate.

"Trust issues, Henry?" Derrick asked.

Taylor made a hmph noise. "More than you know," she muttered.

"Just being safe, Mr. Fletcher," Henry said as he flipped through one of the journals.

Taylor grabbed another stack of books and one of them fell to the floor, a file folder slipping from inside. Derrick watched the pages flutter around and bent to help Taylor collect them, reading them as he did.

"Tay, they have your name on them," Derrick said as he handed a stapled set of papers to her.

Taylor took the papers with a shaking hand. "What the hell are these?" she asked. All the pages were highlighted and covered with notes, the handwriting shaky and barely legible.

"Articles?" Derrick pondered out loud as Taylor shuffled through the pages.

"Yeah," she said, standing. "Articles and printouts and photocopies," Taylor said, shaking her head in frustration. "What the hell am I supposed to do with this?" Taylor looked up at the ceiling and growled, shaking the pages in her hands. "Dammit, Cedric," she ground out.

"Wait, Tay, read it," he said, reaching over her shoulder and flipping back through the papers in Taylor's hand. Derrick grabbed one sheet and look at the article title—"Audio Tooth Implants."

Taylor furrowed her brows and looked at Derrick, shrugging.

"Remember Cedric's autopsy? It said something about a tooth being removed after death," Derrick reminded her.

Taylor's eyes widened in understanding. She leafed through the pages she had pulled out of the envelope. "Henry," she said, handing a page to him with the title "Datura the Mind Control Drug." "Wasn't that the substance found in his autopsy?" she asked.

Henry nodded. "His and Tappen's," he reminded them.

The door opened and Derrick watched Taylor jump at Dr. Mellon's reentry. "Where should I begin?"

"Dr. Mellon," Henry said, grabbing the man's attention, "we found these documents. They were in the box with the journals," he said slowly. "Do you think they in some way pertained to Cedric?" he asked, pushing the file over to the doctor across the table.

Mellon opened the folder and looked at the documents, his eyes scanning them quickly, bringing them closer to try and decipher Cedric's erratic notes in the corners, and then his eyes widened.

"I thought he was delusional," he finally said.

Derrick and Taylor's eyes slid to meet without their heads moving.

"About what?" Henry finally asked.

Dr. Mellon flipped back through the papers he held. "He, well, there was a letter he sent me, after Elizabeth died. It was incoherent. I thought it was his grief, it had broken him, the depression. I tried to call but could not get to him."

"What did it say?" Taylor asked. "What did the letter say?"

"He said someone was controlling him, he said he could feel it, they had done the surgery and now they could hear him all the time, they were listening and talking back. God, the letter was gibberish, and when I couldn't get through to him, I tossed it," Mellon said. "I thought the drugs..." Mellon's face morphed into anguish. "God, I was the only one who listened to him and he came to me. And I thought he was nuts," he said laughing a humorless laugh, shaking his head. "That's rich, the psychiatrist thinking his patient, his friend, was nuts."

But no one laughed.

Mellon continued on. "He wouldn't call me, the last few months when we spoke it could only be emails. He refused to speak on the phone."

"Charlie and Todd told me he hadn't been to the office, he only communicated via email before he died," Taylor said in a haunted voice. "Someone did this to him, for a long time," Taylor said, her voice getting shrill and panicked.

"Taylor," Derrick said, trying to bring her back from the point of hysteria.

Taylor swallowed and looked at Derrick. "Someone tortured him, Derrick," Taylor said. "The Datura derivatives were found in his hair samples, his tooth was removed after he died," Taylor shook her head. "They messed with him, made him do God knows what and when he figured it out, they killed him," she said, a tear sliding down her cheek, "and I just thought he was a spoiled brat, that he took too many drugs and turned into a monster.

"He kept me away," Taylor said. "He found me and kept me away."

The room was silent, so much so that when the air conditioning clicked on it startled them all.

"Well then, Taylor, if he figured it out, then we will too," Henry finally said. "He sent someone to find you and ensured you were safe, sent packages to be given to you, and left messages with Dr. Mellon that you would need answers," Henry recapped. "The answers are here somewhere."

"He's right," Derrick said, standing and grabbing a handful of journals and passing them out to the room's occupants, "let's hit the books."

TWENTY-THREE

TAYLOR CONTINUED to look over the journals, trying to shut her mind off and figure out the order but it was no use. Her thoughts kept circling back to the same recurring thought—everything she knew was a lie.

Her mother was not the woman having a good time at a music festival who happened to meet the heir of a billion-dollar industry. She was a drug addict. One who nearly broke up a family.

Cedric was not a drug addict who was so self-centered he focused on his drug habit instead of his family. He was a peacekeeper who was taken advantage of and tortured before he was bludgeoned almost to death and then murdered.

And Taylor wondered what else she didn't know.

"Hey, let's go to bed," Derrick said as he came over and rubbed her back.

"No, it's okay, I want to—"

"Taylor, it's time to go," Derrick said sternly, and Taylor nodded, saying farewell to Henry and Dr. Mellon. Derrick led her down the hall, along the familiar path to their room. And even in transit Taylor's head spun.

She felt numb. She had tunnel vision. She felt her heart beating and her breath coming faster and the walls closing in around her.

And suddenly she was enclosed in strong arms. "Deep breath, Taylor," Derrick said into her ear. "I've got you, it's okay," he soothed, holding her tight and guiding her into their bedroom. Derrick continued with his soft words, holding her close, and slowly Taylor came back to the here and now.

"What do I believe?" she finally asked. "It's all been a lie, I don't know what to believe, I don't know what's real," she hiccupped.

Derrick put his hands on either side of Taylor's face. "Look at me, Tay," he said softly. But Taylor couldn't focus, she could feel everything closing in on her again. "Taylor, look at me," Derrick demanded sternly, and Taylor settled her eyes on his. "This is real," he said looking in her eyes. "Me and you, us, this is real."

She reached up a hand and laid a finger on Derrick's bottom lip. "I love you, Taylor," Derrick said. "Now tell me what's going on in your head," he instructed.

Taylor shook her head. "I don't know what to do," she said honestly.

"You move forward, Taylor," Derrick said.

"But why all the secrets?" she asked him, tears flowing quickly from her eyes.

"I can't answer that, Tay," Derrick smoothed her hair back and kissed her lips. "But I know that no matter what happened in their past, all the people who were around you loved you and did whatever they thought they needed to do in order to protect you."

"But it was all lies and it hurts," she whimpered. "I just don't understand why it has to be this way," Taylor tried to explain.

"I know, Tay, and we are going to set things straight, get you all the answers we can," he assured her.

Taylor closed her eyes and rested her forehead against Derrick's. "Is this ever going to end?" she asked him, her voice just a whisper. "Is this ever going to end?"

"Yes," Derrick said, and Taylor smiled as his positive voice enveloped her. He sounded so sure, it made her feel like he was maybe, possibly, right. "You know how I know, Tay?"

Taylor leaned back and looked at her husband. "How?" she whispered.

"Because I was nothing without you. I was just moving through life thinking that this was all I got, that I had used up all my chances," he said. "But then I got you. And I realized that this was worth it all, it was totally worth all the shit I went through and put myself through, to get to you."

Her face softened a bit, relaxing Derrick, too. "Why did they lie to me?" she asked quietly.

"I'm sure your mom did it to protect you, Tay," Derrick said. "She was probably waiting for the right time to tell you, but, you know, she didn't get the chance. And I think Cedric, well it seems like he was trying to do the same thing."

Taylor laid her head on Derrick's chest. "My head is too full," she said.

"They loved you, Taylor, that's what's real," he said.

Taylor heaved out a breath. "Can you do something for me?" she asked, looking up at him.

"Anything," he assured her. She was his whole world. He would give it all away to live in a cardboard box with her if she wanted. Well, a cardboard box with cable because he loved movies.

"Can you make me forget all about this for a bit?"

Derrick nodded. "Of course, what should we—" He was cut off as Taylor pulled his hair and made him look at her.

"I want you to fuck me, Derrick," she commanded. "I want you to make me forget all of the shit we are dealing with and fuck me—"

Now Derrick cut her off, claiming her smart mouth and pushing her back against the closed door. His cock had come to attention when the first *fuck* left her mouth. The second one had him aching. He knew she was the one who needed distracting, but he was so hard now that if he didn't get inside of her soon he was going to embarrass himself.

Derrick pushed Taylor's pencil skirt up to her waist, lifted her against the wall, and started rubbing his hard length against her core. Taylor let out a moan at the contact, and it almost sounded like relief. Derrick slid his hands up her body as he continued to grind his hips against her, the friction causing him to sweat now. He tried to push his hands up her blouse, he wanted to free her breasts and taste them, but the fabric wouldn't budge.

Derrick quickly moved his hands and grabbed at the neckline of Taylor's flimsy shirt, and ripped it down the center. It startled her, and Derrick watched her look down in shock at it, and then her eyes met his and they were ablaze. She grabbed Derrick's locks and crushed his mouth to her own.

Derrick continued to move himself against her, and the friction was maddening. He knew if the barrier of his pants was not there that he would be done for. He pushed the cup of her bra down and broke their lips' connection, moving down to cover her nipple.

"Oh God, Derrick," Taylor moaned, pushing her hips forward and moving herself against him. He laved her nipple with his tongue and gently bit, causing Taylor to gasp and then moan.

Derrick pulled his own hips back, and Taylor reached down quickly and pulled at his belt. She fumbled and whimpered and Derrick took pity on the both of them and deftly undid his belt and pants, allowing Taylor full access to him.

She encircled him with her hand, sliding it slowly down his entire length, and when she reversed course Derrick pushed her hand off. It was too much. He took his hard length in his own hand and slid the tip against Taylor's panty-covered core. He could feel the moisture on it, feel her need seeping through.

"Damn it, Derrick, stop fucking teasing me," Taylor griped.

But Derrick couldn't help himself, they were both suffering now, what was a little more of a delay. "What's wrong, Tay?" his voice full of false concern, pulling his cock away from her core, and moving her panties to the side.

Taylor glared at her husband and tried to push herself towards him, but Derrick held her hips in place, removing himself from her.

"Derrick," she groveled.

"Say it," he demanded.

"Fuck. Me." she said through her gritted teeth, and Derrick complied, slamming his cock hard into her wet and ready heat.

Taylor's head lolled back, hitting the door, but she didn't even seem to notice. "Yes," she hissed out, her body relaxing as she finally achieved what she had been seeking.

Derrick moved himself back and then slammed back into her, both of them groaning this time. "More," Taylor panted out begging, "please, more."

Derrick complied, moving quickly in and out of her, kissing her mouth and then her neck. He could feel himself tumbling toward bliss, and he went to touch Taylor's clit and bring her with him, but he couldn't. Because Taylor beat him to it.

Derrick stilled and leaned his forehead against her chest, allowing him to look down and watch as she reached between them, stroking herself, and him at the same time.

"That is so fucking hot," he breathed out as he watched her fingers move where they were joined.

Taylor pushed her heel into Derrick's ass, signaling she needed more from him, and he complied. He pulled back then hastened his pace with each movement of his hips all as he watched Taylor's hand. He looked up when he felt Taylor stiffen, her breathing coming out faster, and shorter.

"Come on baby, let go," Derrick coaxed as he kissed her and swallowed Taylor's cries of release. And continued kissing her so she could collect his own.

TWENTY-FOUR

TAYLOR WOKE EARLY the next morning grateful that she had a husband who was up to the challenge to exhaust her with sex so she could pass out cold. Now it was just before five in the morning, much too early to get ready for work, but going back to sleep was proving unattainable.

She looked over at Derrick and considered waking him, to have him do what he does so well and get her back to sleep his way. But as tempting as that was, he was so deep in sleep she just could not do that to him. He was still recovering from his gunshot wounds—he still needed more rest than he would admit.

Taylor's mind drifted to the journals she had left behind last night, and before she knew it she had silently slipped out of bed and made her way to the office.

She found them stacked in different piles across the desks when she entered the room. Before each pile was a handwritten note. She picked up the one closest to her. *Seems to be most recent books, lots of gibberish.*

Each note seemed to be trying to attach a date and timeline to its stack of journals. At the first stack Taylor found a longer note.

Taylor-

I attempted with Mr. Lowsley to get these journals in chronological order. I hope you find something in them that puts this all to bed for you.

-Dr. X. Mellon

Taylor started in the middle, flipping through, but nothing caught her eye. She kept paging through, occasionally stopping to admire some of Cedric's drawings, but when she caught herself she would move on. She looked through each and every book in the stacks until she had made her way to the last pile. These were the works that showed the troubled and broken Cedric she had lived with. The drawings were amateurish for a grade-schooler—there were arrows and thoughts crossed out. Any words written were in shaky writing, not resembling his penmanship from his earlier entries.

One of the words caught Taylor's eye—*Decree*. She looked over the page that Cedric had written it on, where the word was written and circled. She started to look at the other things on the page. A sketch, not really a drawing, was there, the words "board members" and then "assets" were crossed off.

Taylor flipped back a couple of pages, and she found her name on one, again in the scribbled font, but also crossed off.

"Found you," Derrick said from behind her with sleep still in his voice and Taylo

r jumped, dropping the journal on the ground. "Sorry," he said, cupping her cheek and kissing her, "what are you doing?"

"I couldn't sleep. Look at this," she said, showing Derrick what she had found. "Does it look like a weird checklist to you?"

Derrick tilted his head. "I guess," he said, unconvinced.

Taylor huffed, "I just want an aha moment, you know."

He nodded. "Well, maybe you can have that with your outfit choice for today," he said. "Time for work."

"It's early," Tay said.

"It's after seven," Derrick said, yawning.

"Wow," Taylor said, glancing at his watch. Time flew when you were trying to decipher crazy.

TAYLOR WAS in her office hours later trying desperately to read over the contract before her, but instead it just bled into the drawings that she had pored over that morning. She had flipped page after page and looked at picture after picture. After a while she realized none of it was making any sense to her, and she wasn't sure if it was exhaustion or Cedric's own representation.

She needed to just let things be, give Henry time with what little information they had. But knowing that and keeping her mind on task were two very different things.

There was a knocking on her desk that brought her out of her fog, and Taylor looked up to find Todd before her, his knuckles resting on her desktop.

"You all right?" he asked her.

"Yes," Taylor said straightening herself. "Yes, I'm fine," she answered confidently. "Why do you ask?"

"Well, I had to knock on the desk to get your attention when you didn't respond to my calling your name four times," he answered, "so I thought you seemed a little off. I came to see if you had any questions about that contract before the meeting this afternoon."

Yup, Taylor sure did. She had a million questions, mostly because she hadn't read the damn thing. She had totally forgotten this meeting was even happening, and so what she needed was a recap on all of it. But Taylor was never going to admit that, especially to Todd.

"Nope, I'm good," she said closing the iPad cover in front of her. If there was anything she had learned in her time since taking over, it was that sometimes you had to fake it until you make it. And confidence often trumped ignorance.

Todd gave her a nod. "Okay, see you then," he said turning quickly, his jacket billowing out a bit.

"What is that?" Taylor barked as she saw something under Todd's jacket.

Todd looked around the room. "What?"

Taylor stood. "Under your jacket," she said. "Is that a gun?" she asked, baffled.

"Yes," Todd said flatly.

"Why do you carry a gun?" she demanded. "Is that even legal?"

"I have always carried one, and yes, it is legal."

Taylor was a little horrified. "We have security, Todd, you don't need to be gunslinging."

"Your grandfather asked me to start doing it when I was working with your father. It was before personal security was a big thing," Todd explained. "And so I did. There was a time we all had one hidden in our offices—me, Charlie, your Dad, hell, even your Grandfather. I suppose now it is a habit to have it," he mused.

"Have you ever used it?" Taylor asked, still not completely recovered, looking at the place where she knew it now sat under his jacket.

"Not this one," he answered.

Taylor's office door opened after a quick knock and Henry came in. "Hello, Mrs. Preston-Fletcher, I am here to take you to your lunch date with your husband," he announced.

Taylor furrowed her brow at Henry. She did not have plans with Derrick, "I..." Realization hit as the puzzle pieces fit together. "I am ready," she said, grabbing her purse. She nodded at Todd and followed Henry out of the building, Mick and Ian trailing after her.

They didn't speak the entire way to the garage, and Derrick was just arriving with his own security detail as they made their way to the car.

Derrick leaned down and kissed Taylor. "What's going on?" he whispered to her as they continued to walk to the car.

"No idea," Taylor mouthed back, entering into the door that had been opened for her by Ian. They were alone for a few seconds before Henry slipped into the driver's seat. Taylor examined him and saw he looked just as tired as she felt, dark circles under his eyes and all.

"How are you doing, Henry?" Taylor asked. She was concerned her head of security was burning the candle at both ends. One end being Taylor's problems and the other end his relationship with Marty.

"Dandy," he said, and then turned to face them. "How are you?" he asked. Taylor could tell he was worried about her. She should be worried about herself, too, but unfortunately it wasn't on her agenda for today.

"I'm dealing," she offered and received a nod.

Henry turned forward and started driving. They were all silent until the car exited the garage, and it was Henry who finally broke the lull. "I spoke to one of my contacts about Cedric potentially being involved in something illegal," Henry explained. "He agreed that the trauma to his head was suspicious, but he checked with every contact he had from every gang and mafia outlet he could think of and he got no hits on anyone dealing with Cedric Preston."

"That can't rule it out completely, though," Taylor said. "I mean someone bashed his head in and tortured him, that sounds pretty illegal to me," she said.

"It may be a lower food chain criminal, but my source confirmed that his manner of death was not one that followed with the usual pattern of the crime affiliates in LA."

Another dead end, Taylor thought, shaking her head.

"And something else," Henry said. "You mentioned a house-keeper finding Cedric's body," he hedged glancing and meeting Taylor's eyes in the rearview mirror.

"Yup, that's how he was found," she said.

"My source says he doesn't know anything about a housekeeper."

Taylor furrowed her brow and looked at Derrick, who met her stare with equal confusion.

"How would this person know whether or not..." Taylor stopped herself, hearing Henry's warning in her subconscious about not asking questions. "Never mind."

"You said the housekeeper found him and called the authorities?" Henry questioned.

"Yes," Taylor confirmed.

Henry nodded, then pulled off. Grabbing his phone, he swiped across the screen. "This is the call that came in the morning Cedric's body was discovered."

`Henry tapped at the screen and held the phone back toward Taylor and Derrick so they could hear it.

"911, What's your emergency?"

A deep voice came on the phone, with a gravely quality to it, and they heard the deepness of it vibrate through the phone. *"There is a body at 24 Dartmouth Place, the penthouse. It looks like an overdose."* And then the line clicked.

"Hello?" the operator asked, but the line was dead.

Taylor looked to Derrick. "Maybe the housekeeper freaked and asked someone else to call?" he offered, clearly at as much of a loss as Taylor.

Taylor shook her head. "No, because Todd said—" Taylor stopped, her eyes growing wide. She replayed the conversation from months and months ago in her head. It came into her memory like a blurry photograph.

"Tay, what is it?" Derrick asked.

Taylor looked between her husband and Henry. "They moved the body," she said, barely audible.

Derrick squinted at Taylor's words, and then his own eyes widened in recollection. "Oh my God," he said slowly.

"I need information and I need it now," Henry demanded.

"When I, back when they..." Taylor swallowed and took a breath, starting over again. "When I was brought back, they told me Cedric was in a private morgue. Then they told me they had moved his body, to try and cover up the overdose, and then he was discovered," Taylor explained.

"Who did? Who told you that Cedric was discovered by the housekeeper, Taylor?"

"It was Todd," Derrick said. "He told me when he came to get Taylor."

"He moved the body," Taylor said still in disbelief. "If he moved it, then he would have seen his head," Taylor said, her mind still running wild as the facts filtered in.

"And would have seen that it had a giant hole in it," Derrick agreed.

Henry turned back and put the SUV in drive. "I am going to look into this more," Henry said. "You two need to go back in to work today and pretend that everything is hunky-dory."

Taylor's mind was yet again in a whirlwind, but Henry's demands sidetracked her. "Did you say *hunky-dory*?"

"Yes," the man said curtly.

"That was weird," she said.

"Just go about your day," Henry said tersely.

"What about Todd?" Derrick asked Henry.

"I need to look into it more," Henry said.

"But she is going to be there, with him," Derrick said. He turned to his wife. "Maybe you should go home for the day."

"No, then it will look weird," Taylor said.

Derrick shook his head. "We could say you got sick, or I got sick," he pushed. "I don't think—"

"Derrick, I'm not going to do that," Taylor said. "I'm going to be in the office surrounded by hundreds of people, and I am sure a security detail, right, Henry?"

"Ian and Mick will be with you today. Rog and Sam will be with you, Derrick."

"See," Taylor said, trying to reassure her husband and pretend her heart wasn't trying to beat out of her chest. "It will be fine," she said giving Derrick a small smile.

Taylor watched Derrick's jaw tense. "I don't like it," he said.

Taylor laid her head on his chest. "Me either," she admitted. And they drove the rest of the way in silence.

WHEN TAYLOR RETURNED FROM HER "LUNCH" she felt a little jumpy. Did Todd know something? And why was he hiding it? She had to work overtime to push her mind onto something else, the darker thoughts just too much for her to handle.

"Ready?" a voice came from the doorway and Taylor let out a little shriek of surprise. She turned to Todd and felt her pulse heighten, but he just scowled at her. "What's wrong with you?" he asked.

Taylor shook her head a little too fast. "Nothing," she said in a high-pitched voice, "you just startled me."

"You seem off," Todd said, ever the eloquent gentleman.

Taylor heard Henry's warning in her head to keep a up a front, to be *hunky-dory* in his words. So Taylor cleared her throat, looked at her armed security at the door, and focused on her meeting. "I'm ready," she said, grabbing her iPad and striding out of her office.

Taylor and Todd made their way down the hall in silence, the way she preferred him. When they made their way into the conference room, Charlie was setting up the presentation monitors.

"I just spoke to Mr. Goldfried and they have hit some traffic so they are running a bit behind schedule," Charlie explained to Taylor.

"Traffic is a nightmare at this hour," Taylor remarked, setting her things on the table. The sound of the news station brought her head and attention up to the monitor.

"Apparently someone was using the monitors for viewing pleasure," Charlie remarked hotly as he searched the remote for the button which would switch it to presentation mode.

"Wait," Taylor said before he could change it. A name in the news report had caught her attention.

"Detective Jasper Watts, an eighteen-year veteran of the LAPD was pronounced dead today," the news anchor announced as crime scene video and Watts's department photo were spread out across the screen.

"Watts was shot after he attempted to apprehend a robbery suspect while off duty, the department announced."

"Holy shit," Todd said. Taylor turned and looked at Todd, who looked shocked as he watched the images.

"I can't believe it," Charlie said, as he too watched in disbelief.

"Isn't that the detective who investigated Derrick's shooting?" Taylor asked, attempting to play dumb. Both Charlie and Todd nodded, their eyes not leaving the screen.

Taylor took the opportunity to grab her phone and text Ian, her tail for the day. *Tell Henry I want to speak with him after my meeting, it's urgent,* she sent and got the thumbs-up response she was looking for from Ian's position at the door.

"Good afternoon, so sorry we are late," Mr. Goldfried announced leading his crew in. "Your new security measures did make us a little later, too," he added in agitation.

Taylor was nervous and upset and frazzled, but Oscar Goldfried was such a slimy bastard that he was a good distraction for her while she waited for news from Henry. Goldfried was like a billionaire used car salesman and Taylor was eager to put him in his place today.

"Yes, well someone tried to kill me twice, Oscar, so one can never be too careful," Taylor quipped back to his snotty remark.

"Oh yes, of course, safety first absolutely," he stammered, clearly embarrassed by his lack of tact. Taylor had found that in the business world, which was dominated by men, they were often unsure what to do with a forward-thinking woman. And now that good old Oscar and his crew were uncomfortable, Taylor had the upper hand.

"So Oscar, this contract," Taylor said tapping her iPad, "this is our third meeting about this thing. You know what they say about three times, right?"

"Oh yes, it's a charm, for sure," Oscar said as he took a seat at the long boardroom table.

"See, I am more of a sports girl. For me it's like *three strikes and you're out*," Taylor said smiling, and Charlie chuckled. "So why don't you go ahead and take me to where I will have issues with it and we can fix them right now. Because Oscar, I don't need this deal," Taylor said leaning into the table towards him, "but you do." This was not true either, but Oscar didn't know that.

Oscar played it cool, but Taylor watched the sweat bead at his hairline. *It's what their body says that gives them away*, her father had told her one time. Of course, they were watching a poker tournament and her mom had chewed him out for exposing her to gambling, but it was a life lesson that Taylor felt could be applied here, too.

"You know, I think this is where we both want it to be, for both our companies Taylor," Oscar replied, tapping his iPad.

"I'm giving you one last shot, Oscar," Taylor reminded him.

Oscar huffed, "Okay, okay, let's talk shipping companies." And with that Taylor knew she would get her way and things would be okay. For now. And for the next two hours she was able to keep her mind off the behind-the-scenes mystery that was her life.

DERRICK HAD GOTTEN Taylor's text about Watts during his evaluation from the doctor in his office. It had been one of the deals that Taylor had demanded when he said he was going back into the office. Every other day doctor exams until the wounds were completely healed. He was irritated with it, but he agreed for two reasons. One, he didn't want to argue with Taylor about going back to work, and if this made that a little easier he could take the fifteen minutes out of his day to do it. And two, because she cared about him, really loved him, and that was what he had wanted for so long that he was going to let her be a nagging, caring wife.

Once he got the all clear, he called Henry.

He was not starting to grow on Derrick, but he felt better knowing Henry had his own someone that he cared about the way that Derrick felt about Taylor. Derrick had known deep down that he was being a little bit paranoid about Henry being into Taylor, but he couldn't help it. If he loved her so much, he couldn't imagine anyone else being so close to her and not also falling for her.

"I saw it," Henry said as a salutation to Derrick's call.

"Please tell me it is a crazy, unfortunate coincidence."

"I really don't think it was," Henry answered. "It was three in the morning, and it was in one of the shittiest parts of LA. I have no reason to believe that Watts was just out for an errand at a gas station in Hyde Park then. Also from what I hear, that particular venue has been closed for renovation, so what exactly were these gang members robbing?"

Derrick let out a frustrated breath and wiped a hand hard down his face. "Have you talked to Taylor?"

"No, she was in a meeting, but I am on my way there now," Henry said.

Derrick checked the clock. "I'll meet you over there," he said and hung up the phone.

This was bad. They were no closer to figuring out who the hell this person was and now more people were dropping off the map. He was wondering if he could convince Taylor to go back to working from home, to make sure she stayed safe. But then he pushed that aside. He felt comfortable knowing that Taylor had security, and not just any security but great protection. Henry had gone over the top and then some even before these assassination attempts.

He would keep her safe.

As long as Henry was around it would all be okay.

TWENTY-FIVE

TAYLOR WAS in her office and looked up at the clock as she stretched. It was late, she realized as she looked over her shoulder out the window and noticed the sun was setting. She was just about to call it a night when Henry came in. He nodded to Ian and Mick outside the door, and then closed it behind him. He walked over to Taylor and leaned against the side of the desk.

"Watts was my informant," he finally said somberly. "He was feeding me information."

Taylor felt her shoulders sag. "So it wasn't just a random act of violence?" she said with still just a little bit of hope.

Henry just shook his head.

"And," he said but stopped short when the handle to Taylor's office door started twisting, something Taylor hadn't even heard.

"It's just me," Derrick announced as he slipped in, closing the door behind him, apparently able to read the tension in the room.

Henry crooked his head indicating Derrick needed to come closer. "I just told Taylor, Watts was my informant. And now Dr. Parker is missing," he informed them.

"The Medical Examiner?" Taylor whispered in disbelief.

Henry only nodded. "Someone is figuring out that we are digging. I don't think they know it is us, exactly, but they are taking out the people we used to get this far. I sent someone to be with Dr. Mellon. He was fine last I spoke to him. I need to keep him that way. If he is attacked the silver lining is that my guy will take whoever it is down and we can hopefully get some answers."

"What do we do now?" Taylor asked.

"I am going to take you home," Henry said, "the both of you. You are walking bullseyes right now."

"Okay," Taylor said, her pulse racing.

"There is something else," Henry said.

"Henry, please quit the damn theatrics and just come out with everything for fuck's sake," Taylor demanded hotly.

"I found this copy of the decree in with Cedric's things in the storage area," Henry said reaching into his suit jacket and removing a bunch of papers, folded in half. "In it—"

There was a knock at the door and Henry scooped up his phone, turning the white noise off, and straightened to his lookout position silently.

Taylor cleared her throat. "Yes," she answered.

The door opened a crack and Charlie poked his head in. He was pale. "Uh... Taylor," he said.

"Charlie, what's wrong?" Taylor asked with concern, rising from her desk.

"I have some gentlemen here—"

The door was pushed open by someone from behind and Charlie fell forward grabbing the doorjamb to keep from falling.

Suddenly the room was a flurry of activity. Henry drew his gun as five other men entered the room, drawing their own guns and pointing them at Henry.

"CIA, put down your weapon," one of the men shouted.

"Show me your badge," Henry shouted back.

"Weapon down first," the officer in front demanded of Henry. Taylor looked at him. His voice sounded so familiar.

"How about if you all put down the goddamn weapons and then we can have some introductions!" Derrick demanded, forcing Taylor behind him to shield her as he spoke.

There was a five-second standoff before the officer used a hand to pull forward his badge on a cord that was around his neck.

"Put the gun down, Lowsley," he said.

Henry lowered his weapon and dropped it on the floor and the officers lowered their weapons.

"What the hell is going on?" Taylor demanded.

Charlie rushed forward to Taylor. "They have paperwork," he said, winded. The older man was in an absolute panic.

"We have a warrant and are here to arrest one Henry Lowsley," the officer informed Taylor.

"What the hell for?!" Taylor demanded, her voice rising in pitch and volume.

"We need to question Mr. Lowsley for suspected terrorist attempts against this country and his home country of Ireland. In addition, we understand that he has been working with one war criminal, Jeffrey Benson."

The room started to spin around Taylor. She shook her head, trying to regain herself. "Charlie, go call our attorneys," she demanded of him, as he looked equally baffled just standing in the corner. With a task at hand, Charlie straightened up and went on his way.

"This is ridiculous," Henry said to the officers, but allowed them to take him into custody. "I think that warrant is missing some pages you guys need to find," he said, his brogue getting so thick in his anger it was difficult to understand him.

"Shut up," one of the agents said to him, pushing his head down as he added an additional set of cuffs to allow Henry's arms to be linked behind him. Every time the man spoke Taylor felt like it was a voice she recognized, like she had heard it before. But she had no time to evaluate this fleeting thought.

A walkie-talkie went off in the apparent main officer's hand, "The other members of the security team are in custody."

"What others?" Derrick demanded.

"All of Lowsley's security officers for his company are accomplices to this mess," the agent told them.

They were taking away her entire security force, Taylor finally realized. She was completely vulnerable, totally exposed.

"Ya warrant can not *decree* this be done," Henry announced loudly.

"Shut it," the agent said tensely giving Henry a small shove.

"Yeah, your *decree* is missing pages, I would really check on that," he said. "I'm not sure you should do anything until you find those missing pages," he rattled off, sending a side eye to Taylor.

And then they tased him and Henry went down like a ton of bricks.

"Oh my God! Stop!" Taylor screamed and watched as all of the men worked and hoisted Henry up.

The officer turned the taser at Taylor. "If you take another step towards him, I will assume you are interfering with a federal investigation," he threatened, "and you will also be taken under arrest."

Derrick pulled Taylor back, and put himself between her and the officer. "She's scared, dammit," he barked at him. The two glared at each other as the officers around them worked to move Henry's limp frame through the door. The taser-happy agent left as well, slamming it closed behind him.

"We have to do something," Taylor said. "Should we call the police? I mean this isn't right!"

"I know, Tay, but I think someone is working overtime to get a clear path to you," Derrick said holding his panicked wife to him. "We need to get you out of here," he said finally.

Charlie came rushing back into the room. "I called Kurt and he is getting on it immediately," he said, his face now flushed. "I saw them with Henry, got them to leave through the back door."

"I need to get Taylor out of here," Derrick told him. "Can you and Todd get the company helicopter here?" Derrick asked.

"Todd's not here," Charlie said to Derrick as if this was quite obvious. "Taylor sent him to New York for a meeting," Charlie said.

"No, I didn't," Taylor said mystified. "When the hell did he leave?"

"About two hours ago," Charlie said, flabbergasted. "He said something had happened with one of our manufacturers there and you were sending him because traveling would be too dangerous for you right now."

"I didn't send him anywhere," Taylor said, panic filling her. "Let's get that helicopter and then I need you to find him," she told Charlie and once again he was off faster than one would think the older man was capable of.

"Come on, Taylor, let's pack it up," Derrick said, moving back to her desk.

Taylor nodded and got up, but her mind was darting all over the place. She walked over and went to pick up her laptop, when she noticed a folder she hadn't placed there. She picked it up and opened it and found a copy of the decree in there. It had notes, from handwriting she thought she might have recognized.

"What is that?" Derrick asked, coming to look over her shoulder.

"The decree," Taylor said.

"That's Cedric's copy Henry was starting to tell us about."

Slowly Henry's mouthy babble from just moments earlier filtered into Taylor's head. "Henry was saying something about a decree to the cops just now," she said to Derrick.

Derrick nodded, "Yeah, I think he was trying to stall them for some reason, telling them they were missing pages," he said.

"Yeah but he kept using the word 'decree'. Maybe...," Taylor trailed off as she turned the pages slowly. "Here," she said. "It goes from article number 3 to article number 5."

"Where is your copy?" Derrick asked.

Taylor opened her iPad up, and opened her coded files. "I

scanned it so I wouldn't have it lying around," she told him. She swiped through the pages.

"It's missing here, too!" she whisper-yelled to her husband.

They looked at each other for a moment. "We have to find it," Derrick said.

Taylor picked up the decree from Cedric again and flipped through the pages. There were notes on each page, things were underlined, notes were written on the side. Taylor got to the end of the pages and flipped it over. In small, shaky handwriting it said *Find article 4 for Taylor*, and it had a small box next to it that was checked, as if it had been on his to do list.

"Look," Taylor said, showing Derrick, "he checked it, like he found it."

"Yeah, but then where the hell is it?" he asked, thinking they were no closer to it than they were a minute ago. Derrick took the decree and put it back into the folder Henry had brought.

Taylor felt lost yet again. As she tried to think of a place they hadn't looked yet, Charlie came in. "The helicopter is ready," he said, clearly flustered. "Let's get you home, Taylor," Charlie said.

Taylor nodded and looked at Derrick, attaching herself to his side.

TWENTY-SIX

THE HELICOPTER LANDED at Fletcher Mansion fifteen minutes later. Derrick and Taylor had ridden in silence, not willing to say anything because they didn't know who the hell might be listening.

A butler waiting on the landing pad opened the door for them to the house.

"Tony, can you get Nan and have her meet us?" he asked.

"Why do we need Nan? You cannot possibly be thinking of food right now, Derrick Fletcher," Taylor said to him, completely irritated.

"No!" he exclaimed, and then bobbed his head side to side a bit. "Well, I am a little famished but that isn't it," he said quickly to try and stop his wife from glaring at him. "I think we should tell her about Henry, her nephew, don't you?"

"Yes, I'm sorry," Taylor said. "Uh Tony, why don't you grab Marty, too," she said.

"Why?" Derrick asked his wife as the butler went off.

"Uh," Taylor said, in a conundrum for several seconds. "Well, our security team has been taken into custody—don't you think she should be aware of that?"

"Oh yeah," Derrick said as he and Taylor made their way to the upstairs living space. "You don't think Henry was really part of anything, do you? Like him being in security was all a cover?"

Taylor looked at Derrick with her mouth agape. "No, Derrick, I don't," Taylor said, "do you?"

"He just acts so weird and secretive sometimes, you know, like he is hiding something," Derrick said, then he flicked his gaze to Taylor catching her expression. "Don't get mad at me, everything is so crazy right now I am just looking for answers just like you."

"Answers about what?" Marty asked as she came in the room, totally dressed down in a gray sweatshirt about three sizes too big, and baggy sweatpants that were tucked into fluffy, fuzzy socks. Taylor and Derrick took in Marty's appearance, looked at each other in confusion, and then back at Marty.

"Why do you look homeless?" Derrick asked her.

"Because I don't feel good, numb nuts, okay?" Marty said, totally irritated. "What is going on? Poor Tony is running all around looking for Nan."

"Henry and his entire security fleet was arrested by the CIA, so we have no security team at the moment," Derrick said bluntly, and Taylor watched as Marty crumbled before them.

Taylor closed her eyes and grimaced at her husband's lack of tact. She had been hoping to tell Marty this information a touch more delicately than Derrick had. Taylor rushed to her sister-in-law, embracing her.

"Don't worry, Marty, we will stay safe. We can hire more security if we need to," Derrick said, completely oblivious to anything around him.

Sometimes men were just so dense.

"Derrick, why don't you see if you can find Nan, hmmm?" Taylor said, rubbing Marty's back as she now sobbed in Taylor's arms.

"Yeah, I need something to eat, too," he said as he urgently went off, more likely in search of food than for Nan.

Once he was gone, Taylor pulled back from Marty. "I am going to figure it out," Taylor promised her.

"Was he okay? Where did they take him?" Marty asked through her tears.

"I don't know. We called our lawyers, and I guarantee you I will fix this," she promised.

"Taylor, I love him," she said, her voice cracking halfway through her declaration. "I love him so much," she sobbed out.

"I know, Marty. I will figure it out, I promise you," Taylor said and she held her close again.

Derrick returned to the room with a sub in hand. "Apparently Nan was called when Henry was arrested as she is his next of kin, and she left to try and see what she could do," he said around his mouthful of Italian. "Geez Marty, calm down! Are you hormonal or something?"

Marty lifted her head and stopped her tears. She glared at Derrick, walked over to him, and kneed him full force in his crotch. Then as Derrick folded in half, Marty grabbed the sub out of his hand, took a bite, and left the room.

Taylor watched the whole thing, shaking her head. "You deserved that," Taylor said, as her husband howled in pain. Her ringing phone had her turning away from him to check the caller ID. "Charlie?"

"I cannot find Todd," he answered in full panic before Taylor could even finish saying his name. "I called the New York offices and he never arrived. He should have been there hours ago. So I called the company's travel agent and they have no record of him booking a flight."

"Shit," Taylor breathed. This was totally something that Henry would normally help her with. "Are our lawyers working on helping Henry?"

"I called them right away and told them it was their top priority," Charlie said.

"Okay, Charlie, go home. I will call you later to check in," Taylor said and disconnected. She turned back to Derrick who was breathing like he was about to give birth. "What do we do now?" she asked him.

"I don't know," he wheeze-whined out to her.

Taylor closed her eyes and tried to think. "He wanted to bring us home, right? Maybe he has some information here?" she asked, opening her eyes and looking at Derrick who was now leaning against the wall. "Should we check his room?" she asked her husband.

Derrick shrugged. "I guess it's as good a place to start as any," he grunted out.

Taylor rolled her eyes. "Suck it up and let's go," she said taking off down the hall.

AS THEY MADE their way to where Henry was staying in the mansion, Derrick cleared his throat to ensure his sister had not really kicked his balls into his throat. God, Marty was in a pissy mood, and she had been for a few days now. If only she knew all the shit that was really going on.

When they stopped at Henry's door, Taylor just stared at it. "Do you think it's unlocked?" Taylor asked, just looking at the knob.

"Well, there is only one way to find out," Derrick said dryly, reaching around her and turning the knob, pushing the door open before her.

Taylor looked at the open doorway in front of her. "I was really overthinking that," she said.

"Yeah, you were," Derrick said, "now go in."

They entered the room and looked around. It was in perfect condition. There were no papers on the small desk, the bed was made tight as a drum, and all the drawers were closed.

"Does he even stay in here?" Derrick mused as he bent cautiously and looked under the bed for something, a dust bunny even.

"Look in the drawers," Taylor said, pointing to the bedside table, as she made her way over to the clothes bureau and started looking inside.

Derrick looked in the bedside table drawers but they were all empty, with no sign of anyone ever having used them. He made his way to help Taylor and looked in the other bureau drawers. There were some clothes in the drawers, but everything was so neat it almost looked fake.

"Geez, is he a robot or something? Everything is so precise," Derrick said as he moved some stiff pants out of the way and found a box. It was rectangular, and looked like the box a fancy pen would go in. He picked it up, and it felt light but he heard something move in it. He looked at Taylor, shaking it, and whatever was inside made a rattling sound. Derrick went to remove the lid but Taylor stopped him.

"That looks personal," Taylor said.

"Or it could be something with info," Derrick defended, and pulled off the cover before Taylor could argue. "What the hell is this?" he said out loud as he plucked a white stick with a blue top from the box. He looked at Taylor and saw her eyes go wide and her mouth fall open. "What?" Derrick asked and then he saw that there was a spot on the stick, like a screen with a word—*Pregnant.*

Now Derrick's eyes went wide. "Whoa! Henry's girl is pregnant," he said in a loud whisper and looked at Taylor, whose eyes were locked on the pregnancy test and who looked like she was going to be sick.

"What's wrong?" he asked.

Taylor looked at Derrick and then back to the stick, grabbing it from his hands and putting it back in the box. She threw the box into the drawer and slammed it shut. "There isn't anything here. We need to keep looking," she said, but she was frazzled.

"That's not nothing," Derrick said, looking back at the now-closed drawer.

"Will you focus?" Taylor said, her tone harsh and frustrated.

"Let's go and try to come up with another plan," she said, leaving Henry's room.

Derrick looked back at the drawer, and sadness came over him. They needed to figure something out and quick because now Henry's family was depending on them, too.

TWENTY-SEVEN

AS TAYLOR STALKED AWAY from Henry's room her emotions were in a whirl. But the worst feeling was how pissed off she was at all the unfairness that was currently swirling around them.

That pregnancy test was now at the forefront of her mind. She needed to fix this whole thing for so many reasons, but now she felt like the most important reason was in a drawer three floors below her. Okay, well the reason was actually in Marty's belly, but that was beside the point.

"It seems like Cedric found that page, but where the hell is it?" Taylor asked as she paced around their room. "You would think he would leave it some place obvious," she said in frustration.

"Well, where haven't we looked?"

Taylor furrowed her brow, like it would help her get to a deeper concentration level, and began to think of a place it could be. The brow thing was a fail, though, because she was still coming up blank.

Derrick's phone started to ring, cutting into Taylor's thoughts. Derrick glanced down at the screen but made no move to answer it.

"You should get it—it could be important," Taylor told him.

So Derrick answered. "Yeah," he said. Instantly his forehead scrunched up in agitation as whoever was on the other end spoke. "How the hell did you get my number?" he barked into the phone. "Okay, well I guess that makes sense."

"Who is that?" Taylor asked.

"The beatnik," he answered her. "Yeah, I call you that. Get over it," Derrick said into the phone. "Well then, tell me what you know," Derrick said tersely into the phone. Taylor could tell he didn't like the response, though, as she watched his nostrils flare. "No, you should stay there." Derrick listened for a few seconds more and then rolled his eyes. "Fine, fine, come here then," he said and hung the phone up.

"What was all that?" Taylor asked.

"He said that wasn't the real CIA or anything like it who took Henry."

A shiver rolled hard through Taylor's body. "How does he know that?" she asked.

"Said Henry somehow signaled him when he was taken, and when he started to look into it, he discovered those were not government officials. He said he and Henry had an agreement that if shit went bad, he would help us, and that even though I think he is the lowest life-form on the planet I had to trust him."

"He said all that?" Taylor asked, her head spinning and having a hard time keeping everything straight.

"Not in so many words," Derrick relented. "He asked if we were home, said he's going to meet us."

Home? The word felt like a pop in Taylor's mind, followed by a bright light bulb of realization.

"Derrick," she said slowly. "I think I know where Cedric left that page."

TAYLOR AND DERRICK made their way to the garage and picked out Derrick's Tesla to drive to Taylor's childhood home. Derrick had called back the number Ben had called them from and alerted him of their location change.

"It's quiet," Derrick said, "and no one has ever seen me in it. Paparazzi will be expecting an SUV."

"Okay, good point," Taylor said climbing in the passenger side, taking in the car's pristine condition and overt new car smell. "Wait a second, when did you get this?" Taylor asked Derrick when he climbed in.

"Recently," he confessed.

"When did you have time to car shop?" she asked him. The man had lost his father and been shot, just to name a few things on his busy agenda. How the hell had he found time to buy a car?

"It was pre-ordered months ago, and delivered a couple of weeks ago. This is actually my first time driving it."

"We really need to talk about your spending habits, rich boy," Taylor scoffed as they exited the garage.

"Yeah well, when the smoke clears we can work on the budget, dear, but for now let's just try and find out who the hell is trying to kill you, okay?" Derrick asked as he exited the Fletcher gates, which were oddly deserted.

"It's really quiet," Taylor said quietly herself.

"Yeah," Derrick said. "It works to our advantage right now so let's not question it too much," he advised, and Taylor thought that was a great idea.

The drive to Preston Manor wasn't very long, and tension crept its way into her shoulders as Derrick moved along the remotely familiar terrain. It's funny how even when things change there are still memories ever present. There were some new houses on the route to Preston Manor since Taylor had been there last. A piece of land now had a mansion on it, but it used to be woods where Derrick, Marty, and Taylor would play. A few older mansions had changed their facades, updating their looks to meet the new owners' sense of style. But other than that it was achingly familiar. Every emotion she had ever felt toward this house—good, bad, and in-between—flooded her.

They drove in silence to the mansion, but Taylor clung to Derrick's hand with both of hers as she took in the passing landscape with wide eyes. As they turned down the dark and lengthy wooded drive to the Preston Estate, Taylor's heart hammered in her chest.

The Tesla pulled up to the gate. For a place that hadn't had staff within its walls in years the outside was immaculate, and Taylor was shocked. The huge wrought iron gate before them was black and polished as if it had just been installed. The tall green shrubbery behind it was so well-groomed and thick, there was no way you were seeing through it.

"Taylor," Derrick said, breaking her thoughts from the gates. "Try to get in," he suggested putting his window down and flicking his head to the security box before the gate.

Taylor shook her head as she looked at the security box like it had landed from another planet. "That was put in after I left, Derrick," she said. "I have no idea what the code would be."

Derrick looked back at the device, examining it. "It's print activated," he said. "Try it."

"But how would he get—"

"Taylor, if it doesn't work I don't know how we are getting in," Derrick said in annoyance, "and the longer we sit here in the driveway of an abandoned mansion the more attention we draw to ourselves, so for the love of God just try your hand on the damn thing."

"Good point," Taylor said, and climbed over Derrick to comply. She placed her palm on top of the black screen. Derrick had his doubts that the thing even worked but suddenly a green light scanned beneath Taylor's hand like a photocopier light, there was a series of beeps, and the gate opened in front of them allowing them in.

"Well, I didn't expect that," Taylor said as she pulled her hand back in and crawled back to her seat. "Thanks for yelling at me, babe," she said with a small smile. Something was going right, she thought.

"Anytime," Derrick replied dryly as he edged through the now open gate. He furrowed his brow, "How do you think Cedric got your palm print?"

"You know I don't really want to think about it, because it was probably while I was sleeping or some shit and I can't focus on that creepiness right now," Taylor said, giving Derrick an *I'm trying to keep it together so stop asking random questions* smile.

Taylor's smile fell to the brand-new Tesla carpet as they progressed forward. Where the outside of the Preston Manor gates had been impeccable, behind the gates was a different story altogether.

The grass was tall, the height of the car window in some places as they drove through. The shrubbery was jagged and growing haphazardly, everything in stark contrast to outside the gate. The driveway had started to crack in some areas, and grass grew up through the cracks. The shrubbery that flanked the mansion had latched itself to its exterior and was growing up its side. The facade of the Mediterranean-style mansion was discolored and in some spots the stucco was cracked or missing.

Taylor watched as Derrick looked around astounded. "This is bad," he whispered. "I can't believe it looks like this," Derrick observed honestly as he gaped at the sight before him.

"Wait till you see inside," Taylor said flatly, not shocked at the exterior appearance at all.

Derrick pulled the car around the still, moss-covered fountain, through the circular driveway, and pulled up to the huge, stone front steps.

As they made their way up the steps, Derrick saw that the windows on either side of the door were blacked out crudely with what appeared to be spray paint. Beside the front door there was a print-scanning screen identical to the one at the entry gate. Taylor placed her palm on it, the now-familiar green light scanned, and the locks clicked their release on the door in front of them.

"I was wondering what the hell that was," Ben said, suddenly appearing behind them.

"Holy fucking shit!" Taylor shouted as she jumped at least a foot in the air at his appearance.

Derrick's response, though, was much more dignified—he shrieked like a scared little girl.

The couple both glared at Ben who was definitely trying not to laugh at their responses.

"Why the hell would you sneak up on us like that?" Derrick demanded. Taylor was certain Ben scaring them was not making him Derrick's favorite person any quicker.

"Sorry," he said, shrugging.

"How did you get in here?" Taylor asked.

"I snuck in behind you guys when your car came through. I got here just as the gate opened," he explained.

"You walked here?" Taylor asked.

"Well, I drove and parked down the road and then I walked down here so I could be less obvious," he explained.

"Okay fine, whatever, let's get this done," Derrick said.

Taylor stepped forward to enter, but Ben held her back, his gun drawn. "I go first," he announced, and his tone didn't allow for any arguments. Taylor looked at Derrick who looked all too pleased to have Ben go first, in case something came out and maimed him in some way.

Ben pushed the door forward, and it creaked like a horror movie prop as it moved aside. He did a quick scan and motioned for them to follow behind him.

"Let's just stay close," Ben advised.

"Okay," Taylor whispered, wide-eyed and nodding. "Which way should we go first?"

Derrick looked over to her, puzzled. "Why are you whispering?" he asked in a completely normal-toned voice.

"I don't know," Taylor glared and whisper-yelled at him. "It seems like the right thing to do, okay?!"

"Yeah, well, it's not and it's weird so can you just talk regular? It's like you are in an episode of Scooby-Doo or something."

"You know what," she whispered, and then she cleared her throat and spoke in a loud, stern voice, "I am nervous, okay, and if I want to whisper, I can!"

"Well, now you're yelling, and that's just rude," Derrick said, crossing his arms over his chest and turning away with mock hurt.

"Can you children please get it together?" Ben asked, squeezing the bridge of his nose. "Look, maybe I should case this place before I let you go any further. I'm worried something might be in here."

"We don't have time for that," Taylor said wildly. "My security team has been abducted by some imposter agents, one of my advisors is missing, and someone is trying to kill me," she pointed out. "Time is of the fucking essence, Ben or Jeff or whatever the hell your name is."

"This place is just wrecked, Tay. I don't even know where to start," Derrick said.

Taylor looked around. He was right, it was wrecked for sure. The previously grand and formal entry of the mansion was now just walls smashed open, with their internal components pulled out. Sheetrock dust was everywhere, scattered and dispersed when Cedric had ripped walls down with his bare hands. It looked like someone had started a really low-budget demo and just decided to say *screw it* before the tools got there. Even the floors, the huge marble tile floors, were lifted, like he had pried them up to look under them.

"I think this may be a lost cause," Ben said looking around at the space, too. "It doesn't look like anyone has been in here in a long time. Maybe what you need isn't—"

"There is something here," she insisted. "Damn it, we need Henry. He is so damn huge he could just shake the damn place," she said rubbing her head. She exhaled and started looking around slowly.

"Tay—"

"What is that?" Taylor demanded as she looked across the room. Both Derrick and Ben turned slowly in the direction Taylor pointed.

"Taylor," Derrick said slowly. "I don't know what you are talking about," he said very evenly, like Taylor was an animal that might spook at any moment.

Taylor turned her pointed finger to Derrick. "Don't talk to me in that voice."

"What voice?" Derrick asked her, speaking just as slow.

"The *she's lost her mind, proceed with caution* voice," she said and stalked over to the direction she had pointed and picked up a vase. "This," she said shaking the vase at the two men behind her.

"That's a vase," Ben informed her, in a slow voice matching the one Derrick had just used.

Taylor wheeled around quickly to Ben. "Listen you," she seethed at him through her teeth, "he gets a pass for talking to me like I am crazy. He took a bullet for me." She warned him, "I will kill you with my bare hands, barista boy, if you take that tone with me again."

"Okay, Tay," Derrick said now talking normally to avoid any chaos, "what about the vase?"

"Everything in here is in shambles and this thing is all together, sitting pretty on a table. Wait a minute..." she said, staring at it. She noticed cracks in the vase. "It's been put back together," she said as much to herself as to Derrick and Ben.

Suddenly Taylor's eyes grew large as realization filtered through. "Derrick, I think this is the vase that I—"

Derrick nodded his understanding, going over to her. She was grateful she didn't have to say out loud that it was the vase she had smashed over Cedric's head, thinking she had killed him years before. "You think Cedric put it back together?" Derrick asked, and Taylor nodded. "But why?"

Taylor had a hunch. She wasn't sure she was right but she felt like the best thing to do was follow it even if she was wrong. And to find out if she was right, she threw the vase at a wall and smashed it.

"Jesus, Taylor!" Derrick shouted.

"What the hell!" Ben yelled in surprise.

But Taylor ignored them both and instead walked over to the carnage that had been left by the vase. She crouched down and plucked out a bunch of papers from inside the vase.

Derrick went over to Taylor, "What is that?"

"The decree," she whispered to him as she looked at the pages. She flipped the pages slowly, checking each one until she found the thing she had been looking for. A small penciled arrow was pointing at a paragraph on the page. The page that was elusively missing in her own copy.

IN THE EVENT that there is no living descendant of the Preston family bloodline to take control, or if the descendant refuses to take control of all Preston Corporation holdings, the company therein will be dissolved. At the time of dissolution all employed staff will be released from their positions and offered severance for equal to exactly one month of service.

The company components will then be sold. The components may not be sold to the same company and/or person. Each departmental unit must be sold separately and the clause contracts will depict upon their sale that these companies will not be allowed to use the Preston name or combine these companies for a time of no less than 15 years. This sale and division will be performed by the board in service at the time of dissolution.

If there is no board in elect at the time of dissolution of Preston Corporation then the responsibility of dissolution of the entity falls to the most veteran advisor. This individual would be the only person to have the option to retain control of Preston Corp in a single entity if they had been in said role for twenty years or longer.

THE LAST SENTENCE of the article was underlined, and in shaky handwriting was written: *hired 1988, advisor 1994 (Hammel).*

Taylor pointed to the line in the paragraph and looked at Derrick. "Todd?" Derrick whispered.

"Do you think that Todd did this?" she asked, horrified.

"I don't know," Derrick said equally ruffled. "I mean he's a hard guy to read, but all of this..." Derrick said looking at the paragraph again. "I don't know, Tay," he repeated.

"He moved the body, he bashed his head in and moved it," Taylor said in shock.

"We don't know—"

"God, my father trusted him, my grandfather, too," Taylor said. "He was invited to holidays," she rambled on.

"Tay," Derrick said, but she went on.

"He always hated Cedric, too," Taylor said nodding. "Probably hated him because he was trying to stand in his way, and then he did all of that horrible stuff to him."

"Tay, calm down," Derrick said. "The evidence is damning but sometimes people only see what they want to see. Look at the Tappen thing," he reminded her. "We know Tappen was not the culprit but it made the police and the public feel better to know the high-profile case was shut. So let's be cautious and really look at this from all angles."

Taylor nodded. He was right. Meanwhile Ben was watching them like they were speaking in tongues.

"What do we do?" Taylor asked Ben because she knew that she and Derrick were out of ideas.

"He's right," he said, nodding at Derrick. "The police do not want to look like fools, like they pinned the wrong guy with this huge case. You want to set this right? You need evidence," Ben told them.

"Yeah, no shit, but from where?" Derrick said.

"His office," Taylor said looking between the two of them. "He must have something there, right? I mean if he wanted to take the company over then he must have something there to implicate him."

"It's as good a place to start as any," Ben agreed. "I will head over there," he said. "Give me a head start to make sure there is nothing going on there."

"Why are you helping us?" Derrick finally asked him. "I'm getting a little paranoid about it, to be honest."

Ben was quiet for a moment, seeming to gather the right words. "Cedric was good to me, he took care of me. And I could tell he really cared for you, Taylor," he said, looking her way. "It's not hard to care for you, you're a good person," he said, "and you deserve to be happy. Cedric didn't get his happily ever after, but you should. He wanted you to have it. This is my way of thanking him," he explained.

Taylor stood rooted where she was. "You think he wanted me to be happy, why?" she asked.

"You don't pay that much money to find someone and then not want to know where they are in order to cause them harm," he said. "Wait here, come only after I've called you," he said, and with that he slipped back out the creaking front door.

———————

DERRICK WATCHED as Taylor shook while her eyes skittered around the room. The visceral effect this place was having on her was heartbreaking.

"Let's go outside, Tay," he said, pulling her to the huge door, "we can wait in the car."

Taylor nodded and wasted no time pulling the door open and leaving her former home.

Derrick looked back over his shoulder in the doorway. Seeing it now, he couldn't even remember what the place had looked like. It had been amazing, he remembered that, but he couldn't picture it. The place where so many happy things had happened was destroyed, but it couldn't destroy their memories.

He pulled the massive door closed and jogged down the stairs to the car, Taylor already waiting inside.

"You okay?" he asked her.

Taylor sat facing forward. "It's all just so fucked up," she said softly, shaking her head.

"Yeah," Derrick said, nodding, "yeah it is." He tried to think of something to say to distract her. "Where should we start, you know, when we get to Preston Corp?"

Taylor shrugged, "Todd's office?"

"Do you really think he has stuff in there to implicate him?"

"You know in all my experience in finding criminal masterminds I have found that they do generally leave written confessions in their offices," Taylor snapped and then rolled her eyes. "I don't know, but I do know that is the only place I have access to his stuff."

"Point taken."

"Sorry," she said, grabbing his hand, "I'm a little on edge."

He nodded, "Me too."

Taylor's classical ringtone filled the space, and she fished into her pocket to retrieve it.

"He was supposed to call me," Derrick said.

Taylor looked at the screen and then quickly answered. "Charlie?" she asked, but whoever was on the other end had hung up. "It must have been an accident. I couldn't hear anything." Less than a second went by and Taylor's phone rang again. "It's Charlie again," she said.

"Put it on speaker," Derrick commanded her.

"Charlie?" she asked.

"Taylor?" a hissed whisper came through her speaker.

"Charlie, is that you?" she asked.

"Yes," the older man gasped into the phone.

"Are you okay?" Taylor asked, her eyes staring with concern at the screen.

"Todd is here," he whispered into the phone.

"Where?" Derrick asked.

"Preston Corp," Charlie hissed. "It's bad, Taylor, I don't know what to do—"

The phone clicked and Derrick looked at Taylor's screen to see the call was disconnected.

"Shit, we have to go," Taylor said, looking bug-eyed at Derrick, the pitch of her voice escalating. "We have to help Charlie," she said hysterically.

"Taylor, what are we going to do? If Todd is this insane, he may kill us. He *wants* to kill us," he reminded her.

"We can't sit here and do nothing," Taylor said. "Ben is going there. Call him—he can help us," she reminded Derrick.

Derrick knew it was a bad idea, but he knew they couldn't sit there and wait. He knew it would be worse if they did.

So they left the Preston Manor drive, and headed towards Preston Corp.

TWENTY-EIGHT

DERRICK PULLED the Tesla into the underground garage of Preston Corp and parked. "We stay together, okay?" he said, turning to Taylor.

She nodded, but when Derrick leaned over to open his door she grabbed his arm. Derrick turned back, surprised, and Taylor cupped his face in her hands. "I love you, Derrick Fletcher," she said and kissed him softly on the lips.

Taylor went to slide her hands off his face and Derrick reached up and held them in place. "I love you, Taylor Preston-Fletcher," he said, "and we are going to get this figured out," he pledged.

They got out of the car and migrated to each other before Taylor grabbed Derrick's hand and they hurried over to the elevator. They were halfway there when Derrick stopped, causing Taylor to lurch to a stop too.

"Should we get a weapon, you know, in case Ben doesn't come to help us?" Derrick asked Taylor.

Taylor shrugged, "Do you have anything in the car?"

"Nope," Derrick said. "It'll be fine, we can wing it," he said starting once again toward the elevator and pulling Taylor with him.

Winging it did not seem like a good plan, but it was really all they had.

They made their way up to the office level of Preston Corp. The doors opened and they stepped out, but really had no plan. They hadn't been able to get in contact with Ben. They weren't sure if that was a plus or minus for their situation.

"Should we wait?" Derrick asked softly. "See if Ben comes?" Taylor looked at him in surprise, and Derrick rolled his eyes. "I don't like the guy but there is strength in numbers against crazy people."

"We need to find Charlie," Taylor said. "I need to see if he is okay."

They started off and turned a corner towards Todd's office and as they did a disheveled and shaken Charlie crashed into them, running from the other direction.

"Charlie?" Derrick said in surprise.

"Oh my God, are you okay?" Taylor asked.

"He's mad," Charlie whispered, wide-eyed.

"Who?" Derrick asked.

"Todd," Charlie said in a whisper-yell while he looked over his shoulder. "He has Marty," Charlie said, looking panic-stricken.

"What?!" Derrick and Taylor said together, then looked at each other and set off down the hall at a hastened pace.

"Wait, wait," Charlie cried, chasing them and stepping into their path, "we need to call the police. Please, God only knows what he is capable of."

"That bastard has my sister. I'm not waiting," Derrick yelled as he shoved past the older man. Charlie grabbed at his arm as he went past but Derrick easily shook it off.

"Derrick," Taylor called after him. She got it, he wanted to help but she was panicked for his safety.

"Taylor, please," Charlie said, holding her back, "I think he's after you, you should—"

"Charlie, I can't just let him go in there alone," Taylor pushed him away from her and raced down the hall to Todd's office, where she found Derrick on the floor. "Derrick!" she shouted, dropping herself to the ground beside him. She saw someone sitting in the desk chair in the room and looked up to see Todd slumped over. He was tied to the chair with rope around his arms holding his unconscious frame in place, gray duct tape over his mouth. Taylor looked back down at her husband. "Derrick?" she called to him, soft but shrill.

"He was so alarmed he didn't even feel me inject that tranquilizer," Charlie said, clucking his tongue as he walked in calm and composed, smiling down at Taylor. Quickly his smile morphed into a sneer. "Now get up," he grunted to her tugging her up by the arm.

TWENTY-NINE

TAYLOR WAS SHAKING her head as Charlie pulled her to her feet. "Charlie, what the hell—"

"You stupid girl, have you really not figured it out yet? I must be a much better actor than I thought, huh?" Charlie asked in disbelief. "God, for someone so intelligent you are really, really naive."

"But Todd—"

"Good God, you can't possibly still think Todd is to blame!"

"But how...why—"

"Because when the police come in and find that you have shot Todd and your husband and your sister-in-law and *then* yourself, I will take control of Preston Corp."

Taylor's head spun. "You did this?" she whispered. She shook her head. "But why, Charlie?"

"Why?" he asked in disgust. "Because I deserve this company, dammit!" he announced, stomping his foot on the ground. "I have broken my back and spent my entire life devoted to this company, given my everything to all of it and have gotten nothing, nothing in return. I drove Cedric to rehab twice, got up all hours of the night to bail him out of jail, picked Grant up when he was too drunk to drive.

All so your grandfather wouldn't be caught dead doing it, and that is all in addition to being at your grandfather's beck and call. And for what? What?!"

"Charlie, my grandfather loved you, my whole family loved you."

"You know what your grandfather said to me once? He told me only a Preston could truly care about the business. After all I had done. That was the day he signed the decree for his succession. And that was when I read it."

"What are you saying?" Taylor asked sounding very much like the scared little girl she felt like inside.

"I learned very early on in business if you want something you need to take it."

Taylor felt dizzy as the blood drained from her head. He couldn't really mean what he was implying, she thought. Her breathing came fast.

Charlie's face brightened, "Finally seeing the big picture, Taylor?"

"What did you do?"

"Well it wasn't easy, I will tell you that much," he said. "Years of planning, actually. But I had to eliminate my competition. One. By. One."

Taylor's stomach lurched and it sent bile flooding into her mouth.

The door crashed open from its partially closed position, and four men came in, carrying an unconscious Henry. "Where you want him, boss?" one of the men asked, and Taylor realized it was the agent who had come for Henry earlier, the one whose voice sounded familiar. It suddenly all clicked where Taylor recognized his voice. It was the voice from the 911 call, the one where Cedric's body was reported.

"Drop him over there," Charlie motioned to the corner with his head, and Taylor watched as the men dropped Henry's body in the corner. She was so fixated she didn't see them bring Nan in until they dropped her lax frame on Henry's.

"Oh my God," she whispered, unbidden tears streaming down her cheeks.

"Don't worry, Taylor, they aren't dead," Charlie said in his most gentle voice, "yet."

"We have the other guards tied up in the mailroom like you wanted," the faux agent said.

"Perfect," Charlie said, "and this is everyone, all four of you are here?" he asked looking at each of the men who had just entered, the fake badges still hanging from their necks.

"Yes," the speaker said.

"Great," Charlie said to him, "please proceed to the next step."

The man nodded and motioned his head to the other men, who marched out. As soon as they were out of sight, Taylor heard three gunshots.

Taylor's chest tightened in horror as the scene unfolded. The speaker stepped back into the room, a wide grin spread across his face as he had completed his task. But as soon as he did, Charlie shot dead center in his forehead, sending him to the floor.

Taylor's mouth hung open, and she shook as adrenaline and terror raked her entire body. She jerked her hands up to her ears, and just stared at the sight before her.

Charlie turned back to her, his face and body completely at ease, totally relaxed. "Where was I?" he asked, thinking for a moment. "Oh yes," he said, a joyous smile covering his face, "my takedown of your stupid family.

"At first, I tried to get your uncle to do it, but god damn if that Cedric wasn't a stubborn son of a bitch."

"You said...you said he was an addict."

"Oh, he was and then he wasn't. And then your mother met Grant and it was stars and moons and rainbows and unicorns and Cedric was seeing double he was so mad. And he couldn't clear his mind, couldn't see straight. He was so confused and blind with rage, so I helped him out."

"You gave him drugs again," Taylor accused softly.

Charlie shrugged and smirked, the maniac showing his true colors. "It was so easy," he said with a cruel laugh. "He was so easy to push over the edge, so pliable, it took just a one-finger poke and then he just went into a downward spiral."

"But just the drugs? He had been on drugs before," she said, refusing to believe his tale.

"Ah, but when you pair drugs that make you vulnerable with a voice," he said wagging his finger at her, "then you have a winning combination."

Taylor thought back to the printouts Cedric had put in the folder. "A transmitter," she said to him.

"I put it in myself," Charlie said with pride. "I researched for months the proper product and technique. I had to really knock him out to get it in his tooth just right. The one I used was military grade. I could hear everything he said so crystal clear, and he could hear me just as well."

The puzzle pieces were all jumbling around in Taylor's head, as she thought about the other research Cedric had done. "You gave him extra things too, didn't you? You had his drugs so you tainted them, you put stuff in them."

"Oh, you bet I did," Charlie said in a whisper. "It took me a long time to find the perfect concoction," he said nodding.

Taylor looked at him, trying to find the Charlie she thought she knew. Trying to find him beneath all the evil.

"Charlie, you love this family, you wouldn't—"

"I did though, Taylor! And that is the beauty of it all, no one would ever believe it!" he said triumphantly. "Do you want to know?" he asked. "I have kept it all inside and buried, I would love to share it with you now," he bragged, almost begging to share his secrets.

She didn't want to ask, didn't want to know, but she couldn't help herself. "How?" she whispered.

"Well, your father had his accident," he said, and Taylor could see his high over the explanation. "He and Cedric went for a hike. It was his idea, your father's own idea," he said, his eyes gleaming with excitement.

Tears welled in Taylor's eyes and she subconsciously shook her head.

"Oh no, you definitely want to hear this," Charlie assured her. "Have you ever heard of a West African carpet viper? They are one of the deadliest snakes in the world, residing in West Africa. Importing one to the United States is incredibly illegal. But money can do amazing things, can't it, Taylor?"

Taylor had always been told her father had slipped on rocky terrain. That he had fallen while hiking. It had been a freak thing.

"Oh, he did fall," Charlie replied and Taylor realized she had apparently spoken out loud. "He was bitten after he opened his back-pack. The poison took effect and he fell right off the side of the moun-tain. The difficulty in extracting him allowed the venom more time to work," Charlie explained expertly. "It was my idea to say Cedric wasn't with him. I convinced Cedric that he had brought the snake there and then told him to lie about being there. He was just haunted by what he could remember."

"And then your mother—"

Taylor shook her head violently, "No, that was an accident."

"Oh yes, it was an accident," he nodded, "that was caused by me making Cedric believe he needed to talk with her. He had gotten clean with her help before. And now he had relapsed, so I convinced him to call her, ask her to come to him, had him tell her it was urgent."

"Yes, but she was killed in an accident with a dozen paparazzi."

"Yes, Taylor," Charlie said smiling, "paparazzi who never would have known she was out if someone hadn't tipped them off about her potentially being on her way to a sordid affair," he said, laughing.

Charlie had killed her parents, Taylor slowly realized. The room spun slightly.

"But your Grandfather, he was a tricky one. It was hard to get Cedric to do much to him. I think he was on to me by that point."

Taylor's eyes grew large, and her rapid breathing was making the spinning nearly unbearable. But she shook her head—this could not be true.

"Now you are lying. He had cancer, it ate away at him. I saw the tumors and the MRIs."

"But I replaced the morphine with fentanyl, and the dose was one hundred times the strength of the morphine. It eliminated him much quicker than even I could have anticipated."

Taylor dug her fingernails into her palms, feeling the pain and trying to wake herself up from this horrible nightmare. She had given her grandfather the pain medication he had needed. She and Cedric. She may have potentially given him his fatal dose.

This wasn't happening, this wasn't real.

"It was only you and Cedric after that. And then you disappeared and I thought for sure I could just manipulate Cedric out of the way, but he started to figure it out," he sneered, shaking his head. "He tried to destroy the company, that piece of shit, tried to burn it down to nothing. He tried to dissolve everything Preston Corp had, to close it down all because he knew there was someone trying to get to him. Trying to get to you."

A groan behind Taylor had Charlie darting his attention away for a split second, as Taylor assumed Todd stirred a little.

"And that prick," he sneered at Todd's limp form, "he got wise. He was on me like glue, for years now. And I needed his help. He was useful but it was not without my having to sacrifice," Charlie said. Then a slow-moving smile crept onto his face. "But no one else suspected anything. Everyone thought this was all Todd," he said spreading his arms and doing a small twist. "All of this and even Cedric, just before his last breath, believed it was Todd who was after him," he bragged. "I even had to drug poor Tappen with the Datura to throw him off my scent when Derrick was in the hospital. And it worked. That, Taylor, that is what is called well played.

"And so now that I took care of all of those before you there is just one person standing in my way." Charlie slid his right arm up and pointed his gun at Taylor. "You."

Taylor wasn't sure she was even breathing. It had all come to this. She was literally facing down the barrel of the gun, and whatever happened next would decide her fate.

"It has been such a chore to get to this point," Charlie said in annoyance. "Every time I turn around there is something in the way, always someone in the way. Somehow there is always someone defending you. But not now," he mused, a Cheshire-cat smile creeping across his face as he lifted his gun and used it to brush Taylor's hair to the side, causing a shiver to run through her. "And so who is going to save you now, Taylor?" he asked in mock sympathy. "Now that every person who has ever protected you is out of the picture, hmmmm? There is no one else to take this bullet for you," he said. "They are all tied up," he said, laughing at his own nightmare-inducing joke. "So tell me, Taylor, who is going to save you?"

Taylor swallowed. "I...I don't know." She looked down nervously and slid her hands onto the desk behind her. "But I think that maybe, Charlie," Taylor said, swallowing down her terror, "maybe I will just save myself." She swung the lamp she had grabbed from the desk behind her and hit Charlie's arm, sending the pistol flying from his hand.

Baffled, Charlie watched it fly. Taylor seized the opportunity and kicked her toe right into the center of Charlie's groin, pitching his balls back into his body. The old psychopath gasped, wheezed, and whined like a bitch as he clutched at his groin.

Taylor swung the lamp again and hit the back of Charlie's head as he bent over in pain, knocking him to the floor and unplugging the lamp, plunging the whole room into darkness. She was frozen in place for a moment, then she heard Charlie groan in front of her and a flame of urgency ignited within her.

Taylor edged along the desk toward the door and, hopefully, help. She moved slowly trying to stay out of Charlie's path, but he groaned again and reached out grabbing at Taylor's ankle sending her pitching to the floor. Frantically, she kicked and connected with some part of him, causing him to release her. Taylor scrambled away, crawled around to the side of the desk, and then scooted her way underneath it.

"I am going to kill you, bitch!" Charlie shouted from the other side of the heavy wood.

Taylor held her breath as she listened to him make his way to her. There were thumps as it sounded like Charlie was struggling to stand. And then there was the groan of the desk as he leaned into it for support.

"You little bitch," he grunted, and Taylor started to shake. "I will find you," he growled out.

Taylor closed her eyes as she listened to him get closer. She opened them and noticed that her eyes had adjusted to the dark just enough for her to make out shapes in the room. She pushed herself as far back under the desk as she could, as silently as she could. She lifted her head and it hit something hard and lumpy on the underside of the desk.

Taylor slid her hand up and felt the object, seeing if whatever it was could help her in any way. Taylor realized it was a gun. She flashed back to her conversation with Todd, where he said he used to have a gun hidden in his office. Sweet relief and hope flooded her. Taylor pushed on the gun until she figured out how to slide it free, all the time listening to Charlie come at her, slumping around the desk. Taylor's eyes continued to adjust and soon Charlie's legs stopped in front of her hiding spot under the desk.

Taylor held the gun between her hands. She didn't know if she could use it. Maybe she could just push him down and run out, run fast and far and get help. She didn't even know if the gun was loaded. As she wrestled with her decision Charlie spoke again. "Maybe if I kill your husband first, I can find you," he said softly.

No. Fucking. Way.

Taylor didn't even pause—she shot the gun and a bullet flew into Charlie's knee. Firing it was loud, and the gun recoiled, striking Taylor above the eye. Immediately her head hurt and her ears were ringing. It was an echoey noise, like after a bell has been rung, and everything was muffled all around her. She distantly heard Charlie calling out, but it was hard to tell how close he was, the sound so muted by the ringing in her ears, and the room too dark to make him out.

Taylor scrambled out from under the desk. Staying under there just made her a sitting duck. She was almost at the door when she was yanked back by her hair.

She shrieked as she was pulled flush against a heavy breathing form. The ringing had lessened but the sounds around her were still muffled. She could hear Charlie saying something but it was totally unclear what it was. He was swaying, unsteady in standing, but his adrenaline must have been enough to keep him upright.

He snaked his arm around Taylor's neck and put her in a choke hold. Taylor clawed at his arm but the more she dug, the harder he squeezed.

Is this it, she wondered, *is this how it all ends?* Not just her own life but her family's legacy and her happily ever after.

Hell no.

She brought her elbow up and connected with Charlie's nose, the crack of it breaking so loud she heard it in her muffled ears. The crazed man screamed and loosened his grip just enough for Taylor to jerk back and kick him in the stomach with her three-thousand-dollar stiletto.

Suddenly the door burst open and Kevlar-vested police officers entered the room with their guns drawn, Ben trailing them.

"Taylor," Ben said, going to her, "are you—"

But Taylor couldn't listen to him. Instead she went to her husband lying on the ground. "Derrick," she said as she got down over him, jostling him a little. "Derrick, please wake up," she cried, tears streaming down her face. This was all too familiar, all too reminiscent of the night of the Gala. "Please wake up, babe," she begged and laid her head on his chest.

Derrick groaned and Taylor lifted her head swiftly to look at him. "Babe?" she asked.

"I'm hungry," Derrick grunted.

Taylor's mouth hung open for a beat and then she started to laugh and peppered her husband's face with kisses. She looked up to see EMTs come in and put Charlie on a stretcher, and once on it the police cuffed him to it.

"How did they know?" Taylor asked in relief, looking up at Ben.

"I was here in the building and I saw his thugs carrying Henry, and then I couldn't get a hold of you guys," he explained, "so I called the police."

"He is crazy," Taylor said, "the things he said—"

"Have all been recorded," Henry croaked out from the corner.

"What?" Taylor asked, baffled.

"I put voice recorders and cameras in every office when I took over," he said, sitting up and gently holding his aunt.

"Henry, you are fabulous," Taylor said.

"It is my job, Taylor," he said.

"Tay," Derrick moaned.

"Yes, babe?"

"I really want a pizza," he said.

And Taylor just rolled her eyes, and let the smile spread across her face.

Here it was. This was her happily ever after.

EPILOGUE

Ten Days Later

THERE WERE DEFINITELY DOWNSIDES to being rich. Taylor could think of about five off the top of her head, even with recent events aside.

But deciding that you needed to have a family meeting in a relaxing location and taking your private jet to your own private Caribbean island, well, that did not suck.

Taylor, Derrick, and Marty were lying on oceanfront lounge chairs on the Fletcher private island and leisurely talking over where to go from here.

"Well, the first order of business I am going to take on is restoring Preston Manor," Taylor announced as she sipped her piña colada.

"For what?" Marty asked, peeling her bikini top to the side to check on her tan. "Wait, are you guys moving there?" she asked suddenly.

"No," Taylor said. "I, well, I think I want to open it as a rehab facility," she said shyly, "in Cedric's name." It felt good to be able to say his name now and not have her stomach roll with fear. She still had a lot to work through, but Dr. Mellon had set her up with a great therapist, and she was determined to work her way through all the pain.

"Tay, I love that," Derrick said. "And hey, the demo is already done," he reminded her.

Taylor rolled her eyes at Derrick. "Yeah, I spoke to Dr. Mellon about it briefly, and he is interested in being involved. Dr. Parker, too. He is thinking of retiring from being the ME of LA County," Taylor said. Parker had been found soon after Charlie was taken into custody, hiding in one of the morgue drawers after Charlie's assasins had tried to attack him.

"What about Fletcher Mansion?" Marty asked.

Taylor watched as Derrick tensed a little. "What about it?" he asked hesitantly. This was actually something he and Taylor had talked about, one of the main reasons they wanted to have a family meeting with Marty.

"What the hell are we going to do with it? I mean, it is way too fucking big for us," she said, "and I was thinking of getting my own place."

Relief washed over Derrick's features. "Really?" he asked.

"Yeah," Marty said. "Are you mad?" she asked Derrick timidly.

"No, not at all. We," he gestured between himself and Taylor, "were thinking the same thing. Thinking of getting our own space, somewhere we can start fresh."

Marty's eyes lit up. "That would be wonderful," she said, genuine happiness lighting her eyes, and tears falling. "I'm sorry," she said, grabbing at her towel to wipe her eyes. "I have been so emotional lately."

Taylor gave her sister-in-law a warning look and she cleared her throat. "I think you totally should," she emphasized as she sat up. Marty knew that Taylor had learned her secret, but Derrick was still in the dark about her and Henry, as well as their secret. She was going to tell him, but Taylor asked for her to wait until after their getaway, to let them have a sort of honeymoon they never had before she dealt with the big announcements.

"There is something else," Taylor said to her sister-in-law, trying to change the subject. "We, well, we want to merge Preston Corp and Fletcher Enterprises."

Marty looked between Taylor and Derrick. "Like you two would work together?" she asked.

"Well, we would merge the similar departments and manufacturing systems, but we won't be working side-by-side together," Taylor tried to explain. "But Preston Corp and Fletcher Enterprises would no longer be competitive conglomerates."

"It seems kinda stupid for me to be competing against my wife," Derrick said dryly.

"Yes, especially when I have Preston Corp profits up by 2.3% and you only have Fletcher up by 1.7%," Taylor said, "and we know how much you hate to lose."

"Anyway," Derrick said, shooting his wife a dirty look, "Taylor also bought me a gift and I would like to focus more of my energy on making that work."

"What is it?" Marty asked.

"A production company," Derrick said with a big grin, "so I can finally make movies."

"Derrick, that is great," Marty squealed, and her eyes once again filled with tears that she blinked away quickly. Marty raised her water glass up. "Let's toast to new beginnings and only happiness for us from here on out," she said.

Taylor and Derrick clinked their own glasses with Marty's and they all took a drink to seal the deal.

Ben walked near them on the beach, nodding at them. "Fletcher family," he said as he did his hourly surveillance of the beachfront. Henry had added him to the security team, and he seemed to be in a better place with Derrick now. "You guys need anything?" he asked.

Marty squinted up at him. "What the hell is your name again?" Marty asked.

"It's Jeff Benson, but people call me Ben all the time for my last name so I'm kind of used to that, too," he said shrugging.

"Maybe we can combine it," Marty offered, nodding her head as she thought about it. "Ben-Jeff. How about we call you BJ?" she asked cheerily and then winced as soon as the words were out of her mouth.

"Oh yes," Derrick said, "please, let us call you BJ."

Ben just glared at Derrick, "Sorry D bag, not gonna happen," he said, and continued off down the beach.

"Have you checked on Todd today?" Derrick asked Taylor, and she nodded.

"He is going home tomorrow. Nan is going to stay with him until he is up on his feet totally."

"That woman is tough as nails," Derrick said.

"Damn skippy," Taylor laughed. Taylor felt so bad that she believed Todd was trying to kill her, she had confessed it all to him on one of her visits to him at the hospital. But, in a completely un-Todd-like fashion, he had hugged her.

"I understand, Taylor," he said, "my shitty attitude only made me look more guilty."

"Yeah, you can be a bit of an asshole," Taylor admitted.

"I knew something was going on, and I had a weird vibe about Charlie. I was just trying to protect my best friend's daughter. You were his whole world." he said.

"Your gun saved my life," Taylor reminded him.

"I forgot I even had it," he said, laughing.

Marty stood up, interrupting Taylor's flashback thoughts. "Well, I think that meeting went well. I'm going to take an afternoon siesta," she said, and sauntered off to the beachfront castle that was the only structure on the Isle of Fletcher.

Taylor laid back on her lounge and looked out at the water, not a cloud in sight, and the waves lapping at the shore. She turned to her husband, who was sitting up watching the surf himself, sipping a beer.

Derrick smiled at her. "Happily ever after, Tay?" he asked her.

Taylor smiled back. "Happily ever after," she agreed, and pulled his face to hers, sealing their future with a kiss.

ACKNOWLEDGMENTS

Dave: Thank you for all the time you gave me to write, all the encouragement that it was good and for being my first Beta reader. I love you!!!

Marta: You are amazing. Thank you for texting me while you read the first draft and always encouraging me. You always know the right thing to say and I love you!

Jess: Thank you for being my final beta reader. The fact that you made time for me in your busy life is amazing! Thank you for being honest and for your awesome comments! Love you!

Maria: How can I thank you for your time and patience with me? The covers you designed brought my vision to life and it is perfect! Thank you for putting up with me!

Ann(s): You took coal and made a diamond! Your editing is amazing and I am so blessed to have found you ladies! I am so proud of my work because of what you have done! I can never thank you enough and am so glad you have agreed to keep working with me! Thank you! (I hope there were not too many grammatical errors in this.)

ALSO BY KADE CHAREST

Book One | Inevitable Series

Inevitable Inheritance

Made in the USA
Middletown, DE
25 July 2019